Seeds in the Desert Wind
A Novel by T. P. Graf

Book III
From the Trilogy - The Life and Stories of Jaime Cruz

ISBN 978-1-7352332-7-7

Library of Congress Control Number: 2021900774

amazon.com/author/tpgraf
TP Graf on Facebook

Images BYLO AI

This is a work of fiction. While some of the public places and
institutions exist and events in relation to time may be real, the
characters and context involved are wholly imaginary.
The opinions expressed are those of the characters
and should not be confused with those of the author.

This trilogy is dedicated to
the generous hearts and beautiful creatures
living under the vast West Texas skies.

T.P. Graf's Writings & Awards

As the Daisies Bloom - A Novel

PenCraft Awards - 2020 First Place, Cultural Fiction
Book Excellence Awards - 2021 Finalist, Friendship
Chanticleer IBA, 2020 First Place, Somerset Book Awards

A beautiful telling of life's trials and tribulations, always overcome by the love of family and of something greater than oneself. - Reader's Favorite

*Enchanting as it is charming … intimately and poetically told …
like a well-written symphony - Literary Titan*

*A powerfully written character-led novel; stark and unsettling but often funny too.
Highly recommended! - A 'Wishing Shelf' Book Review*

August Kibler's Stories for Tyler
Voices of Context from Eden to Patmos
(Companion to As the Daisies Bloom)

Firebird Award - 2021 Winner, Christian Poetry
American Book Awards - 2021 Finalist, Religious Poetry
Royal Dragonfly, 2021 Honorable Mention, Religion/Spirituality

*A compelling and thought-provoking study of the bible and Christian history. The writing style is almost angelic! It's the sort of book you want to discuss; that stays with you for a long, long time.
- A 'Wishing Shelf' Book Review*

*Graf has crafted a masterful work of modern literature that takes on some very complex topics…in a format that any reader can engage with and glean wisdom from … entertaining … highly recommend.
- Reader's Favorite*

The book offers fresh ideas … absorbing … thought-provoking and evokes a positive emotional connotation. - Literary Titan

Roots, Branches and Buzz Saws
More Stories of August Kibler

"Celebrate who you are, even if it is quietly…". That is what this book is, a celebration of August's life and a reminder to the reader to celebrate their life, who they are. - Literary Titan

Graf manages to keep readers enthralled with Jaime's day-to-day experiences chapter after chapter ... a beautifully penned tale of self-discovery and a strong main character who stands out in a crowd.
- Literary Titan

A gripping story filled with colorful and often captivating characters.
- A 'Wishing Shelf' Book Review

An immersive journey of self-discovery and a sense of home ... you find yourself invested in the lives of the people and the friendships that are made. - Readers' Favorite

Night Air Descending (Book Two)
From the Series - The Life and Stories of Jaime Cruz

A cleverly-crafted, character-led family drama set in Texas. I got so immersed in it, I started to feel like one of the family too!
- A 'Wishing Shelf' Book Review

Whether you're in the mood for a slice-of-life drama or a study of eclectic characters, Night Air Descending by T.P. Graf is a memorable read.
- Readers' Favorite

This is a beautifully written book that has a grounded and authentic feel so much that it feels like we are reading someone's diary ... heartwarming ... [with a] distinct literary aesthetic. - Literary Titan

Seeds in the Desert Wind (Book Three)
From the Series - The Life and Stories of Jaime Cruz

Every quirk, every nuance, and each daily challenge make this story relatable and enjoyable...a book that wraps around you like your favorite blanket and touches your heart in a unique way. - Literary Titan

Graf again delivers interesting, full-bodied characters that we can relate to and want to follow through to their conclusions... a story that will entertain and move you. - Readers' Favorite

A powerful, often thought-provoking end to this excellent trilogy. Highly recommended. - A 'Wishing Shelf' Book Review

A Cowgirl's Stories
Companion to The Life and Stories of Jaime Cruz Trilogy

Days in the Desert
Food for Body and Soul

Part I

Chapter One

While Sallie was mostly retired from her ranch duties, one chore she hung onto, without objection from Billy or me, was shoeing the horses. Since Billy had done his share during his years in Van Horn, I was her official helper. Billy thought I needed to learn the skill while I had the master teacher to show me how. Shoeing five horses every month or so is no easy task. It certainly was always a reminder to me just how tough Sallie really was.

I say five horses because Billy always shoed his own horse. "I need to do it enough to remind myself how," he would say.

Sallie would say back to him, "Like riding a bicycle, Billy. Like riding a bicycle. You'll never forget how."

She rarely smoked her Swisher Sweets anymore, but when it was time to shoe a horse, she'd light one up. "Lifetime of habit, Jaime. I wouldn't know how to start if I didn't have my Swisher Sweet to get me motivated."

Noah had come into our lives just shy of two and a half years ago. What a boy! When I was his age, I doubt very much that I had even an iota of either the maturity or discipline he possessed, which he certainly did not inherit from either parent but clearly exhibited once Sallie and Billy came into his life.

As I lined the three of them up in my mind—daughter, grandson and great-grandson—I could picture old man Geermann standing on one end of the line with Grandma Geermann on the other as the perfect bookends of the shared characteristics passed on to the three generations between them. On one end, the crazy, witty, great formulator of plans in an instant. On the other end, the gentle and generous soul that permeates their very beings.

Just as Sallie, the great lover of birds, had taken Billy under her wing when he was a boy, she took this latest fledgling and nurtured him. While I could shoe a horse as good as Sallie could these days, she had in her mind that, once she had to give it up for good, Noah needed to be ready to assume the role.

Noah wasn't quite so sure. "Aunt Sallie, these horses look mighty big to my little skinny self."

Sallie smiled at him while saying, "Noah, you'll grow into it by the time you need to. In the meantime, you've got Jaime and me to guide you along. You're a good helper already, and that's all you need to be for a few more years."

Our time with Noah on the ranch had been as splendid as one could ask for. Not only had healing come from having his father, Brett, restored to the family and Noah rescued from the tragedy of his childhood, the rains of the past summer had made for an exceptional year across the region of the tallest grass we'd seen in years. It was lush and beautiful. But as I learned in the spring of 2011, such a gift from nature can turn rather brutally and rather quickly on the land and its creatures in this desert place.

Noah, Billy and I had gone into Fort Davis for the food pantry distribution on a very windy April Saturday. It was miserable— there's no other word for it. The winds were near steady at sixty miles an hour, which were damned irritating—even to those of us toughened to the spring winds that can beat you silly.

As Billy was driving in, we felt the wind trying to push the pickup off the road. He said, "If I thought Rosalinda had plenty of help this morning, we'd have stayed home. I suspect only us tough cowboys, and the few die-hard volunteers, are gonna get out this morning to help."

Noah suggested, "Could be the people wanting food might not show up either."

I responded, "I guess we'll see who really needs it—that's for sure. I know if my kitchen was stocked enough for a couple more weeks, I'd skip this one."

When we got to the pantry, we saw how right Billy was. It was clearly a slim group of the faithful there to help. As we walked toward the building, we felt like we were being sandblasted with the dust and grit pelting us from all the surrounding bare soil.

I hollered to the other two, "Hang on to this door or it will blow off the hinges!"

It took some doing to get it open against the force of the southwest wind. Once inside, Billy said, "Lord, I don't know how we're gonna get back and forth carrying bags of food for people."

Rosalinda heard that and said, "Boys, meet the dedicated door opener and closer."

Ernesto replied, "You can see, I've got my marching orders for the day. *Jaime*, at least we're not out on that ridge laying up adobe with a norther blowin' in the snow."

I noted, "I'd much prefer the snow over the grit blowin' out there."

"You've got a point," he replied. "Just think of it as a spa treatment—peeling off your dead skin."

Then he feigned in a serious tone, "We'd better keep Noah inside working this morning. The wind will pick him up and carry him all the way to Balmorhea!"

Noah replied in an equally serious tone, "It tried to already, but it blew me against the building instead."

We made the best of it, and we all decided to skip our usual outing to the Slo Poke Cafe and just get back home and out of the wind. While there we swept up what dust and grit had worked its way into the building, which was substantial. Then we stayed and visited a while before braving the wind again.

As we got into the pickup and headed up the road to go to the post office Billy said, in an unusually subdued voice, "Oh, shit."

I glanced to see what brought that on and saw him looking out the side window. I asked, "Is that what I think it is?"

He answered, "Drive a little further into town. Yes, that's what you think it is—if you think it's a fire."

Noah asked, "Do you think that is some building on fire?"

Billy replied disconcertedly, "That's way bigger than a building. The ranches are on fire."

I said, "And with last year's grass it has lots of fuel. This ain't good."

Billy added, "With this wind there's no way they can do anything but watch it burn until they get enough help and equipment. If it gets into town, Fort Davis is gonna burn to the ground. Forget the mail—let's get back home."

We turned on the Alpine radio station on the drive back to the ranch, to see what they might be saying about it, and had it on in the house once we were back home. The fire had started at a house south of highway 90, west of Marfa, and quickly jumped the highway. It caught a railroad trestle over a little arroyo on fire just north of the highway, and had the Sunset Limited parked indefinitely east of Marfa. They were calling it the Rock House fire as it apparently started as an electrical fire at an old rock house just outside of town. Billy called his folks to be sure they had the radio on and knew about the fire.

This was the second time I saw real worry in the Geermann-Schlatter household. The first, of course, had been for Brett and Noah during the months leading up to Noah's arrival at the ranch and Brett rebuilding his life in Alpine. Now, there was worry—not just for their own homes and animals, but for every rancher, animal and resident in the fire's path.

I called Chuy and Lupe to see if they were okay. Chuy answered the phone. I said, "You're home and answering the phone. I guess that's a good sign."

Chuy responded, "We might get evacuated. We're not sure if it's gonna hit town directly or not. We're gonna know in the next few minutes that's for sure. We've heard some houses out at Mano Prieto are burning down as we speak."

I noted, "I'm not going to keep you on the phone. Stay safe."

Chuy replied, "We'll let you know how things pan out."

"Okay, friend."

Billy asked, "What'd he know?"

I relayed what he'd said. It wasn't an hour later that Chuy called back. I told him, "Chuy, I'm putting you on speaker. Billy and Noah are here with me."

Chuy explained, "It looks like Fort Davis mostly got lucky. The firefighters stopped it from gettin' all the way into town. It's burned to the east, and it did catch several homes on fire on the south side of town. We hear they are gone—burned to the ground or still burning."

Billy, thinking out loud, added, "I need to be gettin' in touch with the fire department or that forest service bunch at the observatory to see how I can help. I've got some experience from my Van Horn days, and they are gonna need all the help they can get."

Chuy said, "Call Ernesto. He's already talked to them. He can fill you in on where to go if you're gonna help."

4

"Will do," Billy replied.

When we hung up, Billy looked at me and said, "And no, if you think you should, you are not going to help. You need to be here and ready to move cattle, dogs and people."

I noted, "Your folks and Sallie will be worried sick if you go fight this fire."

He replied, "I know that, but I don't see I have any choice, though I thought maybe you and Noah might be a little worried for me, too. I guess not."

Noah suggested, "Jaime, I guess we could chain him down— maybe then he'd be convinced we're worried too."

I said, "That's what it'll take to keep him here, I'm afraid."

I asked Billy, "Are you tellin' your folks or am I?"

He answered, "I thought we'd let Noah do it."

Noah shook his head, "I don't think so."

Billy sighed, "Hell, I guess I have to do it myself then."

I mentioned, "It isn't gonna help that you're likely to be without a cell signal to call and let us know how you're doing."

Billy explained, "The way this thing is burning there are gonna be a lot of people without any electricity, and I suspect cell phones may bite the dust along with the landlines."

"I suppose that's true. I'd not thought about that."

Billy made his call to Ernesto who was about to head out. He told him, "Billy, sit tight. Let me come and pick you up. They want us to the north anyway. It's headed towards the observatory and looks like it will be burning for days. It's only gettin' bigger every hour this damn wind keeps on."

Billy instructed Ernesto, "Pick me up at Mom and Dad's. We're heading over there now to tell them what we're fixin' to do."

"Okay, *amigo*," and Ernesto hung up.

We keep fireproof coveralls just in case—and had never needed them until now. Billy got suited up and ready to go.

I said out of obvious concern, "Your mom's gonna shit when she sees you in those coveralls."

He replied, "I know, but even she's got a pair, doesn't she?"

"I guess that's true. Insurance we never hoped we'd need to collect on."

He said, "Let's hope we still don't. You know I need to do this."

"Yes, I know," I replied.

Chapter Two

We saw very little of Billy for the next twenty-plus days. He and Ernesto were in the thick of it with firefighters from across the state, and other states as well, trying to protect the ranches and the subdivisions outside Fort Davis. Every day passing where we'd heard no one had died was both a relief and a blessing.

I suppose it's not too surprising that a few folks pitched a fit about decisions made by the county on how best to deal with an out-of-control fire. After it was finally under control, they would press on with their complaints, but overall I had a hard time finding any fault—not that I went looking. The two dozen or so homes lost went down in those first hours when no one could do anything but get out of the way. And while it ultimately burned for nearly a month and scorched almost five hundred square miles, no one died —and even the cattle losses were much less than any of us thought possible, given its fast pace across the arid land.

When he was first home for good, Betsy had a welcome home dinner for Billy. Jean, Mary-Alice and Brett all drove out for it.
He told us, "Those flames could get at least thirty feet high in the air as it moved, and whatever was in its way was gonna burn. We just tried like hell to keep it in the mountains and off the ranches."

Bill noted, "Y'all managed to keep it off the observatory even though it seemed to be burning all around it by the images I saw online. And frankly, I was surprised Limpia Crossing made it through. I sure thought we were going to have it bearing down on us for several days there. Jaime, Sallie and those dogs of yours got the cattle moved to the sections where I felt like they'd have the best chance if it hit the ranch. You'll have some reshuffling to do now that you're back home."

Sallie noted, "Some of these ranchers lost miles of fence and water lines. They're gonna be busy for the next two years or more gettin' things back in shape."

"Some will probably think it's a lot easier to sell them and retire, Betsy added. "The big-money buyers don't care if most of the ranch isn't supporting cattle anyway."

Sallie agreed, "Too true. Too true. I'm not sure ranching is gonna make it another generation. It's a dying proposition."

Noah said, "I don't like the sound of that, Aunt Sallie."

"Well, I don't either!" she exclaimed. "It's gonna be up to you, Jaime and Billy to figure out how to beat the odds. Your granddad, sittin' here, has certainly passed along as fine a stand o' grass as there is west of the Pecos. You got that much goin' for ya."

Bill mentioned, "Oil's ridin' high right now. I'm sockin' away what I can for the ranch trust. Money won't be your biggest problem, but raisin' and sellin' cattle certainly isn't gettin' any easier. The news is good at publicizing anything negative on beef that they can, whether it's based in fact or not—almost always not."

Billy observed, "Dad, we've been organic without advertising it. Could be we need to see what it really takes to get that label so we can work on some direct sales to people interested in that kind of beef. And you know my view to slappin' a label on something or somebody. In this case, we might ought to do it."

Sallie said, "I have wondered about that myself, but didn't figure it was mine to do at this point—and I didn't want to put you boys to where you felt like you had to do it because I brought it up."

Bill added, "It's crossed my mind, too. I guess if we're all thinkin' it, maybe it means we should be gettin' around to doin' it."

I said, "I guess that means I ought to get to looking online for what all that's gonna take."

Bill responded, "Jaime, that would be great. You are our official researcher, after all."

Jean commented, "You've got three markets in one if you do it. Organic, grass-fed and grass-finished. I was showing Mary-Alice the price of that kind of beef last time we were in El Paso."

Mary-Alice added, "I don't know what the rancher is getting out of it, but they are sure proud of it in the store."

Bill suggested, "If you're really gonna do all the cattle that way and not do any feed finish-out, it means leaving 'em on the grass long enough to get some marbling on 'em—not that the grass is costin' us anything. What we'd add in months, we'd make up in feed costs."

Sallie chuckled, "Look at how old I am. I still ain't got no marblin'. I don't know how you expect these cattle to fatten up."

Billy countered, "You don't spend your day eatin' nonstop like the cattle do."

She sighed, "Too true. Too true. I guess that would make a difference. Maybe I should try it. Sister, I think I'll start eating from the time I'm up until I go to bed. You'll need to see to me gettin' marbled up some."

Betsy concluded, "Marbled up or not, you aren't gonna bring anything at market. You might as well stay thin. You can spare Nellie the extra pounds. She's not getting any younger."

Sallie said, "Every time I saddle up the ole gal she says to me, 'It's a race to the finish now, old girl.' And I say back to her, 'Nellie, if you beat me to it, I'll see you get a good Christian burial up on the ridge.' That threat of burying her seems to keep her pluggin' along from one ride to the next."

Noah asked, "Aunt Sallie, is that why you pointed out to us on our ride to the ridge where your folks are buried, and why you said where Nellie's hole was to go?"

Sallie replied, "That's right, Noah. She said back to me that day when I was brushin' her down, 'I approve if that's where you wanna put me. I'm just glad I'll be far enough from you and upwind of those Swisher Sweets.' She always snorts at me when she gets whiff of those. The older she gets the more she snorts though I hardly ever smoke anymore. She throws a fit when I do."

Betsy stated flatly, "I'm with Nellie."

Noah suggested, "I guess when I turn sixteen, I'll take up Swisher Sweets."

Billy jumped in, "I guess you won't unless you're moving to Alpine or El Paso. But what's being sixteen got to do with it?"

He answered, "Uncle Billy, that's when you decided you were grown up enough to leave. I figure I'll be grown up enough to smoke."

Billy responded, "I figure you still got some figurin' to do, and when you get it all added up, I'd just as soon it not include your grandpa or aunt's proclivity for tobacco."

Noah asked, "What's proclivity?"

"Being hell-bent to have it—of a kind."

9

Noah said, "Memo to self—no smoking or chewing around Uncle Billy."

I responded, "Memo to Noah—no smoking or chewing around Uncle Jaime, either."

Brett added, "Memo to Noah—no smoking or chewing around Dad, either."

Noah shouted, "All right! I get the message!"

Jean observed, "We sure have strayed a long way from the future of cattle raisin'."

Sallie responded, "Not really. We just got some boy raisin' thrown in there while we were at it."

Jean added, "I guess. I thought Dad and Billy had the market cornered for wandering off topic, but I see it runs through the Geermanns as badly as the Schlatters."

Betsy reminded her daughter, "You are both, you know."

Jean replied, "Yes, but I'm a CPA, and we like things neatly in columns."

Billy said, "I don't know what recessive gene got in there for that, but you got a healthy dose. You surely are persnickety compared to the rest of us."

Mary-Alice added, "And don't look at me. It's a full time job keeping her loosened up at all. I do my best."

Betsy noted, "Daddy loved numbers. You get that part honest."

Jean questioned, "I guess you're sayin' I didn't get being persnickety honest."

Betsy noted dryly, "I'm not saying anything about that."

Sallie said, "I will then. That's straight from your momma. She's just loosened up over the years."

When we all looked at Bill he asked, "What are you lookin' at me for? I'm stayin' out of this one."

Then he said, "I think I'll steer us to a new topic. Girls, what's that drive from Marfa to here look like after the fire? I've been meaning to take a ride down there, but haven't gotten around to it."

Jean commented, "In one word, depressing."

Mary-Alice explained, "More like two words, depressing and filthy. And that black earth is really making the afternoon dust devils stir up like I've never seen before. One afternoon on the way back from Fort Davis to Marfa, we saw eleven at one time—

carrying all that soot, ash and dust to the people out at Mano Prieto whose houses made it through the fire."

Jean added, "The couple from church who live out there say they get a fresh layer in the house every day that they have to clean up."

Bill observed, "There hasn't even been rain to help settle the dust or wash the soot into the soil. I can imagine it's pretty bad."

Mary-Alice continued, "One of those eleven about blew us off the road. Not only have I never seen so many, I've never seen them so strong. I know it's the black earth heatin' 'em up. But the smell is another thing. Our car reeked of soot for days just from that one dust devil."

Sallie said, "I'll bet that fire made a few newer arrivals wonder if they really wanna live out here."

Billy replied, "It was some of those new arrivals that griped about how we went about fightin' the fires, but they weren't out there doing it either."

"Typical," I said.

Bill added, "And it's some of those new arrivals that opened up their pocketbook to help those that lost everything to start again. A lot of poor families are gettin' a new home from their generosity."

Betsy acknowledged, "It's amazing what they've raised to help the people out. It certainly drowns out the grumblers with the community's generosity—old and newer arrivals."

"Amen to that!" Then Sallie added, "Let's just hope when the rains come that we get some gentle showers to give the grass a chance to come back before any heavy rain comes. If the first rains are gully-washers, it will indeed wash out a lot of land and make for a lot of black mud."

Betsy responded, "For their sakes, I hope that's not one of your intuitions you're trying to hide behind wishing for the gentle rain."

"If I'm on Sallie's wavelength, I'm afraid you're right, Mom. Something tells me it's gonna be a hard dry spell followed by a deluge," Billy agreed.

Sallie sighed, "I confess, I'm afraid so, too."

It was mid-July before any rain came. When it did the *Puertacitas* and some other spots got over six inches of sideways rain in less than two hours and another deluge after that, according to

Jean's report. Gully-washers everywhere, along with black mud and the stench of wet ash—the last great act dumped on those in the torched-earth areas before new life would finally spring from the ground and heal the land.

On hearing the telling of it, Sallie said, "Still, the rainbow came."

I looked at her and smiled, recalling how she and I had talked about Noah's rough landing into the family. I echoed, "And still, the rainbow came."

Chapter Three

I've rubbed off on Noah a little bit, I guess. I'd always sung in the shower, though soft enough even Billy never really noticed. And I'd always had my theme songs. "Tumbling Tumbleweeds" suited me well enough for years. I'd been on the hunt for a new one, but nothing had really hit me yet. Noah had his, and he liked to sing it every time he took a shower. He didn't know the song until Billy taught it to him. He wasn't raised heathen like me, but darn close during those years in El Paso.

About as soon as the hot water would hit him, we'd hear him start up.

Noah found grace in the eyes of the lord.
Noah found grace in the eyes of the lord.
Noah found grace in the eyes of the lord.
And he landed high and dry.

He learned all the verses to go with it, and as he put it, "I just sing it with the same instructions as on the shampoo bottle. Lather, rinse, repeat. I sing while I lather up, I sing while I rinse and when I'm done with that, I start again."

Billy noted, "Those directions are just to make the shampoo company rich. One lather and rinse is all you need, and once through the Noah song is all Jaime and I need in a day, too."

"But you say you like to hear me sing," Noah stated rather matter-of-factly.

Billy replied, "Yes, we do, but a good musician has more than one song. You're stuck on that one."

Noah responded, "I guess you know you must mumble, 'hidimie-pidum,' about thirty times a day. I don't even know where that comes from or what it means."

Billy answered, "I don't guess I do either. I'm not sure I can lay that on Sallie. That's my filler to give me time to think. I must be doing a lot of thinkin'." Billy looked at me. "Do I really say it that many times a day?"

I chuckled, "Thirty is just where Noah and I lose track."

"Huh," he said. "Noah, I guess you need to add to your repertoire, and I need to cut down on my mutterin'."

Our little band of musicians had grown by one. In addition to Billy on harmonica or fiddle as well as vocals, me on guitar and vocals, Bill on mandolin—we never could get him to sing—we now added Noah for vocals, and he was learning to play keyboard.

It must be said, he had a pretty good haul that first Christmas on the ranch. We made it clear it was catching-up time and not to get used to it. Billy and I got him the pencils, paper and watercolors he expected, but we also threw in some acrylic paint and canvas in case he got inspired. With Brett's finances still tight, he went in with us on the bicycle Noah was pretty sure was still on the list. Bill, Betsy and Sallie got him two nice Yamaha keyboards, one for home and one "for school," along with a paid membership to an online piano teacher. We suggested to Jean that she and Mary-Alice could throw in some good headphones to go with them—mostly for our sake. She was kind enough to comply. Of course, the school keyboard resided over at the new house. The only lugging Noah would have to do was to get it from Bill's office into the house on the nights we sang for our supper. Thus far, he was not ready for a public performance and stuck to vocals.

When we asked him if he wanted to go to Fort Davis to school in the fall, his response was, "If it ain't broke, don't fix it."

Billy asked, "That's all you got to say about it?"

Noah answered, "I don't know what else I'd say. Jaime gets straight to the point, and so do I."

I smiled. "I'm glad you noticed."

Billy didn't want him to go into town to school any more than Noah wanted to go, but he had to keep at it a bit more for his own amusement.

He asked, "Jaime, are we gonna let this boy make such a poorly informed decision without any further discussion?"

I replied, "We could give some consideration to whether there is anything else worth considering, but you know how we do once we try to start considering all the possibilities."

Billy agreed, "We never did get good at that. I guess, we'll just have to let the boy be schooled here and hope he can pass the GED at least by the time he's thirty."

14

Noah asked, "Is that how long it took you, Uncle Billy?"

Billy responded, "If I was a better lier, I'd tell you yes, but I can't even exaggerate to my satisfaction on this one."

Noah asked, "How old were ya?"

"Seventeen," was all Billy said.

I could see Billy frettin' if he had to admit he winged it—afraid it might send a bad message to Noah.

Fortunately Noah concluded, "I guess I'll have to try for sixteen then. If I can't smoke then, I might as well graduate early."

"I like the sound of that," I said, "but if it takes a year or two longer, that's okay, too."

Noah asked, "You won't love me less?"

Billy answered, "Now you're just askin' questions you already know the answer to. You can't get smarter that way. You gotta ask what you don't already know, so Jaime and I can pass along our wisdom to the younger generation."

I could see from the sparkle in his eyes, Noah was pleased with what he was going to come back with. "For wisdom, I go to Aunt Sallie, for current affairs, to Grandpa, for proper English, to Grandma and for bullshit, to you two."

Billy protested, "Hey! You don't know that word yet. That word can't come out of that mouth until it's eighteen."

I said to Billy, "You always say boys grow up quick on a ranch, and we are pretty good in the bullshit department."

"You're a big help." Then Billy added, "Noah, you best keep the bullshit lessons on this side of the ranch. Your Grandma isn't gonna want you taking what you learned here over there."

Noah replied, "I sorta figured that already." Then he added, "Of course, you're both pretty good at teaching a boy how to work hard and work smart. As best I can tell from Grandpa's history lessons, I'm pretty sure a lot of boys never learn that."

"Never was a truer word spoken," I said.

Noah added, "And I think you're both pretty good at raisin' boys and dogs. You got one good boy and two good dogs."

Billy echoed my words, "Never was a truer word spoken. Jaime, you ought to be popping some popcorn so this good boy can do his popcorn throwing chore for the dogs."

"I'm on it!" I said.

15

I was just dumping the popcorn into the big bowl we all three eat from on the couch when the phone rang.

I answered, "I believe this is my sister calling. Am I correct?"

"Hey, Jaime. Mark wanted me to call just to be sure you got our train schedule in the mail."

"We got it," I replied. "We'll be meeting the Sunset Limited in two weeks. We're glad you've decided to take us up on the offer to spend a month. Billy says if he gets tired of us, he'll go stay in the bunkhouse."

Zoey explained, "Mark will be working some, and you don't have to entertain us the entire time. We thought we might even borrow your old truck if it's okay and spend a week down in Big Bend on our own. Of course, you could join us. I just wasn't sure you could get away for a week."

I responded, "We really can't, and you'll enjoy the freedom of doing whatever, whenever, when you're down there. The truck is yours any time you want to take off and explore ... Zoey, hang on. Noah's wantin' to say somethin' to you."

"Hey, Aunt Zoey. I've already told Dad he's confined to the bunkhouse while you're here. We'll have your same room as last summer ready and waiting."

He handed the phone right back to me. "Hey, Zoey. I'm back. He's as bad as Billy—grabs the phone, says whatever's on his mind and hands it back—no hello or goodbye."

Zoey said, "He's adorable."

I asked, "He gets it honest, doesn't he?"

She replied, "Yes, he does. I guess we're done, too. Should I just hang up or say goodbye?"

I said, "Let's try their approach."

I was waiting for her to hang up and she was waiting for me. She laughed, saying, "We're not very good at this."

"No, we're not," I said, and we both hung up.

Billy figured out I was off the phone and hollered from the living room, "Are we eating popcorn in my lifetime?"

I walked in with the big bowl heaped up. I said, "If you weren't so disagreeable you could have gotten up and fetched the bowl yourself."

Noah, beating Billy to the punch asserted, "It's more fun to fuss at you."

I shared, "I just told Zoey, you get it honest. You and your uncle are cut from the same cloth."

Noah asked, "Why did that come up with Zoey?"

I explained, "Because, like your uncle, you came in, grabbed the phone to say what you had to say without a hello or a goodbye, and then handed the phone back to me."

Billy admitted, "That does sound a little like me."

"Yeah, just a little," I said, adding, "I can't talk and eat popcorn at the same time. I say we focus on what's important here, like the two red heelers down there catching every piece Noah throws their way."

I got up to go back in the kitchen. Billy asked, "Whatcha gettin?"

"La Croix. Who else wants one?"

Billy answered, "You might as well bring two for me. I know you're gettin' two for yourself."

Noah added, "I'll take a Bud Light."

"Okay," I said. I came back in with five La Croix cans, and when I handed Noah his, I said, "Here's your beer." Then I handed him an unwrapped Tootsie Roll. "And here's your Swisher Sweet."

Billy said, "Noah, I can tell you from experience, that Tootsie Roll tastes a lot better than Sallie's Swisher Sweets."

Noah bit off a chunk. "It's pretty good with popcorn. Too bad you old men can't eat 'em anymore."

I clarified, "We can. We just choose not to before some doctor tells us we can't."

Noah said, "I've never known either one of you to go to a doctor. When's the last time you went to one?"

I looked at Billy and he looked at me. It's funny, we'd never talked about it before. I thought about it a while. "I'm not real sure. In California before you were born."

Noah asked, "Uncle Billy?"

Billy answered, "We must be tougher than most. I can't remember going to one. I must have when I was little somewhere along the line. You'll have to ask your grandma."

Noah suggested, "Next time the vet's out, you two might need to get your shots. Dogs get 'em every year. You're bound to be overdue for something."

I replied, "Well, tetanus for sure. In fact, I wonder if your dad knows if you've had one or not. I guess we'd better check. We should have your dad get your medical records sent out here to the doctor in Fort Davis."

Billy added, "I'm surprised Mom hasn't said anything about vaccinations. I guess doctors aren't on any of our minds."

Noah said, "I used to get swollen glands and sore throat, but I haven't since I moved out here. I probably got sick from other kids at school."

I said, "Yes, you probably did. Did you ever get lice?"

He said, "No, I never had cooties in my hair."

I noted, "I thought calling something cooties probably died out with our generation. I guess cooties live on."

Billy commented, "I thought we couldn't talk and eat popcorn at the same time. Now, we're talkin' about lice and cooties. I already feel like I got cooties crawling all over me!"

I felt a little shiver up my spine. "Now that you mention it."

Chapter Four

The next Sunday, all the family were in attendance for the chapel service and lunch. As we were finishing lunch, Bill said, "I have an announcement to make. Mother, Sallie and I are finally going to make that trip to El Salvador. I've already been in touch with Chuy and have settled on a mid-January trip. Now, we need to get busy getting our passports and tickets in order."

With vaccinations fresh on our mind, Billy asked, "Do you have to get shots before you go there?"

Betsy answered, "I'll have to ask Rosalinda about that. I'm not sure."

Noah pointed to me and Billy. "These two need their shots. Neither one can remember the last time they've had a tetanus shot."

Brett said, "I don't guess I've had one in ages, either. Did Olivia get you properly vaccinated?"

Noah answered, "We think we'd better get my doctor's records from El Paso. I don't know either for sure what I've had or haven't had."

Bill observed, "Looks like the whole bunch of us may give the doc in Fort Davis some business for a change in the next few weeks."

Sallie interjected, "I'm not going unless required for the trip. I'll take my chances from here on. I had a tetanus shot once that had me so sore, I couldn't move for a week. I told Mother, 'I'm never getting one of those again!' I guess I'm allergic to them."

Bill asked, "Did you ever tell the doctor you had that kind of reaction? It could be, he might have been able to do something about it."

Sallie gave her head-bobbing chuckle. "I don't guess that ever occurred to us. No, I suffered in silence."

Betsy said, "I remember that, though not the silent part. What I remember is my big sister moaning and groaning every day for a week. I think you even skipped school two or three days."

Sallie admitted, "I might have done some moanin' and groanin', and I know I stayed home from school for three days. Mother sent me the first day, and I must have moaned and groaned there, too, because the teacher sent me home with a note telling Mother not to send me back until I was feeling better."

That memory gave her sheer delight in recalling it for us.

Billy reckoned, "I'm not sure I want a tetanus shot now after all. Could be such reactions run in the family. Jaime'll put me out in the barn if I start moaning and groaning. Noah, don't think he won't put you out there, too, if you get to moaning and groaning."

I clarified, "I'd probably let Noah stay in the house, and I'd at least be sure you got a nice blanket to lay over your hay bed in the barn. I'd even tend to all the chores. The dogs and I would handle things until you both were feelin' better."

"Too kind," Billy said.

Jean interjected, "Enough of your domestic affairs. I'm wondering how you get from point 'A' to point 'B' when you're trying to get from Fort Davis to where Chuy is."

Bill replied, "As Chuy rightly pointed out, his mom and dad have that routine perfected. We're going to talk to Ernesto and Rosalinda rather than reinvent the wheel."

I said, "That's pretty exciting. I know it will mean a lot to Chuy for you all to get down there."

Betsy observed, "I know it will be an eye-opener for us on how good we've got it here. I don't think we can anticipate just how much going in—even knowing such is the case."

Jean agreed, "I'm sure that's true."

Billy suggested, "As part of Noah's education, he should probably have an international experience in a third world country. Maybe he should go with you on this trip—or Jaime, Brett and I should take him on a trip in a year or two."

I was surprised he actually thought about Brett so naturally as part of the trip.

Bill responded, "As his history instructor, I'd agree that would be a good experience. I suspect it would be the richer experience to go with the three of you rather than three old farts who aren't going to be all that active once we get there."

Betsy reaction was immediate. "Oh, thank you, dear. I don't believe you've ever called me an old fart before."

Bill stated flatly, "Of course, I meant it in the nicest way."

Sallie chuckled. "Bill, there's no coming out with clean boots after steppin' in it as deep as you just did."

Bill acknowledged, "I'm afraid you're right about that."

It didn't take me long to observe just how good Bill was at making history interesting for Noah, so much so that Noah was often telling us about what he'd learned. As often as not, it was at an awareness level new to me and Billy on any given number of events in history.

We knew Bill had a collection of books, and as best I could tell he never pinned himself down to one ideology. Billy said as long as he remembered, his dad subscribed to *Harpers, Time, National Geographic* and *The Economist*. A few others would come and go as well, but those seemed to be the ones he kept year to year, and which still showed up in the mail bin. When he was done with them, they'd come home with us.

In heavy use for Noah's US history lessons was Howard Zinn's *A People's History of the United States.* While Bill almost never mentioned his brother, he did say to Billy and me, "My brother would label me commie-pinko for teaching a boy from this book. As far as I'm concerned, not to do so would be like reading the Bible while skipping all the prophets. If you ever want to even try to sort the victor's story from the rest, you've got to look critically at everything.

"I barely lucked out of the drafts between Korea and Vietnam, but if there were two wars early on in my life that made me wonder what the *hell* we were doing as a country, it was those two. As it turns out, they were just the start, as we see now. I'm not going to teach Noah some idealized America. We're a great country carrying an enormous burden of sin right alongside our prosperity."

When Billy and I talked about this, Billy said, "We always say Sallie and I don't like labels. Well, as pertains to politics and economics you're never gonna hear Dad attach to any label either. I remember before I left home asking him, 'Are we Republicans or Democrats?'—as though a family was one or the other like we were Protestants or Catholics."

I interjected, "Or heathens, though that was not applicable to your childhood at the time."

Billy continued, "Well, we knew heathens but, of course, that didn't apply to us. Anyway, Dad's answer was, 'As a family we are not attached to either one. I'd just as soon you, as my son, not attach to one or the other either.' Why is that? I asked. He said, 'Don't outsource your thinking, whether it's to the preacher or the politician or anyone else. The powerful love to suck you into their games.'"

I commented, "That's outstanding advice to give a teenager. A little risky, I guess, given a boy could use those words against sound fatherly advice. It suggests he thought you were mature enough to hear and understand it."

Billy said, "I never forgot it!"

"We've long agreed, we can't argue about politics like most people because we agree on politics."

Billy responded, "Built on our shared understanding—dumbasses abound."

"Dumbasses abound," I repeated. "Noah's lucky. He's probably getting a more balanced education than most people get even in college. I can say with the little bit of college I did get in my California days, such is certainly the case. I had some core history course where the professor might just as well have been a robot. He'd lecture for an hour—completely oblivious to the fact that half the class was asleep. Since he gave, basically, the same tests from one year to the next, you could buy the tests from other students for next to nothing. When people picture the lazy, tenured professor—he epitomized it."

Billy asked, "Did you buy the tests?"

I answered, "I was heathen, remember? I had no problem getting an 'A' in a course where I learned absolutely nothing. It was also the main reason I dropped out when I did. I thought, why am I shelling out money for this? I suppose, I limited my employment opportunities by not having the degree, but I was chasing great opportunities all the time in those days—and sitting in a classroom just seemed to be delaying my achieving greatness."

"I wouldn't have been your mess in those days. I'd have steered clear of you."

"And rightly so," I said, "but I'm doin' all right now."

"But you're doin' all right now," Billy repeated.

Chapter Five

When it was time to drive to Alpine to pick up Zoey and Mark, we decided the three of us, with two dogs, was getting a little crowded. Billy suggested he stay home and Noah ride in with me. We didn't have any compelling reason not to do that, so it was Noah and I standing on the train crossing as our guests stepped down from car one of the Sunset Limited.

Zoey smiled, "Getting off this car is almost like having a platform." Then she looked to her left and said, "Oh my, there is a platform! Such progress!"

Mark asked, "No Billy?"

Noah answered, "He's home with the dogs. He thought last year was a little crowded with all of us in the pickup. He wanted to tie me in the bed in back."

I noted, "The boy is wandering into the Geermann-exaggeration gene a bit there with that last part."

Zoey looked fondly at Noah. "You're adorable, Noah, just like your uncle."

As we drove into the mountains, Mark let out a long sigh, "Ahhh, I already feel at home. In fact, I felt so the second I stepped off the train. I've missed this place."

"We both have," Zoey said. "Brother, I have news about your brother."

"Oh?" I asked with obvious curiosity.

She explained, "I've actually had news for a while, but given its lack of being earthshaking, I just decided to tell you about it when I got here. I ran into him."

Mark interrupted, "No, he ran into you."

"I could have phrased that better. Yes, he literally ran into me. He rear-ended me on Highway 101. Traffic came to a rather abrupt stop, and this car behind me bumped into mine—hard. I got out to look at the damage, and there he was getting out of his car. It took us both a minute to realize who the other was."

Mark commented, "I'm surprised they knew each other without producing some ID. It had been well over ten years."

She replied, "It was only the sorta startled look we gave each other that confirmed we knew each other."

I said, "I gather since you said it wasn't earthshaking that it hasn't led to a close connection."

She answered, "Not even close. He'd had a few beers, and wanted me to let him get on his merry way and not wait for the police. He assured me he'd pay for the repairs."

"And did ya?" I asked.

Mark answered for her, "Yes, she did. No Sallie tough love from Zoey."

She added, "I thought maybe he'd try to connect after that, at least on some superficial level, but I've not heard a peep from him. His insurance company worked with my insurance company, and that was that."

"Did our parents even come up?" I asked.

"There was no time for that kind of conversation in the middle of the highway," she rightly noted. "I was going to be brave enough to ask when I heard from him. He knows where I am, and how to get a hold of me should the spirit ever move."

Then I wondered about the address I had for him. "Does he have a new address different from the old one I had when I mailed my letter?"

She replied, "He hasn't moved. I'm sure he got your letter."

"I guess that seed blew in the wind only to land on hard rock," I observed.

It was Mark who answered, "I would say so or, maybe more accurately, into the weed thicket of a drunken, sorry life."

"Out of curiosity, how'd he look?"

Zoey replied, "Like I remember our father looking at that age, though I don't remember our dad looking like an alcoholic, and I'm pretty sure Mason is one. It was barely noon when he'd already had his 'few beers.'"

"That is sad," I said.

Mark added, "It wouldn't surprise me if the 'few beers' weren't really something stronger, and he just thought beer sounded like something Zoey wouldn't take as seriously."

She said, "I certainly didn't get close enough to pick up on his intoxicated breath to be able to tell what he'd been drinking."

Noah asked, no doubt recalling his despairing years with his own mother, "Does he have kids?"

Zoey answered, "I don't know the answer to that."

I added, "From the little we know, I hope not."

Mark said, "I've started a weekly check of the two online news sites where we assume your parents still reside just to check the obits to see if either one ever pops up.   I guess they are alive if not well."

Zoey explained, "Of course, we mean 'not well' in a mental or spiritual sense, though if they appear in the obits, it would certainly indicate their body had succumbed to their toxicity or some accident had intervened to put them out of their misery.

"Sorry, Noah, this is little heavy."

Noah said, "I lived through murder. This is nothing."

I'm sure what was his "truth" hit the others just as it hit me in that moment.

Back at the ranch, as we walked in the patio door, Billy asked, "Jaime, did they ask how their favorite cowboy was?"

I answered flatly, "They didn't have to.   They could see I was fine."

Zoey joked, "We're not about to start choosing favorites. One of you, including Noah, is apt to cancel any further reservation requests."

Billy said, "Memo to self—cancel Caribbean cruise tickets for Zoey and Mark."

Noah exclaimed, "How about that!   I am a gen-u-ine cowboy, now."

I responded, "Memo to self—measure Noah's head before buying next cowboy hat—head could be swelling some."

Billy said, "Apparently, no one laid across the tracks this trip. You must have gotten in nearly on time."

I replied, "About five minutes late was all.   And you won't believe it—Alpine now has an actual concrete train platform!"

Billy said, "I guess once we got into the twenty-first century, they thought they ought to at least catch up to the eighteenth. They've got a ways to go to catch the Schlatters though.

"Mom says we should sing for our supper unless our guests would rather have the first night here at home."

Mark looked at Zoey who gave an affirmation to the invitation. "Sounds good to us."

Then Billy added, "I would talk to you about a proposition that came up earlier today, but Dad thought it would be more believable if he laid it out rather than me."

Noah looked at me, and seeing him look at me, so did Zoey and Mark. I said, "I have no idea what he's talkin' about, and it sounds like I won't until I've sung for my supper."

Billy said, "Too true. Too true."

We sang a few songs that evening while Zoey puttered in the kitchen with Betsy. Sallie sat in her favorite spot on the couch, just listening.

Bill announced, "The mandolin player is gonna drop out now. Sallie said she thought it seemed like a good night for old fashioneds."

Billy asked, "Sallie, you goin' 'round the bend? It's a long time till Christmas."

"This is to celebrate Zoey and Mark's return to us," she replied.

I said, "I'll drink to that."

Betsy suggested, "You boys can take the rest of the night off and relax."

Billy laughed, "It must be a peanut butter sandwich dinner if we're getting off this cheap."

Bill asked, "Who would like something besides Noah? It doesn't have to be an old fashioned, but the bar is limited and the bartender even more so."

Zoey said "An old fashioned is fine."

"Fine by me, too," Mark said.

Billy and I just nodded our heads in agreement.

When he brought the drinks around, he handed Noah what looked just like our cocktail, complete with a cherry and orange slice.

Billy asked, "What have you given the boy, Dad?"

Bill answered, "That's between me and Noah."

I took one sip of Noah's and recognized orange La Croix and suspected food coloring made the bourbon color.

I thought the drinks would kick off "the proposition," but we just visited—with Bill talking about the upcoming trip to El Salvador and Mark talking about Zoey's run-in with the drunken brother.

"Good lord," Bill said.

Sallie remarked, "He's lucky you let him make a clean getaway before the police arrived."

We heard Betsy announce, "Come to the table."

We made our way to a table spread with brisket, turkey, sweet potatoes, a cauliflower-broccoli salad and her latest creation—what she called her hot pan bread which had no flour or cornmeal but tasted a lot like cornbread. It was popular on both sides of the ranch—having sworn off the starchiest foods.

Betsy had more help than usual with this meal. As she explained, "Ernesto was kind enough to smoke the brisket and deep-fry a turkey for us. He told Bill he might like the turkey. He said, 'If he doesn't, it won't hurt my feelings, and I've given him plenty of brisket.' I was going to send Billy in to pick up the meat, but Ernesto insisted on delivering it as well. So tonight, we toast the founder of the feast, Ernesto."

She raised her water glass while we raised what was left of our old fashioneds and Noah's concoction. "To Ernesto," she said.

"To Ernesto," we all repeated.

Then Betsy added, "For our blessing tonight we're going to sing the Doxology."

We seemed to have all the parts covered—soprano, alto, tenor and bass—and we filled the house with our harmony. It was beautiful. Sallie obviously thought so, too.

She said, "I don't know why we haven't tried that in here before. Jaime, you and I could retire the blessing business if we sing that when we get together."

We started passing food and waited to see if Bill took any turkey. Bill saw us looking in his direction and said, "Yes, I'm going to take some turkey. If anybody could cook meat that I'm not crazy about and make it taste good, it would be Ernesto."

A couple of minutes later he took his first big bite, chewed it for a bit and then concluded, "Well, it's a moist gunnysack. Not as good as beef, but pretty good for a bird."

Sallie remarked, "That is high praise comin' from you!"

Bill asked, "I wonder what he can do with a can o' tuna?"

We'd obviously not clued Mark in on Bill's dislike of canned tuna, and he remarked, "Oh, I love canned tuna."

Bill gave the first hint to the proposition when he responded, "Billy, that shoots down our earlier idea."

Billy explained, "Dad's least favorite foods are canned tuna and kale. Mark, I think he was hoping to hear how much you like a beef brisket."

Mark said, "I love that, too."

Bill replied, "Well, maybe there's hope, then."

He seemed content to leave us all in suspense.

Zoey and I offered to help clean up after we'd all finished eating, but Betsy said, "Sallie and I will clean up. The rest of you need to hear what Bill and Billy have to say."

Bill added, "It's a nice night. Shall we go out on the porch?"

He started that way and we followed. He waited until we were seated and then pulled his chair around to face us.

Bill started in, "Mark and Zoey, Billy seems to be under the impression that you would consider leaving California at some point and settling here. Now, if the boy is off his mark on this, stop me now, because the rest would be irrelevant."

Mark said, "We're all ears."

Zoey nodded in agreement.

Bill continued, "None of us here are too confident that, between the news media, politicians, plant zealots and land prices, ranching has any future in it. Noah seems to be of a mind that we should try to beat the odds for his sake. We're all willing to try. As Billy rightly noted a while back, we are already an organic operation getting non-organic prices for our beef. With the right minerals and such, we could market grass-fed, grass-finished organic beef.

"We know the livestock side of what that takes inside and out. The idea Billy had earlier today, which his aunt immediately endorsed as their common premonition for things that generally occur, was that we need a good urbanite or two to help dumb cowboys and an old cowgirl get their high quality meat to market.

"Let me be clear, we aren't after a quick profit. This would be a long-haul strategy. Mark, I know you work some online. I don't

28

know if you could do that full-time here or not. If not, then this might be a little tougher to launch than we thought it would be otherwise. Zoey, we're wondering if you would consider taking over Jaime's job of being our chief researcher and devoting at least half-time to it, though full-time is an option if you'd be open to it. We'd want you to explore how we can get this marketed, and then manage that part of the operation once it gets going."

Bill paused to get some reaction from any of us. I know I was surprised by the proposition. I was sure they were in shock.

He continued, "I suppose I left out a couple important details which are, we'd want to do this within the next year, but not immediately. What we would want to do immediately, if you are on board, is to have Ernesto build a small home for you on the ranch. We could scope out some possible spots not too far from water and power while you're here. The house would be part of your compensation, but we'd still pay a modest salary also. And Mark, if it grew to where it could support you both, that would be all to the good as far as we're concerned."

Zoey was the first to respond. "I don't even know what to say. You worked my brother into your lives—I can't believe you'd work our lives into yours as well."

Mark added, "I suppose the sensible thing is to say, 'We'll think it over.' I'm more inclined to say, 'Let's see where Ernesto is going to build that house Jaime designs.'"

Bill replied, "I'll take that as a maybe."

Billy said, "You can see why I thought you needed to hear it from the headman himself with his wife and the head cowgirl within earshot."

I chuckled, "When I had to declare my intentions, Billy gave me about a minute. Maybe he will at least give you ten or so, since I was already living in town and not eleven hundred miles away."

Bill said, "You can take all month. We don't need a decision even while you're here. We're not out recruiting for this. If you want it, we'll work on making it happen. If you don't, that's fine, too."

Betsy came out from the house, walked over near Zoey, and said, "It could be we are just too far from civilization out here. After your illness, you might want to be a lot closer to doctors."

Zoey replied, "I'd just as soon put some miles between me and doctors at this point."

Sallie came out, leaned against one of the stone columns and lit up a Swisher Sweet. She took a long drag reflecting, "It wasn't that long ago the only company I had out here was Bill showing up when he did. The family keeps getting bigger. It seems to me, it's gonna get bigger by two more when Ernesto gets that house built."

Just then a cactus wren hopped up on the porch looking up at Sallie. She studied the bird as each bobbed their heads back and forth a bit. Then Sallie said, "You're right.... Okay then." And the wren flew off to her nest in the yucca.

Bill asked, "What'd she say?"

"She heard me say I was alone a lot all those years, and she was just reminding me that she and the other birds were always here. But now, they are all real happy to see such a nice family growing. They weren't sure what riffraff might come after me. Then she said, they think these last two would be good additions to the family, and I said, okay then."

Zoey looked at Mark and he at her. After an affirming look from Mark, Zoey asked, "Is this where we stand up and hug Billy?"

Chapter Six

Back home, we all plopped in our usual spots. I looked over at Billy. "I did not see that coming. Where and when did you even come up with the idea?"

"You and Noah wouldn't have even been over the cattle guard, when I said out loud to the dogs, 'We could use some urbanite help rolling out our organic beef.'"

Noah asked, "What'd the dogs say?"

Billy looked a little perplexed. "You know, I forgot to listen. I was already two moves ahead thinking I needed to go over and talk to Mom, Dad and Sallie before y'all got back."

Noah said, "That explains why Kola said you'd been ignoring them."

Mark asked, "Did she say anything else?"

Noah jested, "I thought I caught something about they knew just the spot for a new house."

I replied, "I don't know about that. It might be a little bit beyond their pay grade."

"I might have embellished a little bit," Noah confessed.

Mark said, "I felt like I was Jaime standing out on that ridge with Bill that day when he felt his whole life changing before his eyes."

Billy asked, "Are you both really all in on this?"

"We have a month to start exploring," Zoey answered. "At the end of our visit, you may change your mind or we may. Somehow I doubt it. Sallie and the cactus wren have spoken."

"I would concur," Mark said.

Billy said, "I have some ideas on where to build, and I'm pretty sure Jaime will get inspiration from at least one of them. How big a house do you want?"

Mark noted, "We live very modestly in California. Our condo is 850 square feet. We don't need anything bigger than that, do we, Zoey?"

"No. That is quite adequate."

Billy confirmed, "We'll just round up to a thousand then."

To confirm the basics of the building I added, "That would give you two nice bedrooms and two full baths. You can put up our brother that way if he shows up."

"Generous of you, Jaime," Zoey said.

Mark laughed, saying, "Rounding down to five hundred is sounding better."

Noah jested, "We'll just stick him in the bunkhouse."

"I guess that would work, too," I said.

Billy suggested, "We'd all best retire for the evening. Tomorrow morning Jaime and Zoey will need to be up early cookin' our breakfast before we head out to look for homesite inspiration." With that, he was off to bed without a "good night" or "see you in the morning" as per usual.

It must be said, our routine, morning and night, even now that Noah is living with us, consists of just going to bed and just getting up without any need to say anything. I can't help but greet Billy in the winter months—when he shuffles like an old man into the kitchen in the morning in his slippers and bathrobe—when I say, "Good morning, sunshine." He rarely responds and when he does, he mumbles, "Of a kind, I suppose."

Even in the dark, winter mornings when he's exercising his one time of the year to be lazy, he can't turn off the magnetism that is Billy. There is something about this quasi "old man Billy" that suggests to me that even in old age he will still have that inherent ability to draw people to him—a trait, I suspect, is from Grandpa Geermann and certainly present in Sallie.

After he'd gone to bed, and the rest of us were thinking about doing as advised, Zoey said mostly to Mark but to Noah and me as well, "This unexpected offer may preclude our plans for a week in Big Bend."

Mark replied, "If we decide it should, we'll need to cancel our rooms down there ASAP."

I said, "I think you should still go. We've got a few days to consider the next steps, and it will give you a little time to reflect on everything. Then you'll still have two weeks after you get back."

Zoey agreed, "That makes sense. We'll stick to the plan in that regard. We scheduled it so we would be here for Quiet Day. We both really enjoyed that last time we were here."

I said, "Betsy is still doing them, and the little faithful group shows up every first Saturday."

While we were talking, Noah had gotten up and gone to his room to call it a night. "You'll note they go to bed the same way they get off the phone."

Zoey said, "It was a little odd to us the first time we stayed here to see Billy just get up and go to bed, but we're used to it by now. It's rather amusing to us."

I stood to retire as well. "I'll say 'goodnight' now myself. When you're here is the only time there's anyone left in the room for me to say 'goodnight' to."

Late summer is *not* Billy's lazy season and he, Noah and I were all up at the crack of dawn to muck the stables and feed the horses.

Billy laid out his plan for the day. "When we first head out after breakfast, I want to stop at the shed to show Mark and Zoey what we're doing with the supplements with the herd now to get truly grass-finished beef. Then at some point, we'll take them along when we replenish the feed in the sections where we've got the cattle."

I concurred with the foreman. "That's a good idea. They'll see what inputs are going into making this a really high quality meat."

Zoey and Mark came out to the pens with their mugs of El Salvadorian coffee just as we were finishing up.

Mark asked, "Does moving out here include a rotation in horse shit management?"

Billy paused long enough from his chore to say, "It could, I suppose. And it would've if Noah hadn't shown up. Now, Jaime and I are inclined not to deprive the boy of such a fun chore."

Noah observed, "It looks to me like we might need to become an eight-horse family. We could let them muck the two new ones."

"There's a thought," I said.

Billy added, "I'm more hoping they get some chickens at their place so we can start having our own eggs. We can attend to their two horses unless they want to keep them over at their place."

Zoey jumped at the suggestion. "I'd love to have some chickens!"

"Well, there you go!" Billy said.

I commented, "Another Billy proposition born on the fly, and adopted just as quickly as it was conceived."

"It is one of my gifts."

"Yours and Sallie's," I said.

Zoey and I headed in to make breakfast while the other three gave a quick brush down to the horses. The dogs, knowing bacon would soon be heating up in the skillet, followed Zoey and me into the house.

Zoey smiled, saying, "I see they still drive you in with their noses on the back of your ankles. That is just too cute."

"They are a little lazier doing that with us since they have the cattle to move on a regular basis, but when it comes to breakfast time, they're still all in on herding me into the kitchen."

I had the oven already preheating so that I could pop a large pan of bacon in rather than try to do batches in the skillet. Zoey started cracking the dozen eggs we'd scramble and fry up with a little grated cheddar and my homemade salsa on top. With the eggs ready to put in the pan as soon as the bacon came out of the oven, she got a fresh pot of coffee going.

She remarked, "I sure like this coffee. It ranks up there with the best dark roasts we can get in California, it seems to me. Have you thought about doing a special custom blend that you could market in whatever brandname you end up using for the beef?"

"That has never crossed our minds. See, your urbanite mind is already coming up with ideas. You'll have to try your idea out on the foreman when he gets in here."

A minute later, the other three were in making themselves comfortable at the large kitchen table where we always eat. Billy and Mark filled their coffee mugs, and I handed Noah the hot chocolate I'd made for him.

I said, "Billy, Zoey had a thought about our coffee."

She shared her idea, and Billy, with his usual enthusiasm for new ideas, responded, "I can see my profile image with cowboy hat down to my boots on the bags now!"

"Your profile image, huh?" I asked. "You're just trying to show off that hind end none of the rest of us have around here."

Billy responded matter-of-factly, "Sallie says, 'Share your gifts.'"

I couldn't disagree altogether with his assessment. "I'm not sure that's what she had in mind, but I suppose a hot cowboy on the label wouldn't hurt sales any."

Noah suggested, "You might want a younger model."

Mark, inspired by the idea added, "You might want two blends —one featuring the old cowboy and one the up-and-coming cowboy."

Billy said, "I'm pretty sure the artist can make me look older or younger according to what our urbanite marketing manager thinks will sell. I do like the idea of two blends—a lighter and a darker roast—not too light, though. If it's gonna be our ranch blends, both need to kick butt."

Noah smiled, saying, "That sounds like a good name for the darkest one—kick-butt coffee blend."

Zoey exclaimed, "That might work!"

Billy added, "Kick-butt morning blend and kick-butt espresso blend. I think it covers both."

Mark said, "We should see what the artist in residence comes up with. Noah, you could get those pencils out and create your first product labels."

I pulled the bacon out as Zoey started the eggs. "For now, we'll get our protein fix for the morning and be on our way. It sounds to me like ideas abound for keeping this old ranch alive."

Just as we sat down, with the windows of the house all opened up, we heard the curve-billed thrasher out singing her beautiful song.

Billy turned his head to the window. "Listen to that thrasher singing her heart out."

One was soon joined by another as they traded their calls back and forth.

He said, "You can bet Sallie's listening with great delight, right now, to the same songs next door."

Noah smiled while saying, "We don't really need any other blessing for this food this morning with those birds offering the gratitude for life."

I agreed, "You've got that right, Noah."

We all went silent giving our ears to the morning songs filling the air.

With breakfast over and everything tidied up, we were preparing for the day's exploration. Billy said, "These dogs are gonna wanna come along. I guess they could ride in the back of the pickup since we're not gonna be going but a few miles an hour."

I assessed the needed accommodation for us all. "I'll throw a bale in the back and sit back there with them."

Noah, always eager to be with the dogs, declared, "I'll ride back there, too."

Billy overrode the plan. "Noah, I had in mind that I'd navigate and you'd drive."

Noah exclaimed, "Uncle Jaime, you're on your own!"

At twelve, Noah was quickly catching up to Billy and me in height. He was already over five feet tall—though just barely. He was almost certain to be at least six feet tall by the time his growing spurt ended. He was nowhere near to the end point of that yet. As soon as he could reach the pedals, Billy had him driving around the ranch. The first couple times was quite entertaining, but by now I was sure our guests would be surprised at just how naturally he could drive better than most with licenses.

As we started out the patio door, two dogs sat looking to see if they were coming along or not. I was the last out the door and turned to them—making them wait in anticipation—amused by their pitiful look. "Come," I said softly, and they tore out the door and did their business including getting a good drink. I jumped up into the back of the pickup and gave two taps to my leg. Both were instantly up in the back with me.

I hollered to the boy behind the wheel, "We're all settled in back here. Drive on, boy."

Chapter Seven

Noah drove the three miles to the cattle guards and crossed over to where the bunkhouse, pens and shed were located. Billy pushed the shed door open all the way to let in plenty of light.

He started in with his explanation of what we'd implemented in the past year. "Once Dad was connected to the internet, he began doing a lot of research on what ranchers were doing to finish organic and grass-fed. Some are just marketing smaller animals and pushing their meat as more lean. Some are grass-fed but not grass-finished, and so those are still feeding grain off grass to get some marbling. The ones Dad was most impressed with are keeping them on grass and getting them marbled. These guys are still getting two to three pounds a day in weight gain, which is very good, with their steers coming in at over 1,100 pounds."

I interjected, "Even the feedlots we all hear about only get two and a half to three pounds a day, and they're spending a lot of money on feed."

Billy said, "And it's damn hard to do anything organically when you're bringing in feed and having animals confined in any close proximity. Spread out, like they are here on the ranch, they are naturally less susceptible to disease."

Just then, Bill and Sallie pulled in. Bill said, "Sallie thought you'd probably start here. We thought we'd chance it to see if she was right. Have you already explained all these barrels to them?"

Billy replied, "No, I just told them about how a lot of the grass-fed is sold lean and others still finish with grain. Why don't you take it from here."

Bill said, "Now, you're gonna look at some of this and wonder why cattle would eat it, but as I'm sure you'll see at some point during your stay, they do indeed eat it up. It's quite a mix of things that offer some surprising benefits.

"First, we've got these ground minerals and volcanic ash which have copper and iodine and other trace minerals that are good for the health of the animal. He went to the next barrel and scooped up a handful of flax seed pellets. "These are flax seed pellets which they love, and we use them to sweeten the minerals and diatomaceous earth, which is this next barrel. The diatomaceous earth actually creates a natural insecticide which kills off any flies or lice that get on the animals. Some will contend it kills internal parasites as well."

Noah interjected, "It's the cootie killer."

Moving along to the apple cider vinegar, Bill continued, "Yes, this and the bags next to it are just what the labels say. You could use them in your kitchen. The vinegar helps keep their rumen naturally acidic, avoiding any bloat problems which is common enough in the feedlots. The baking soda also helps their digestion and the sea salt from Utah salt beds is just for the salt any animal needs."

Billy said, "Ranchers workin' things this way say their bulls are able to breed for nearly twice as long, and they're keeping their best cows for well past a decade."

I added, "And on the grazin' side of things, we move them around in larger herds in smaller pastures to do what they call 'mob grazing'—so they are eating the tops off the shoots and not eating the grass down to the nub."

Bill continued, "And they fertilize as they go and work it into the soil with their hooves. I've long depended on this grazing practice to keep the grass healthy here. Sallie and I just never tried to get them all finished out on grass. Now, we're getting steers and heifers every bit as big as we were getting with grain-finished."

Sallie scooped up a handful of diatomaceous earth and let it filter back into the barrel through her fingers. "When I first was skeptical about this, I said I'd never got marbled up and didn't see how the cattle were going to, but Billy pointed out, I don't eat from morning to night and the cattle do."

Bill concluded, "So, in a nutshell, we have some costs associated with bringing in these barrels and bags, but we're still netting a savings over the feed we were buying or the money we were giving up selling off the calves for someone else to fatten out. The grass is free, and the extra time on it only costs us our labor. I don't see how it's anything but win-win for us and the animals."

Sallie added, "We've never seen our stock as healthy as they are now. The vet isn't getting any business from us."

Bill echoed, "He never did do too well off us, but we sure haven't needed him since adding in all these supplements. They just make for healthier animals."

Mark was nagged by ever-present news reports. "I sure hear a lot on NPR and other places about methane from cattle. What do you do with the argument that plants are a better source for protein than meat if we're going to save the planet?"

Bill answered, "Meat and fish offer the most dense protein there is, so you'd think that would give some merit to them. But to your point, it might not be a surprise for you to hear me say, I don't think they're looking at the big picture.

"Animals thrived by the millions upon millions on the plains and savannas on every continent for millions of years. Methane goes up, fairly quickly turns into CO_2, comes back down in the rains and is returned to the plants as food. Few things can sequester carbon or absorb water as well as a good stand of actively growing grass. We always want the cattle eating off the top third of the plant.

"I've yet to drive by a ranch and smell shit other than from a horse stable, but every time I drive to El Paso I can see the green smog and pollution that hangs over it and Juarez while I'm a good thirty miles from town. It's damn convenient to blame the rancher who's out of sight for their pollution.

"Moreover, every time you turn the soil you let loose CO_2, and other gases for that matter, and that's the very premise of most plant production. Layer on top of that the irrigation required, importation of very seasonal foods from around the planet and the exploited labor needed to keep it all going, and I just don't see that they have a sustainable model there despite all the positive press they are gettin'."

Zoey said, "I can see this marketing is going to be about educating consumers along with selling your brand."

Bill agreed, "I'd say that's right."

Sallie added, "There's a good case to be made. There are more and more who get it. Most of the land is grass and scrub already and it's a lot more sustainable to build on what's there than trying to live off the ever-dwindling arable land which needs constant fertilization and ever-increasing irrigation."

Mark said, "We Californians know well enough about the water wars between farmers and urban areas."

Billy asked, "What's big-Ag gonna do once they've got the aquifers and reservoirs sucked dry?"

Zoey said, "And we know well enough about farm labor too. It's only worse in many of the countries exporting their fruits and vegetables to keep our stores stocked as though all that grows year-round in quaint, little, organic gardens by happy, little farmers."

I commented, "That's where just the label 'organic' doesn't cut it. It could still be from a monoculture crop shipped halfway around the world. It seems to me our beef needs to be sold with the real local connection to the rancher intact."

"Like I said to Zoey, I'd say that's right, too," Bill stated.

Billy was ready to move us onward. "I suppose that's enough to take in for one day in your cattle 101 course. We might just as well go scout out some homesites."

Bill said, "We'll leave you to that. Sallie, Billy and I have already discussed ideas we had. Noah, are you riding along with these dogs in the back, or you wanna come back with us?"

Noah said, "I'm drivin', Grandpa. Jaime's in the back with the dogs."

Sallie gave her customary chuckle, saying, "Noah, don't you be runnin' over any jack rabbits. They just wanna live, too."

"I'll steer clear, Aunt Sallie."

As we walked to the pickup, Billy asked, "Do you want to go from how I would rank the sites, or just how they fall leaving from here and driving straight from one to the other?"

Mark responded, "You're the navigator. However you see fit."

"Okey-dokey," Billy replied. "We've got one this side of the cattle guard and two across the other cattle guard. Noah, drive down a mile and cut to the right." Then to Mark and Zoey he said, "I'm not going to give my ranking when we get there. We'll just look at all three and then either return to whichever one you might want to see again or talk through the pros and cons."

Zoey said, "I think finding any cons out here is going to be a challenge."

Soon after the turnoff, Billy instructed, "Noah, turn in here."

We all got out of the truck including Kola and Koala. Billy said, "See, we've got a well and electricity here already. That's the biggest constraint in building just anywhere on the ranch. Just wander around, and we'll see what, if any, inspiration comes to the resident architect of a kind while he and the dogs look around."

I suggested, "I think you work in 'of a kind' more than I do and that takes some doing."

"I do like it of a kind."

I could see he was pleased with his response, and I said, "It doesn't take much to amuse you."

We were there about twenty minutes when Billy asked, "Ready for site two?"

"Sure," Mark answered for both.

We left the west side of the ranch and headed back towards home. Again, we turned off on a little used ranch road and stopped by the first well. No one said anything this stop, but just did the same relaxed walk-around as before. After about twenty minutes, we loaded up and were off to the final spot. This one was the deepest into the ranch and within sight of the ridge of the family cemetery.

After another twenty minutes Billy asked, "Is there one you'd like to go back to right now for second look, or do you have your mind made up, or do you just want to ponder a bit?"

Mark looked at Zoey. "There was one where Zoey took my hand but didn't say a word. I might be wrong, but I think that's the one that connected with her."

I asked, "Did it connect with you, Mark?"

"It did."

I said, "I saw her take your hand, and I can say if that's what it meant, I had the same feeling."

Noah interjected, "Kola and Koala told me, there was no contest. They thought the second one with the hills on both sides was the one."

Zoey smiled, saying, "I did see both of the dogs were eager to get up on those rocks to have a look around."

"They like bein' high up on things," Noah said.

Billy responded, "Noah, drive us back to site number two then. Let's take another look."

When we got back to the site, Billy said, "For sure this was Sallie's first pick. She said there are bats up in a little cave up the mountain that keep the bugs down. I hope you're not afraid of bats. Like other creatures out here, we let them live as long as they leave us be.

"Now what I thought we'd do, on whichever site, is enclose an acre or so of ground to keep in any dogs or chickens and keep out any coyotes or javelinas. We can't do much about critters that can jump a fence or a wall, but we've never had much of a problem in that regard at the other houses. We'd put a cattle guard here off the road so as to keep the cattle from coming in if the gates are left open. What say ye?"

Both nodded their agreement to his plan.

"Jaime, any ideas coming to mind?" Billy asked.

"I definitely see a small porch looking off to each side of these hills, which will also catch the sunrises and sunsets." I asked Mark and Zoey, "Do you like the adobe blocks at the new house or the plastered look of the old house?"

Zoey asked, "Wouldn't the plaster be a lot cheaper to build?"

Billy answered, "That ain't your worry. If you want adobe just say so. If you prefer the more minimalist, contemporary look just say so. You can ponder on that. I can't think it impacts the floor plan other than the wall thickness."

"That's true enough," I said. "You can let me know what you decide when you decide."

Mark responded, "All right, we'll ponder it then, unless Noah has a directive from either Kola or Koala."

Noah registered the dogs concerns, saying, "They just want you to be sure to include an outside dog water bowl for when they come callin.' They're both gettin' thirsty, and we all left without putting any water in the truck."

I added, "It could be the boy's gettin' thirsty, too."

Zoey said, "It could be a girl has to pee pretty soon, too. You boys have found a convenient spot to relieve yourselves. I'm still holding mine!"

Chapter Eight

Back at the house, I asked Noah, "You wanna get your pencils out and join me in the office to see what you can draw for kick-butt coffee, while I draw a house that's comin' into my mind?"

"Sure."

"I think we might need the dogs to help us, don't you?"

Noah answered, "They can tell us if we're on the right track."

"Well then, the other three of you are going to have to make your own entertainment for a while."

Billy asked, "Aren't we eatin' lunch?"

"How about an early supper instead?" I countered.

He said, "It's all right with me if it's all right with the newcomers to the family. They might not be acclimated to only two meals a day like we are."

Mark responded, "Then it's time we get that way."

Zoey added, "I gather neither artist wants an audience other than the dogs while they create."

"I can guarantee that's the case," Billy replied. "I'm always sent off on my own when either one of them gets their head down into their creative process."

Mark stated flatly, "Boundaries. We all need them."

Billy said, "While they're cooped up inside, I'm going to sit outside. You two can sit wherever you want, and talk or not talk— it's up to you."

Noah kept a sketchbook of things he would draw. Sometimes he would show us one or two and more often he would draw away, close up the sketchbook and put it in his drawer. Neither Billy nor I ever pressed him to show us his work. On this particular day, he quickly sketched out something and set it aside and got his watercolors out. I took that as a sign he must be moving right along with an idea.

I was doing much the same. I hoped they would go with adobe and set the wall depth accordingly. I started with an idea of a very simple structure with a single-slope, low-pitched roofs to give it a more contemporary look—not minimalistic, but certainly simplistic. I was sailing right along with my idea as was Noah with his. I glanced up in the corner of the computer screen to realize four hours had passed, and if we were going to have an early supper, we'd ought to be getting it around. With my latest CAD software, I could pretty easily generate a 3-D elevation, so I did a view from the right front corner showing the front and the end with the chimney for the fireplace. Noah heard me kick off the plotter as it started to print the floor plan and the rendering of the elevation.

He said, "It looks like we'll both have something to show them. I've done all I'm going to on these for now."

"Let me get these two sheets printed, and then we'll trade homework before we show the others. How's that sound?"

"Like a plan," Noah responded.

He had three nice drawings with black-pen and watercolors. I thought it was perhaps the most serious effort he had given to his paints. He had one drawing of the older cowboy profile, clearly Billy, for the kick-butt espresso, one with a boy-cowboy that certainly appeared to be a self portrait for the kick-butt morning blend, and a third watercolor of a logo that could be used for both the coffee and the beef marketing. The logo included the ranch name he'd condensed to GS Ranches, Fort Davis, Texas, and in the center, on a horse, an older cowgirl that was certainly a tribute to Sallie.

He explained, "Showin' Sallie on the label would let people know we respect women."

I said, "We'll see if the urbanites pick up on that without us telling them."

To my plans he said, "These look real nice!"

"Time to show 'em to the world, then."

The other three were in the kitchen. I had suspected as much about fifteen minutes earlier when the dogs scratched at the door to get out of the office. I said to Noah then, "Either they need to pee, or they smell meat coming out of the refrigerator."

Noah replied, "I can tell by lookin'. Kola smells meat."

Kola was right. Billy had steaks out getting them to room temperature and Zoey was starting on a big salad.

Billy saw us with papers in hand. "The art-eests have returned. Whatcha got for us?"

I responded, "Noah and I will take over dinner from here. Y'all can look at our handiwork."

Billy added, "The grill is ready if you are."

"I realize my drawings are just rough ideas," Noah explained. "I'd expect some professional designer to actually make 'em into something if you like 'em at all."

I asked, "Noah, you wanna do the steaks or the salad?"

"I'll grill," and he headed out with the five ribeyes.

Billy noted, "Between his drivin' and grillin' there's less for me do around here all the time."

I added, "I don't think you're bored just yet."

Billy said, "I might not let him drive my black Jag if I ever get one, but I'm glad to ride around the ranch with him driving the pickup."

Mark looked up from the plans long enough to say, "Black Jag? I never pictured you as a Jaguar enthusiast."

Billy explained, "The gay guys who bought the old house in town had a black Jag before they moved here. They've gone for boring now, but Dad and I both liked that car. Dad said we could get him one of the convertibles just to drive around the ranch at night with the top down, though he figured that was a bit of a waste of horsepower.

"They still had the kitty on the hood back then. Now that the new models don't have that leaper on the hood, they've sorta lost most of their appeal."

I repeated my oft clarification. "We don't know that the guys from Dallas are gay, but that's never stopped the great non-labeler from speculating such is the case. I'll grant, it probably is accurate, but we don't know that. All we know is they run an upscale bistro in Alpine and send Bill their mortgage payment like clockwork."

Billy added, "We used to see them in the Slo Poke Cafe a lot, and Rosalinda would always say that Jaime and I looked more gay than they did."

Zoey responded, "From what we've heard about you two in the Slo Poke Cafe, I can understand why."

Billy said, "I like these three drawings of Noah's."

I commented, "I thought you would, given that three Geermann generations are represented."

Zoey said, "We should add somewhere the year the ranch was established."

"You'd think I'd know the year, but we'll have to ask Mom and Sallie," Billy stated. "We'll ask both to see if they agree."

I said, "Your dad probably knows, too, but that is a good idea, Zoey. I'll bet it's pushing a hundred years if not more."

Billy continued, "I know it's over a hundred. It was started by Great-great-grandpa Geermann. In those days it was pretty common to will things to the oldest son. Great-grandpa was both oldest and the only boy. I don't know what his sister got out of it. I'm not sure Sallie would even know that."

Zoey said, "I see Noah has paid homage to Sallie as the central figure of the logo. I like that. Sends an inclusive message."

"I happen to know he'll be thrilled to hear you picked up on that. He said when he was showing these to me, 'Showin' Sallie on the label would let people know we respect women.'"

Mark had barely taken his eyes off the plans since I laid them out on the table. "Jaime, I have one major problem with these plans."

"What's that?" I asked.

"Layin' on this table isn't going to get it built. What're you waitin' on? I like them a lot. I guess we'll see what your sister thinks."

She answered, "I feel like my head's spinning. I can't believe what has transpired just since we stepped off the Sunset Limited yesterday afternoon!"

Billy jested, "Procrastination isn't a trait that runs in this family."

I agreed, "That's an understatement. I didn't even know you knew the word."

Billy said, "It's an ugly word, isn't it? About like optimism and pessimism. I don't like those words either."

Mark asked, "What is it about those two words you don't like?"

Billy answered, "Those words are too much like Mom's fundamentalist days when I had to hear about who was sure they were going to Heaven while the rest of us were consigned to Hell. Optimists are the ones preordaining that the future will fall to the good of its own accord, and pessimists are the ones preordaining the future to fall to the bad. Neither requires any effort of stewardship, which is the only way anything falls to the good."

Mark replied, "I'll never hear those two words the same way again."

Zoey said, "Ditto that."

I added, "Also, you might want to be sure you never use the word 'pride' in any GS Ranches marketing. Nothing drives Bill crazier than this obsession with everyone telling everybody how proud they are of everything."

Billy said, "He has a fit when PBS has some company sponsor— 'Proud sponsor of *Masterpiece Theatre*'—or whatever show is coming on. He says, 'I guess they don't want money from any humble sponsors, so I'll keep mine.'"

Noah had come in with the steaks, hearing just enough to pick up on the topic. He added, "Grandpa says if you want to understand the sin of pride, all you have to do is study any empire and look at anything going on in Washington."

Zoey shook her head, lamenting, "That's for sure."

"Clear the table," I said. "Let's eat. After dinner I'll try to call Ernesto and see if he has any time to build a house before too long. Maybe he can drive out and take a walk-around while y'all are here."

Billy commented, "If he shows up with a John Deere backhoe on his trailer to drop while he's here, you'll know he does."

I said, "We did assure the Mendozas that they have time to mull all this over without any pressure from us."

Billy grinned at Mark and Zoey. "No pressure ... of a kind."

"That's about right," I said.

Mark added, "We're enjoying the ride. I don't think we'll jump off while it's moving."

Zoey laughed, "Ditto that!"

After dinner I rang the Cardonas' number.

"Hey, Rosalinda. It's *Jaime*. How are you?"

"We're well. What can we do for you? Did Bill like the deep-fried turkey?" she asked.

I replied, "He said for gunnysack it was pretty good. That is high praise from Bill for any turkey. Is your husband still working for a living, or has he retired?"

She said, "If it's work for you, I'll see to it he doesn't retire just yet. What you are up to?"

"There is a possibility we might build a casita out on the ranch for Mark and Zoey."

Billy grabbed the phone from me. "Hey, Rosalinda, this is Billy. Just take out the word possibility and put in high probability."

Then he handed the phone back to me. "Hey, Rosalinda, it's me again. I suppose we have to go with the foreman's orders. I was calling to see if Ernesto could run out here tomorrow, or a week or so from now, since Mark and Zoey are going down to Big Bend the day after tomorrow for a week."

"Hang on. He's in the back yard." I heard her holler, "Ernesto! Come to the phone. It's *Jaime*. He's got a project for you."

"*Qué pasa, muchacha?*" Ernesto asked.

"Hey, *loco*. We wanted to see if you could work in a thousand-square-foot adobe in the next year or so."

He asked, "Is Billy throwing you out? Did you jilt his advances once too often?"

"Something like that. We'd be building it for Mark and Zoey, if they decide to move here."

"Hey, that would be great! Mark and I could do a drag act together sometime," he replied.

"I can see from the smile on Mark's face that he heard that, and it wouldn't take much convincing either."

Ernesto asked, "When you want me out there?"

I replied, "They're going to Big Bend for a week starting day after tomorrow."

He asked, "*Mañana está bien*? I could be out there by ten or earlier if you need me there earlier. I know you got your morning chores to do.

"Ten will work. Just come to the house, and we'll go from there."

"*Bueno, muchacha*. See you then."

With that he hung up. I said, "He almost says goodbye."

Billy responded, "The plan rolls on!"

"Speaking of plans, if he's coming out here tomorrow, I need to do some more on these and print him a copy. Mark and Zoey, you might leave cleanup duty to the foreman and his apprentice and come back with me to begin tweaking things as they come to mind."

Billy added, "The foreman and crew have everything in hand out here. Get to it, you three. After all, we've got a ranch to save for the boy here."

Noah smiled, pronouncing, "No pressure."

Chapter Nine

Ernesto came circling around the drive right at 10:00 the next morning with trailer and tractor in tow. When I saw it, I just shook my head at Billy.

Ernesto left the diesel engine running but cranked down the radio as I approached. I said, "You don't have the job yet. Whatcha doing hauling this tractor out here?"

He replied, "It just happened to be hooked up, and I didn't feel like messin' with it this morning."

Billy was there too by now and said, "Just as well. You'll want to start loading up clay from the pit."

Ernesto responded, "This may be my last adobe. I'm seriously thinkin' retirement."

I asked, "I don't guess your crew could keep it going, could they?"

"I'd be glad to sell them everything at the yard plus the tractor with good terms if they wanted to, but so far I haven't had any feelin' they want to take it on."

I asked, "What are you workin' on now?"

"If you want to know when I could start, I'd say in about two weeks. I'm doing some rock work now, but I don't need the tractor anymore for that, so I really could drop it at the pit while I'm here, if you think this is gonna fly."

I replied, "For that we'll have to wait and see. We've dumped a lot on Mark and Zoey just in the past two days. I'm not sure it's sunk in yet."

Billy added, "We're asking them to leave California and help here with direct marketing our beef."

Ernesto said, "Then I take it, they didn't know this was on your radar before they got here?"

I replied, "This wasn't on the radar when I left to pick them up in Alpine. Billy thought of it after I left, and he had already talked to Betsy, Bill and Sallie by the time we were back home."

Ernesto laughed, "That almost seals the deal, doesn't it? One of Billy's quick plans rolls into action."

Billy said impatiently, "The plan ain't rolling into action as long as we sit here. Jaime, round up the strays and let's get going! I'll ride over with Ernesto. Y'all meet us over there."

I knew Billy had updated his folks on the site visits and initial plans including Noah's designs. When we arrived at the site, Betsy, Bill and Sallie were there waiting. Ernesto and Billy had just arrived and Ernesto was shaking their hands.

I asked, "Do you think that handshake is a greeting or sealing the deal? I recall on that Saturday when we went tractor shopping and ran into Bill, within a few minutes Ernesto had the house deal and a new tractor all sealed with a handshake."

Mark said, "I'm pretty sure Bill will wait for our intentions to be confirmed."

I assured them, "He will. He's not compulsive like his son and sister-in-law, but he doesn't flip-flop on any decision once it's made."

Noah interjected, "You can take what Grandpa says to the bank."

"Amen to that," I agreed. "He'll certainly respect whatever you decide, as they all will, but I think you know that."

Zoey said, "Yes, we do."

I nodded my head in their direction. "They're staring at us wondering why we're still sitting in the truck. Shall we?"

I waved everyone over to Billy's pickup, let down the tailgate, signaled the dogs to stay and rolled the plans out for them to take a look. I had a second copy rolled up to give to Bill and Betsy.

I handed the second set to Betsy and said, "I told them how you marked up the set of plans for your house, and Mark and Zoey wondered if you'd give some thought to these as well."

Betsy replied, "We'd be glad to offer some ideas."

Ernesto looked over the plans. "I like 'em. I don't have to tell you if you want to do this, we ought to start while we got the fall to get all the adobes made and laid up."

Bill asked, "So you could take this on this fall?"

"I can start in two weeks, and I could have Mando and Tanya hauling clay from the pit between now and then."

Bill replied, "When and if we can start will be Mark and Zoey's to decide. But we'll not leave you hanging."

Billy, Sallie, Betsy, Zoey and Noah all wandered over to imagine exactly where the house might sit.

Mark confirmed their intentions. "We'll give you a decision as soon as we're back from Big Bend. I'm trying to work out in my mind what my own work is going to look like if I'm doing it all remotely from here. That's really our only hurdle to saying 'yes' right now."

Bill said, "That's totally understandable."

Ernesto asked, "Mark, what kinda work do you do?"

"I'm a tech geek. I support large database systems—a DBA as they say. I almost never have to go into data centers where the actual hardware is running anymore, but right now, they also know I'm less than an hour away. I'll have to convince my clients they don't need me there even if they think they do.

"I would probably have to get two different satellite providers out here just to have the redundancy. Jaime and I already looked into that last evening."

Bill said, "I've been thinking about talkin' to Ma Bell or Big Ben Tel about running fiber out here and getting rid of the satellite, but I'm not prepared to say that's any kind of option. I know fiber runs out along the highway, but I don't know where they could tap into it exactly, or how proud they'd be of it to run it the few miles we'd need to get to all three sites."

Ernesto added, "They'll be proud of it. You can count on that."

Bill responded, "It won't cost me anything to check into it. That's the top item on my to-do list."

Mark suggested, "It's possible they'd be interested in putting a tower on one of your peaks and might cut you a good deal with microwave or wireless."

Bill clearly liked that possibility. "I hadn't thought of that!"

Ernesto added, "You might get free service out of that deal if they can use the tower for cell service."

Bill replied, "As long as no one has to really look at it, a tower would be all right by me. Good idea, Mark!"

Ernesto rolled up the plans and handed them to me. "*Jaime*, your to-do list will be to get me the usual sets of copies I need once it's a go."

"Sure," I said.

Then Ernesto said, "Mark, the first New Year's you're out here you and I should dress for *Nine to Five*. Of course, I'll be Dolly and you get your pick between Jane Fonda or Lily Tomlin. It would be a good way to introduce you to Fort Davis."

Mark replied, "I don't know. I haven't been in a dress for over twenty years."

"You can pull it off," Ernesto assured him.

"Good lord," Bill said. "Mark, you'll fit in around here better than I realized."

Ernesto said, "Bill, I don't know why you don't ever come in to ring in the New Year."

Bill answered, "I go by the Swiss clocks of my ancestors so I can get to bed at my usual time. I don't like seeing 12:00 more than once a day and when the sun's up."

Ernesto laughed, "You don't know what you're missing."

I commented, "With Billy's account of the evening, it's the next best thing to being there."

Bill concurred, "I can agree with that."

We wandered over to where the others were. Ernesto asked, "Are we ready to strike a line where the front wall will set? Bill and Betsy knew just where they wanted theirs."

Zoey instructed, "Billy and Betsy go to your corners."

They each walked in opposite directions, stopped, turned and faced each other. Zoey said, "That's where they stepped off and suggested as their possibility. I like it. What do you think, Mark?

He considered the lay of the land for a couple minutes and said, "Ernesto, string your line."

"Hot damn!" Billy exclaimed.

I said, "I'll get the stakes, mallet and string from your truck, Ernesto."

He replied, "*Gracias, muchacha.*"

Noah commented, "Sallie taught me *muchacha* was a girl."

Ernesto said, "I call all my helpers *muchachas* or *chicas*. I won't say what they call me."

Billy reached up to put his hand on Ernesto's shoulder. "Pope Chuy has been such an influence on you, I'm not even sure I can still call you badass Ernesto anymore. You could teach Sunday School for the Baptists these days."

He responded, "Suggest that to Rosalinda and Lupe next time you see them. I'm sure they'll agree."

As I walked by I nodded for Ernesto to follow. "I'm pretty sure they'll agree badass Ernesto lives on and will have to disappoint the Baptists."

Ernesto snickered, "Those Baptists would interfere with my barbecue watching, too. They'd be ridin' my ass for missing one Sunday. I'll stick with the Catholics. I've gotten them all broken in."

We set the line for the house. Ernesto asked us to follow him to the pit and help unload the tractor.

Bill asked, "Isn't that gettin' a little ahead of ourselves?"

Ernesto replied, "It can sit out here as good as it can in Fort Davis. Either way it's comin' off the trailer today. I need my trailer. I'd just as soon risk it, given I know how this family makes decisions—including the Cruzes who become part of it."

"Amen to that," I said.

The next morning, Mark and Zoey were off for what they'd thought was going to be a week of relaxation and exploring in Big Bend. Now, we'd layered on a massive dose of reflection time to their agenda. We agreed to phone-and-email blackouts both ways during their stay. Mark intended to touch base with his clients, but otherwise they too were going "off the grid."

Bill thought he'd better bring Brett, Jean and Mary-Alice up to speed on the quick plan that had come together over the past three days. They all came out to spend the weekend—the girls and Brett in the bunkhouse since Mark and Zoey had been using Brett's room at the house. We had offered to get it ready for him, but brother and sister agreed to sharing the bunkhouse.

Billy stated, "That almost falls into the category of a bonafide miracle."

I said, "I'm sure since we've given him a regular room here, Jean figured it was the right thing to do."

Billy added, "He's not a bore anymore; it's no real sacrifice on their part."

"True enough," I agreed.

When we arrived at the house, all three were surprised that Mark and Zoey weren't there. They had thought this was probably a welcome dinner for our guests. Little did they know the family dynamic was about to be altered, yet again. I didn't drop any hints. I just said that since Mark and Zoey were going to be around for a month, they wanted to spend a week in Big Bend. Beyond that, they didn't even seem curious as to why there was a family dinner a week ahead of the usual Quiet Day weekend when they would all be there anyway.

For the first time since this all began, I had a bit of a panicked feeling. I motioned for Billy and Sallie to follow me back to her office and closed the door.

I asked, "I don't know why I'm just thinking of this, but are either of you concerned that Brett or Jean—mostly Jean I'd say—is going to wonder why one of them wasn't considered for taking on what's been offered to Zoey?"

Sallie replied, "Jaime, your frettin' about this just ain't necessary. Bill has sunk money into getting Brett set up in real estate, which is the thing he likes to do and is good at. You know, as well as I, that ranch life isn't his life. I'd be all too glad to remind him the debt he owes his momma and daddy if he even thought about saying anything about Zoey doing this. I think he's come along enough; she'll be welcomed by Brett.

"Where Jean is concerned, she's said it herself. She wants everything neatly in a column. We say she's persnickety, and she doesn't deny it—Mary-Alice even says it. I love those girls, but they are strictly numbers people. Jean gets her head for numbers from my daddy, but she didn't get anything of his personality. You can look at their home and see neither one has a creative bone in their body. The only bold thing they ever did was hang that neon Corona beer sign back over their gay bar in the backyard.

"And, Jean and Mary-Alice both like risk and change about as much as they'd like a hole in the head. Jean wouldn't know where to start with something like this, but Zoey could see right away where this could head."

Billy interjected, "Jaime, she's got your gift for seeing what can be. I've been around her enough to see that."

Sallie added, "That's what inspired Billy in the first place—and when he came over here to talk about his idea, it didn't take any persuading. We see it, too."

"Everything you say makes sense, as usual," I said. "I feel a lot better than I did when I saw them all in the room just a bit ago."

Sallie chuckled, "Leave it to your Aunt Sallie's gift for being tough in theory should any intervention be needed. When necessary I can speak my mind, as you well know!"

"Really? Mild mannered Aunt Sallie?" Billy joked.

Sallie said, "They'll be wondering what we're up to back here. We'd best get sociable."

When we joined the others, I'm not sure we were really missed. Bill had them engaged in the newest family plan to keep the ranch alive, and he was spelling out exactly how Zoey's role fit into that.

I breathed a huge sigh of relief when Jean said, "That sounds like a fantastic idea," and Brett added, "I agree with that."

Bill said, "There's one other thing I've been thinking about that we still might want to address, which is being sure that we can get all this meat processed exactly how we want it. That may take some investment up front to help the processor we've always used, or one or two others. We've got to ensure quality all the way through. But that's all mine to do. I've been ponderin' on this the last few days, and I will start doin' something about it in the next week or two."

Billy asked, "Have they seen Noah's ideas for the logo and the coffee labels?"

"I hadn't gotten around to the coffee yet. Noah, fetch your drawings. They're out in the office."

Billy commented, "We thought we could market two special blends of the El Salvadorian coffee under our ranch brand."

Jean asked, "What are we calling all this?"

Bill noted, "Noah just called it GS Ranches. I guess we'll need to see if that's already registered, or if we want to call it something else."

Noah was back with the three drawings.

Brett commented, "These models look rather familiar."

Jean exclaimed, "Kick-butt coffee—leave it to the foreman and his sidekicks to come up with a name like that!"

Noah noted, "We still want to add to the logo what year the ranch was established. None of us knew."

Sallie said, "That one I can answer—1887. Next year will be 125 years in the Geermann family."

Billy had another sudden inspiration, "We should create 'The 125 Summer Sausage' brand to market with our online sales of the coffee. That way it's tied to the year we launched all this."

Betsy said, "I made Momma's sausage a few times but haven't for a long time. I'm not sure why. I just forgot about it."

Bill added, "We might want two varieties—125 Tame and 125 Kick-butt that's got some good heat to it."

Noah had a big grin on his face. "I might have to marry early and start having kids right away to keep all this going."

Billy expressed his dissatisfaction with such a notion. "You don't need to be thinkin' about your breedin' program just yet."

Bill concurred, "I'll second that. No need to get an early start!"

Betsy said, "You don't need to race with your brothers and sister to see who makes me a great-grandmother first."

"I'm in no hurry for any of my kids to start on that," Brett said. "I hope they've learned from my mistakes not to rush into marriages where you don't even know who you're marrying or why. Have you learned that, Noah?"

Noah said, "I suppose I have. I guess a nice boy might come along I'd have to give proper consideration to, like Uncle Billy and Aunt Jean gave consideration to, of a kind."

"Noah, that's right for a start," Sallie agreed. "And I never married and never regretted not gettin' married. Whether you do or don't doesn't matter. If this ranch dies out before the next 125 years that doesn't matter either. We can't worry about what might happen down the road. All we can do is tend to it while we're here."

Bill said, "The old gal is right about that."

Sallie noted, "Just as a reminder, I'm not that much older than your granddaddy here, but he likes to think I am. I'm old enough, I'll grant that."

Betsy, pleased to ribbed her husband, quipped, "And, as you will all recall, your father says the three of us are old farts."

Bill lamented, "I'm still payin' the price for that. These two work in all kinds of comments to remind me of my transgression on an almost daily basis."

Chapter Ten

Zoey and Mark were back in time for our customary Friday night family dinner before the September Saturday Quiet Day. When they arrived at our house, I figured Billy would be beside himself to get their decision. Noah beat him to it.

They no sooner were out of my pickup when he asked, "Are you leaving California to join us cowboys?"

Mark ruffled his hand through Noah's hair, which I realized in that moment was long overdue for a good trim.

He said, "Noah, you're gonna have to get used to two more people out here on the ranch."

Billy exclaimed, "Hot damn!"

I asked, "Billy, do I call Ernesto now, or do I wait for the family to know."

"I'll call Mom and Dad, and then you can call Ernesto. We said we wouldn't keep him hangin'."

While Billy shared the good news with his folks, Zoey, Mark and I sat down on the chaises. I asked, "How was the park?"

Zoey replied, "We loved it. It was just the place to wrap our heads around all this, and we know it is the right thing to do."

I asked, "Mark, what's your family going to think about you taking off for West Texas?"

He said, "I don't think they'll be all that surprised. We've talked about this place so much that my dad even said he wasn't sure why we didn't just move out here."

"Oh, that's good. And, between the second bedroom and the bunkhouse, we can certainly accommodate any Mendoza family visits."

Mark added, "The only emails I did all week were with my clients, and when I laid out what Zoey would be doing out here, they decided they'd rather keep me from afar than replace me. It looks like my client base is secure for the moment. I also have enough head-hunters chasing me all the time so, even if I had to, I could always find work."

I replied, "That's great. By the way, Bill shared the offer with Brett, Jean and Mary-Alice. Their exact reaction was, 'Fantastic.'"

"Oh, that's good to hear," Zoey said.

Noah came out to summon me. "Uncle Billy says to get on the phone to Ernesto."

"*Jawohl*," I responded. "The *kommandant* has issued the order. I'll be back in a minute."

It was more like five minutes. By the time I was off the phone with Ernesto, Billy and Noah had settled in on the patio as well.

Noah said, "We was just tellin' 'em about 125 Tame and 125 Kick-butt summer sausage."

Zoey commented, "What a great idea! And launching all this on the 125th anniversary of the ranch is a happy coincidence."

Noah added, "Nobody seems to have thrown out my drawings yet, but they were just to get ideas going. I want to work on them some more."

I said, "We'll see where the spirit takes you."

He responded, "I'll take things along to Quiet Day. It might help in the inspiration department."

"I'm not sure kick-butt artwork aligns too well with Quiet Day inspiration, but I guess we'll see. We still need to nail down whether we can call it GS Ranches—or if someone's had an idea for some other name. I did a search of the US trademark database, and it looks like it should work. I assume Jean would be the one to know about what we have to do to set it up as a DBA in Texas."

Noah asked, "What's a DBA? I thought Mark was a DBA."

I responded, "You're right, Noah. Mark is a DBA. This DBA predates Mark's kind of DBA. Since the ranch is its own trust, and we want to do business under another name, we have to set up the name as 'doing business as,' which is what this kind of DBA stands for. In this instance, it would be the Geermann-Schlatter Ranch Trust doing business as GS Ranches. *Capiche*?"

Noah reasoned, "I don't know what capish is, but I'm guessing 'yes' is the right answer."

I said to Noah, "The next order of business before we head over for supper is for you to get your hair cut. Grandpa will be gettin' the cattle shears out if we don't trim up that mop. I'll get the clippers. You get the cuttin' cape."

Zoey and I had decided, while we were together and at Quiet Day, that we'd once again cast out seeds towards those estranged in California. We thought they ought to at least know that she would be moving here when the new house was done, and we weren't sure if there was much to say beyond that. She had her laptop with her, and would bring it to Quiet Day. We'd both attempt to write something and then put it together as a letter from both of us. Then I'd print it up and get it in the mail.

Between the 7:30 service and the 10:00 service in the chapel, we didn't make any headway. We would look at each other, and I'd stare down at my still-empty page and she at her empty screen. Between the 10:00 service and noon, we didn't do any better. Maybe after lunch we'd finally make some headway. Or maybe trying to do this without talking, as was the way of Quiet Day, just wasn't going to work.

We made one last run at it after lunch. Zoey pieced together my scribblings with her thoughts. Of course, we let Billy and Mark read it after Quiet Day was over.

Mark commented, "You thought of more to say to them than I could have ever come up with."

Billy added, "You both have beautiful thoughts."

Dear Strangers,

We can't pretend as a family that we are anything other than that— strangers. For the two of us, that is no longer the case. Our lives have moved beyond the empty, hollow shells we occupied for so long, and are now conjoined into a new kind of whole that neither of us conceived as a possibility just a few short years ago. One's solace and acceptance in his West Texas desert home led to the healing and acceptance of the other. Soon, we shall both call this place home.

The Geermann-Schlatter family has embraced us in an affection we never knew as a family—though they, too, had years of wounds to heal. We have healed with them, and this has led the Mendozas of Oxnard, California (Mark and Zoey) to plan to move to Fort Davis with the one Cruz who settled here more than ten years ago. Neither of us would be recognizable to the three of you on most any level.

It is our hope that you have found solace and happiness in your lives through events beyond yourselves just as we have. If you have not, then we pray such may still come to you one day.

Now, we take life as it comes to us—and know that gratitude for the simple joys of life and for all creation is the great calling of us all. We wish you peace and joy.

Your daughter and sister; son and brother,

Zoey and Jaime

Noah was back in the house with Kola and Koala and found us all seated at the kitchen table. He asked, "Whatcha doin'?"

I answered, "We just let Mark and Billy read a letter Zoey and I have written for our parents and brother."

Noah said, "You'd better read it out loud to me and the dogs to see if we have anything to add. Remember, they were born in a shelter, and you know what I lived through."

I smiled at him and read the letter aloud.

Noah commented, "You didn't cry or even get choked up."

Zoey asked, "Do you and the dogs have anything to suggest?"

Noah looked at the two contented red heelers and said, "We're in agreement—it's good as is."

I said, "The cosmic force of love has spoken. We shall toss the seeds to the wind."

Noah smiled, saying, "If that means you're gonna mail 'em, that's good."

Part II

Chapter Eleven

Bill, Betsy and Sallie made their ten-day January trip to El Salvador to visit the village and surrounding communities and farms that were so much a part of their generosity and Father Chuy's home and life. Chuy met them at the airport in San Salvador and drove them on the two-hour drive west to his mountain parish.

Betsy reflected, "The lushness of the mountains and beauty of all the small coffee *fincas* were just incredible."

"Here we struggle to get the grass to grow," Sallie added. "There you need a machete to cut back the jungle before it takes over."

"Sallie got halfway acquainted with a dozen new birds including several big colorful parrots," Bill said.

She chuckled, "Well, their Spanish and my Tex-Mex varied some so we were limited in our conversation. I'd need more time there to get really acquainted. Billy, you might be kin to those Geoffroy's spider monkeys down there. You've got their big black eyes, and they like to show off their hind end, too."

She was most amused by her connection of the spider monkeys to Billy.

Bill added, "Billy, they'd give you and Ernesto both a run for your money in the entertainment department, that's for sure. Between all the different calls they chatter to each other, they also can shake the trees like crazy when they don't like what they see coming their way."

"Of course, they liked Sallie," Betsy said.

Sallie chuckled again. "Chuy and I both had one riding up on our backs half the time I was there—their arms hangin' on around our necks. I said to Chuy, 'I hope he doesn't decide he's had enough of this particular *gringa* and ring my neck.' He said, 'Clearly, he thinks you're a kindred spirit.'"

"Clearly, Chuy is a kindred spirit with those people," Betsy observed. "They have *such* affection for him. He's got Elma's faith, Ernesto's charm and Saint Francis' humility."

Bill added, "We went to every Mass he did which meant at least one a day, and when those people would come forward for communion, they looked like it was Jesus himself passing out the bread."

Sallie stated, "Well, that is his name. He's *Jesús* down there, not Chuy. He couldn't be more suitably named."

"That's for sure," Betsy said. "There was a time in my life when I would have judged anyone for naming someone after Jesus. Now I looked at Chuy and thought Jesus isn't just in Chuy's heart, he's in his hands, and smile and every fiber of his being."

Bill said, "They all call him *Padre Jesús*, of course, which sounds a little funny to me only because he still looks like a boy. He always did have a boyish look, and that hasn't changed at all."

"And Rosalinda is right—you never saw such happy people," Betsy added.

Billy inquired, "I guess the new school is all done by now."

Bill replied, "Oh, yes, and it's simple like everything is down there, but they just think it's wonderful. Noah, your history teacher really ought to assign an international education assignment sometime. I would like all of you to get down there one of these years."

Sallie noted, "Billy, you're not going to get a hot shower while you are there. I don't think we saw a hot water tank anywhere including where we were put up."

Billy reflected, "The appeal of the place just plummeted."

I said, "Well it is the tropics. They're probably looking to cool down more than heat up."

Bill said, "It's that and their natural inclination to frugality."

"And yet, they are such artistic people," Betsy added. "Their weaving and carving and painting—so much indigenous arts and crafts that they use for both practical things and things clearly for the joy of it."

Bill added, "With such welcoming and loving people in such a beautiful place, you wonder how governments in these countries can be so inept and corrupt. Of course, our own government is only too happy to stir the pot at every opportunity."

Sallie said, "At least Chuy's parish is well away from the violence."

Noah asked, "So how are the farmed fish? Did you eat some?"

Bill replied, "That's *mostly* what we ate and they were good. They have a-dozen-ways-to-Sunday on how to fix 'em."

Noah asked, "No canned tuna, gunnysack or kale?"

"I'm delighted to say none of the above! I did eat fruit I'd never bothered much with in this country, and the avocados were huge."

Billy asked, "Any more projects comin' up that Chuy needs money for?"

"He's no money-grubber that's for sure." Bill continued, "I asked him exactly that, and he said they didn't really need anything right now. With the fair trade coffee going well and the fish they can now market, they are on a sustainable course. He said if we wanted to make another gift, he could talk to the bishop and with his fellow Franciscans to see what other needs could be met."

Sallie added, "I'd gladly give if I thought the money was going into hands and hearts like Chuy's."

I commented, "That's the great unknown always when you don't have a personal connection. Are you helping or funding the corruption?"

"Jaime, you hit the nail on the head," Bill said. "Chuy seems to be pretty confident with the work of his Order, but even he said he had some concerns, given the widespread corruption. As he put it, even the best intentions can be undermined if you are not right there in the middle of it."

Billy asked, "So how'd you leave it?"

Bill replied, "We'll still rely on him to tell us of a need, though we aren't going to hold it against him if what we give it for doesn't ever come to fruition."

Noah said, "If it's anything Elma is prayin' for, it seems to come about."

Sallie smiled at the boy, "Too true. Too true."

As with the first house, Bill served as project manager for the build of Zoey and Mark's abode. Technically, I covered for him during his brief time away in January—but with his management skills, I didn't really have to do anything while he was away. He had it all in hand before he left.

This time, I wouldn't be part of the crew building it, but Billy and I had no lack of things to work on. With Ernesto's tractor, we dug down enough to bury a good portion of fence to be sure the javelinas and coyotes couldn't dig in under it. We decided that with the rise the house sat up on, we could put up a game fence, and it wouldn't be an eyesore. As with both existing houses, we made sure we had some gravel around the structure as a firebreak. We got the pipe to fabricate the cattle guard, and we built a nice solar-powered, automated gate for the entrance to their drive.

I put the few carpenter skills I had acquired while working with Ernesto to good use. With Billy and Noah's help, we built a chicken coop complete with laying nests, automated waters, roosts and a large outdoor run. We had critter-proof barrels for Zoey to store the feed.

Billy said, "We do need to warn them to look in the nest before they go reaching in for an egg. Our fence isn't going to keep rattlesnakes from looking for a fresh omelette."

Noah asked, "Since God made cattle dogs, did he make chicken dogs, too? Maybe they need a couple dogs to keep the snakes away."

Billy answered, "There ain't no chicken dogs that I know of. I've heard foxes and raccoons help keep snakes away, but they'd both rather eat the chickens than the eggs. I guess she could try a few guinea hens in the yard. I've heard a flock of those will go after snakes. We'd have to figure out something higher up for them to roost in at night. They don't wanna be cooped up, but if you don't have someplace for them to call home, they'll go shopping for one. Sallie will end up with Zoey's guineas roosting in that big desert willow outside her room."

I concluded, "It sounds like looking, before you go reaching, is the best first step."

Bill got his hilltop lease for a communications tower, and we all got faster Internet. We decided for Mark's redundancy needs to move our dish over to their place, and Bill got rid of his altogether.

I was emailing Mark and Zoey pictures of the progress as it went along. By the end of March, my email simply read,

Move-in ready, whenever you're ready. Jaime

Their plan was to rent a large moving truck and tow their car. We didn't need to worry about furniture—they had enough to adequately furnish the new house. Betsy had coordinated with them for all the appliances needed. They'd have everything new in that regard.

The email back from Zoey read,

We'll be there before your birthday! Zoey

I said to Billy, "I'm not exactly sure when they'll roll in but it will be before May 6."

Billy replied, "We can make it a joint birthday and welcoming party with the Cardonas and Elma, too."

"I'd like that," I said. "It will be good to see Elma again, but I think we should give them time to settle in. Instead of my birthday, how about a joint party when Elma and Noah's birthday rolls around?"

Billy said, "Even better!"

A couple days later I got another email from Zoey.

Jaime, Billy and Noah,

We can't stand it. We're heading your way. We should be there by Monday the 9th. See you in a week!

Zoey

Noah said, "They're missing me."

I replied, "You *and* Billy, I'm sure."

On Monday morning, the 9th, I got an email time-stamped 6:05 AM.

Just left the hotel in El Paso. Zoey

Billy asked, "Is that time stamp showing Central or Mountain time? El Paso's an hour earlier than here, you know."

"That's a good question. I'd assume El Paso time."

Billy said, "If that's the case they should be rolling in around 10:30. I'd assume with the truck and pullin' a car, it'll take them an extra half hour or so."

"I would think so."

Billy noted, "We can wait for them as easy over there as here. We'll head over right at 10:00."

"Okey-dokey. Is this boy drivin' himself to school, or are we givin' him the day off?"

Noah said, "Seems like you might need my help."

Billy replied, "Seems like you should keep your teachers occupied so they don't think they have to come unload a truck."

Noah agreed, "I suppose they might feel obligated. I guess I'll go to school today, Jaime."

"Okey-dokey," I said again. "Get goin' then."

Apparently the faculty had other ideas. We were at Mark and Zoey's abode by 10:00. Bill, Betsy, Sallie and Noah rolled in right at 10:05 with Betsy carrying a big pan of tamales, and Sallie a big bowl of guacamole. Bill had a set of plates and silverware, and Noah the chips and salsa and a twelve pack of La Croix drinks.

Betsy said, "A bit off the diet, but by way of celebration."

I didn't object. "Those tamales smell wonderful!"

She popped them into the oven to keep them warm.

Almost on the dot, Mark and Zoey pulled in at 10:30 and looked no worse for wear after their long drive. Before we started to unload, they naturally wanted to wander through their new home.

Mark exclaimed, "I smell tamales! "Oh, those smell good. I certainly wasn't expecting that!"

Bill said, "Brett used to tell people to boil some cinnamon sticks before people came to look at the house they were selling. I told him, if you want me to buy the place, pop some tamales in the oven!"

Zoey looked out in the back corner of the property. "I see I have a chicken coop! You never sent me any pictures of that."

Noah said, "We wanted that to be a surprise."

"Well, mission accomplished. I'll take a good look at it later."

Bill said, "I hope it was an uneventful drive over."

Mark replied, "Almost. We had the truck parked as near to our room last night as we could, and about 2:00, I heard an alarm go off. I bought one of those locks for the truck and another for the hitch for the car that goes off if someone tries to tamper with them. I jumped up, and I saw two guys running back to their pickup and then take off."

"Good thing you had 'em alarmed," I noted.

Zoey said, "That's for sure. It certainly would have ruined the trip if the car or the stuff in the truck was gone this morning."

Sallie joked, "I don't suppose the alarms came with a built-in Taser to give 'em a good jolt for their efforts."

Mark replied, "No, just a hell of a noise. I had to go out and reset it, of course, and the rest of the night was quiet."

Zoey added, "As quiet as it gets when you are a hundred yards from I-10 which isn't very quiet. Between being keyed up already, and that alarm and the traffic all night, we didn't get much sleep— but we didn't want to drive out here in the dark either. I'm sure we'll be turning in early tonight."

Billy pressed us onward. "To that end, that truck ain't gonna unload itself. Let's get to it!"

Sallie chuckled, "The foreman has spoken. Welcome to our world!"

Chapter Twelve

Billy decided it was getting too confusing which house was which. We used to refer to the new and old house. Now we had two new houses. He thought we should have names for each.

I said, "You're the one who came up with *La Capilla de la Rosa* for the chapel. You have anything in mind this time? Hopefully a little shorter than that last one."

Billy deflected, "Noah, let's see how you're coming with your Spanish lessons. What name would you give all three houses if they were Spanish names?"

He thought about it a while. "Maybe *Vista Grande* for Grandma, Grandpa and Sallie's place because of that view off the ridge."

I said, "That sounds about right to me."

Then he continued, "And maybe *Cielo Lindo* for Mark and Zoey's because of the way that sky gets framed between those two rises."

Billy pronounced, "I think you're on a roll. What about here?"

"That's easy. *Perros Locos*."

I said, "I don't know about that. I'm pretty sure I just heard Kola say, '*Hombres Locos*,' maybe."

Billy suggested, "I think we'll need to keep workin' on that last one but I like the other two. I guess we'll have to see if the occupants approve."

I agreed, "We wouldn't want them thinkin' the foreman was dictating the names of their own homes."

Billy commented, "Comin' from Noah I doubt they'll get that idea."

When we shared our naming ideas with their occupants, Bill said, "Noah, if you draw something out for *Vista Grande*, I'll get one of those UV-protected, carved signs made and one for anyone else that wants one for their house."

Sallie added, "I'm with Kola on the name for y'all's place. *Hombres Locos* is a lot more fittin' than *Perros Locos*."

"I suppose it should be a name that can live past its current occupants anyway," Billy noted.

Sallie said, "It is the old house. You could just call it *Casa Vieja.* It ain't gonna get any younger."

"I like that," I concurred.

Mark said, "We like *Cielo Lindo.*"

Zoey added, "Noah, if you want to design a sign for us, that would be wonderful."

Sallie said, "We never have put a sign out on the road comin' back here. I think we should get one made for out front where the road splits that has 'GS Ranches' and the names of the three houses with arrows pointing in the right direction."

Betsy noted, "They sure are trying to keep you busy, Noah."

Noah replied, "Between homework and chores, I get plenty to do, that's for sure. Child labor, and I don't even get an allowance."

Billy asked, "What would you do with an allowance? The only place we ever go is the Slo Poke Cafe, and we always buy. Out here you get everything for free. I guess Jaime could pay you an allowance, and then I could start chargin' you rent."

Noah answered, "I wasn't gripin'. Just statin' fact." Then he added, "Hadn't we oughta get goin' on Elma's and my birthday party and Mark and Zoey's welcome to the neighborhood party?"

Betsy agreed, "Yes, we do need to do that. It'll be here before we know it, and the Rodriquezes may already have something planned for Elma."

Sallie said, "We could always shift a day or two if they've already lassoed the 10th."

I offered, "Let me go call Lupe right now and ask her."

I went in to use the phone in the kitchen at *Vista Grande* and told Lupe what we had in mind.

She replied, "That will make *Mamá's* day. I haven't heard from any of my siblings that they were doing anything yet so consider the 10th confirmed!"

"Wonderful," I responded. "It's a Sunday so let's plan on after-church lunch here at Bill, Betsy and Sallie's, which Noah has named *Vista Grande.*"

"Oh, that's a good name for it. You know we'll bring eggs and cake."

I replied, "And you know they'll be greatly appreciated and gobbled up."

She asked, "Did you know Chuy was coming home for a short visit? I'm not sure of the dates, but I think he may be coming home about that time."

"My next call is to Ernesto and Rosalinda. I'll find out shortly. It would be wonderful if he was here then. I just hope our plan doesn't stomp on their run to El Paso to pick him up."

Lupe said, "Just let me know if we have to move the date. I'm sure they'll want to be there."

I decided before I updated the family on Lupe's confirmation, I'd better call Rosalinda. We chatted just long enough to get things confirmed. I went back to give my report.

"Chuy, Lupe and Elma are confirmed for after church on the 10th. They will bring deviled eggs and the cake. Ernesto and Rosalinda will bring one other guest with them. *Padre Jesús* is coming in on the 8th for a week's visit."

Bill exclaimed, "Oh, that's wonderful!"

I added, "Rosalinda was going to call us about getting together but just hadn't gotten it done yet. They just found out he was coming home yesterday. She said Ernesto will bring brisket and chicken if we are interested. As he put it, 'The Schlatters can host— I'll cook.'"

Bill inquired, "I assume you accepted."

"I did."

Billy said, "We've got brisket at *Casa Vieja* we can drop off next time we're in town. At least we can contribute the beef."

Sallie noted, "Noah, you becomin' a teenager is turnin' into quite a celebration!"

Billy, wanting to rib Noah, said, "I suppose becomin' a teenager he'll be thinkin' a new pair of cowboy boots and hat are in order."

Zoey commented, "I take it surprise parties and wrapped gifts aren't big in this family."

I clarified, "Billy, Noah and I like to announce gifts well ahead of time in case we need to threaten their withdrawal."

Noah added, "I'll hear half a dozen times between now and then Billy or Jaime sayin', 'Memo to self—cancel cowboy boot order for Noah,' and the other one sayin', 'Memo to self—cancel cowboy hat order for Noah.' It don't take much to get somethin' on or off a list around here."

Sallie said, "These boys do a lot of verbal corresponding by memo—that's a fact."

Billy added, "Memo to Zoey—get up to speed on ranch communications."

"Memo to Billy—consider it done," she responded.

At Noah's 10th and Elma's 93rd, the two had been matched in height, and as Ernesto had said, one was going to tower over the other soon enough. Now, Noah was a foot taller, and while still lanky in stature, he looked so much larger than tiny Elma.

Billy, Noah and I all went up to hug her ever so gently, and we asked her how our favorite *abuela* was. She had always just said in return that she was ancient. This year she had a different answer, and one that caught all three of us slightly off guard.

She smiled at us with her still-bright eyes. "This is your *abuela's* last birthday. I'm not going to see ninety-seven."

She didn't seem a bit distraught by such news. I naturally wondered if this was some prognosis from the doctor.

Lupe said, "*Mamá* is convinced that her time has come. She's been saying for the past month, 'Lupe, this cake will be the last one you ever bake with me. You'll have to do it on your own from here on.'"

Elma smiled and touched Noah's cheek. "Noah, I've had so many prayers answered in my life. My last one is that I die peacefully in my own home. You'll pray for me, won't you?"

"Of course, I will, Grandma Elma," Noah assured the old woman.

Billy added, "We all will."

"Oh, thank you boys. You're all such nice boys. Lupe understands. My other children pretend I'm going to keep living. I know my time is done. I'm ready."

Billy said, "Mom says when she looks at you while you two pray together in the chapel, she sees a saint."

"I do want to go in the chapel with your mother. Do you think we could do that now? But I'm no saint."

Lupe stated, "*Mamá*, if you aren't, no one is."

"Amen to that!" I said.

Billy spoke to say, "Noah, go get your Grandma. I'll walk Elma to the chapel."

Elma asked, "Lupe, why don't you see if young Chuy would come pray with us, too?"

"Okay *Mamá*," Lupe replied, and was off to retrieve *Padre Jesús* who was there in his brown Franciscan tunic.

We always left the two of them alone together when they went in to pray. We never knew if they sat silently or prayed out loud together. Since neither ever said, we never wanted to ask. We urged Noah not to ask as well. This time they were in there longer than usual. Perhaps the humble *padre* was the reason. We began to wonder if we should go ahead with the meal, as neither would want any fussing over them and, certainly, none of us were going to go call them for lunch.

Sallie ordered, "None of us are starvin'. We'll wait."

A full hour had passed when the three emerged with Elma on Chuy's arm as they slowly walked to where we were. Betsy was behind with her handkerchief in her hand. Whatever had transpired in the chapel had clearly moved her to tears, though the look of all three now could only be described as beautiful—their countenance glowing—I don't know another way to describe it.

We quickly got everything ready to serve. Ernesto said, "With the voices here, I guess we'll be singing the Doxology for our blessing," and without confirmation he started it off with all of us joining in.

Of course, he would lead the English and Spanish versions of the birthday song when it was time to cut the cake.

Zoey took my hand, saying, "This is what love looks like. Our poor family had no idea what we were missing out on all those years."

I replied, "And what the rest probably are still missing out on."

When Elma and the Cardonas had headed back to Fort Davis, Betsy asked Noah, Billy and me to join her in the chapel.

She said, "I'm sure you wondered what we were doing in here for so long. Elma and I prayed together as we always have. Then she asked Chuy to lead the Rosary, and they prayed that together. I started to join in, too, if you can believe it. After that she wanted to talk about her memorial service. She knows there will be a Mass in the church, but as she said, 'It's the graveside where I want to see if your boys will do something for me. I've already told Lupe what I want. She'll ask Ernesto to sing "How Great Thou Art." I'd like Billy to play *"Ave Maria"* on his violin, and I'd like Noah, Billy and *Jaime* to sing "Abide with Me." *Jaime* could play his guitar with that song. Do you think the boys would do that for me?' I assured her you would. Chuy composed a nice prayer—well, part prayer, part eulogy—while we were in there that she wants me or Bill to read at the graveside as well.

"Then she laughed at herself and said, 'It probably sounds like I'm going to drop dead before the day's over. I'm just getting prepared. I know I don't have long.' Then Chuy placed his hands on her head and gave her a beautiful blessing. That's when I couldn't hold back the tears any longer."

Noah was perplexed. "I wonder why she thinks she's going to die soon."

Betsy replied, "I don't know, Noah. Some people seem to know. I'm not surprised she would be one of those people. I have little doubt my sister will know when her time is coming, too, unless Nellie gives her a boost into the hereafter the same way Daddy's horse gave him."

Noah laughed, "Sallie says Nellie tells her it's a race to the finish now, so it might be Nellie bucks her just to get free of those Swisher Sweets."

Billy lamented, "That sounds like something I'd have come up with."

I commented, "You're gettin' slow in your old age. The teenager is outpacing you on entertaining us."

He recovered, saying, "I was just being reflective while in the chapel. We've never talked so informally in here before."

Betsy stated, "That's certainly true. Still, the roof hasn't caved in on us, but we'll not make a habit of it just the same. Let's go join whoever's left in the house."

Everyone had gone. It was just Bill and Sallie.

I said, "The foreman and crew will head home, too. Enjoy what's left of your Sunday."

"Bye, boys," Bill said. "As I recall, we'll see you tomorrow morning for the first official GS Ranches staff meeting in the school room."

"Eight sharp," Billy confirmed.

Chapter Thirteen

As designer in residence, Noah, along with the dogs, was included with the rest of us in the first staff meeting. Mark also came along, as Zoey wanted him to talk about hosting services for the online marketing site. He was first on the agenda, so that he could get back to his own work. Jean came out as well to talk about getting everything set up properly with the state. We had a remarkably well-rounded, in-house team.

It took no convincing on Mark's part that we shouldn't try to maintain our own hardware. He had plenty of data center contacts to work out a well-supported, redundant service where all we had to do was manage the content. Even there, he showed us tools and services that would make managing an e-commerce site doable with the skills we had between himself, Zoey, Noah and me.

We spent the entire morning going over all things logistical, and the afternoon brainstorming on all that is related to product development and marketing.

Jean excused herself after lunch, saying, "Where creativity is involved, I'll have little to say. My time will be better spent going back and working on all the logistical things we approved this morning."

Sallie looked at me and I at her. Our smiles confirmed what she'd said to me that evening when I was so concerned about Jean— "neither one has a creative bone in their body."

Right after lunch, Noah showed us all his latest renditions, now complete with an updated GS Ranches logo bearing the banner, Est. 1887. All drawings were black-pen sketches with some acrylic paint fill and a creative wash of watercolors.

I said, "I don't know that I have any marketing expertise—in fact, my failed business in California would probably bear witness to that fact, but I think these are fantastic! I'm eager to see how they scan and print."

Zoey agreed, "I'm with Jaime. Noah, these are wonderful."

Billy exclaimed, "Well done there, young man!"

Sallie added, "Praise all around."

"Hear, hear!" Bill intoned.

Noah observed, "It's like Jaime says—I just moved my hand where it seemed to wanna go."

Bill said, "I move we adopt them for immediate use. Is there a second?"

Zoey added, "I'll second that."

Sallie said, "If Zoey, who has to make it work, seconds it, I don't think the rest of us need to vote, but for the record, I vote 'Aye.'"

Billy and I repeated, "Aye!"

Bill said, "Run with it, Zoey."

By now, Billy had the grass-finished beef mastered. We'd had processed a few just to check it out, and we were all very pleased with the result. Bill had worked out the quality and quantity of processing with the old reliable source he'd worked with over the years to handle everything, including the two types of 125 summer sausage. We also had the two kick-butt fair trade coffee blends we liked from the co-op in San Angelo. It looked like they would get that part of the business.

By 4:00, Bill stretched back in his chair and gave a big yawn. "I'm about meetinged-out. I think we've covered all we need to for now, wouldn't you agree, Foreman Schlatter?"

Billy said, "Meeting adjourned. This boy will want to be gettin' home to muck stables, and these dogs will be wantin' some supper."

Sallie noted, "Kola and Koala have been ready to go home for a while now. They thought all this was boring compared to runnin' cattle."

I said, "I'm sure that's right."

Billy said with an increasing volume, "We gen-u-ine cowboys and cowgirls need our fix of sunshine and wind in our face, ain't that right, Noah?"

Bill commented, "He's out the door with those dogs. I don't think he heard that was addressed to him."

I added, "I guess him rushing out of here answers it well enough."

"Too true. Too true," Sallie said with her head-bobbing chuckle.

The next two weeks, Brett was taking his first real vacation since moving to Alpine. The business had grown enough that he and

Annie shared an agent who worked both the Fort Davis and Alpine offices covering for whichever one might need the help. She was also bringing in some of her own listings from people who knew her. Things were going well, and Brett had paid off everything he owed to his mom and dad. They had surprised him by revealing that they had long ago set up college funds for all the grandchildren. Jaxon had just finished his freshman year, and Brett had been shocked that he'd chosen Sul Ross in Alpine and majored in Industrial Technology. He had wanted to live on campus in the new housing rather than with his dad, but it was clear the two were becoming closer.

During Brett's vacation, his two other kids, Quinn and Aiden, would be staying out at the bunkhouse which is where Brett and Jaxon planned to stay as well. Brett was going to spend days taking them down to Big Bend. He left it up to Noah as to whether he wanted to join them or not.

When Noah told us of his dad's plans, he asked, "Do you think I need to go?"

I asked, "Do you want to go?"

"Not really."

Billy asked, "Any reason in particular you think you should go, and any particular reason you don't want to go?"

Noah answered, "My particular reason for thinking I should go is not hurt Dad's feelings. My particular reason for not wanting to go is I don't want to go."

Billy said, "Your dad left it up to you, so he shouldn't get his feelings hurt—and if he does, he shouldn't have pretended he wouldn't if you turned him down. As to not wanting to go, you're gonna have to decide if you want to get closer to your brothers and sister or don't really care. I can't tell you what to do on that, and neither can Jaime. We've never gone out of our way to get close to anybody we weren't naturally drawn to."

I agreed, "I guess that's true enough. I was thinkin' I should encourage you to go to get closer to them, but Billy's right as usual. It isn't anything we'd do, if we weren't inclined to do so with some idea towards enjoying it."

Noah said, "I guess I'll wait and see if the spirit moves when Dad's ready to head down there."

I said, "You'll have a few days after they get here and dinner over at *Vista Grande* to decide how the week's going before deciding for sure if you want to go along or stay and work."

Billy added, "That's your 'out' if you need it. You can take on some task that needs getting done instead of taking off to the park."

"I like that," Noah responded. "Better have something good lined up in case I need it at the last minute."

I said, "I'm pretty sure we'll find something. By the way, I can't help noticing these past couple weeks your voice is doin' a lot of crackin'. You're about to lose that boy soprano voice of yours."

Billy noted, "I guess one of us needs to sit down and tell you the facts of life, then."

Noah smiled, "You're a little late for that. I figured all that out a few years ago."

I said, "Growing up on a ranch will do that."

"That's right," Billy noted. "I do recall you talking about your early breeding program to populate the next generation. Just to confirm—Sallie said you needn't bother to do that on any of our accounts."

Noah said, "No breeding program any time soon."

"Good," was all I said.

Billy continued, "Our serious moments are usually just silence, and we have plenty in that regard. But seriously, you can talk to me and Jaime anytime about anything. You do know that, right?"

Noah said, "Grandpa said the same thing. I'm well taken care of across the board."

"Well, all right then," Billy said.

Noah was growing up in an adult's world. Even with our Saturdays at the food pantry, he rarely saw kids his own age. Ernesto's grandkids lived elsewhere, so we rarely saw any of them. If Noah didn't want to spend time with his own brothers and sister of a kind, was this because he was uncomfortable with any kids or just them? He was certainly a mature young man, and so we often brushed off any concerns in that regard. But it was on our minds now.

When Noah was back on his keyboard with the headphones on, Billy asked me, "Do we need to rent a boy or two for him to make friends? Are you worried about that?"

"I don't know that I'm actually worried, but as you know I do wonder. Even if he goes with his older siblings, it's not going to be the same as having a friend his own age. He's anything but socially awkward, and he's certainly made it clear, he isn't lonely anymore."

Billy responded, "I think we just need to trust him to say if and when he wants to try to make some other friends. I never had any before I came back and met you. I turned out all right."

I said, "I never had any before I met you either, and I turned out all right, though I had a lot more turnin' to do than you ever did. Also, I've seen no indication that Sallie has had a single friend other than Norman, who was gone for fifty years."

Billy noted, "He gets it honest then. I ain't gonna worry about it."

I added, "I don't see anything that could ever push him to leave for twenty years."

Billy said, "Like I said before, dogs are a lot less worry."

I chuckled, "And we forgot them—boy's best friend. Those two dogs are certainly that boy's best friends. Sallie and her birds and Noah and his dogs."

Billy, imitating his aunt, added, "Too true. Too true."

Noah spent the first few days of Brett's vacation and his half-siblings' visit staying up at the bunkhouse. He'd drive my pickup back and forth when it was time for chores. On the night before they were to leave for Big Bend, I asked Noah, "Come to any conclusion yet whether you're going along in the morning or not?"

"Yup," he said.

"Care to share?" I asked.

He replied, "I told Dad I wanted to stay here. I didn't even exaggerate having to work on something. I wanted to see how he reacted."

I asked, "And how did he react?"

"He said, 'You've been down there, and they haven't. I thought probably you'd stay home. I'm sure those dogs are already wondering where you are every night. You don't have to stay in the bunkhouse when we get back unless you just want to.'"

"That's pretty nice of him to understand, isn't it?"

Noah smiled and said, "He's comin' right along!"

81

Chapter Fourteen

From Zoey and Mark's first tutorial on the supplements and quality assurance that were going into beef production on the ranch, we all agreed to worry less about getting certified as organic, and focus more on educating the retail sources on our ranching practices. Zoey had managed to get a number of farm-to-table agreements with restaurants in San Angelo, Austin, San Antonio and El Paso. By fall, we were supplying them exclusively with GS Ranches beef. In each case their menu gave credit where credit was due, and we were soon being contacted by other clientele, both commercial entities and direct consumers. We had a fledgling website to help manage interest on the consumer level. In those cases, we were directing them to work with the processor for the meat.

All in all, things were off to a good start. We had both the coffee blends and 125 summer sausages stocked in all the local grocery stores, including Pecos, Fort Stockton and up in Carlsbad. Within the year, we hoped to be stocked as well in a few Midland and Odessa stores. Bill and Billy were persuaded that once at that level, we'd have to manage the client base we had and not go looking to expand further. None of us had any interest in managing multiple ranches in order to go statewide or national. We had a "local market" as Texas miles are measured, and that was the goal. We had a model other ranchers could duplicate if they were interested in doing so. If other ranchers were successful and greedier, they could certainly cause GS Ranches competitive problems, but it was a risk we seemed okay accepting. This was always about stewardship of the land and its cattle first and foremost. Quality and care would not be sacrificed.

Billy never knew the true bottom line of the ranch before the GS Ranches brand, and he and I were pretty sure that neither did Sallie. Bill wasn't dropping any hints about how much he might be subsidizing the business through his oil revenues, but we had a real sense it must be decreasing. All he would really say is, "In a year or two, we should really be able to assess the degree to which this has worked."

I said to Billy, "That sounds to me like we're less of a drain."

Billy replied, "I know for sure we're getting more per head than we ever have and feeding less. That is all to the good. Of course we have new overhead expenses for Zoey, marketing, and all the data related expenses. I'm not sure how that all nets out."

I added, "I know your dad is hesitant to oversell anything including the possible success of this venture. I respect that a lot."

As we were talking, I heard the phone ring and went into the kitchen to answer it. I saw it was Chuy and Lupe's number. We had just finished breakfast, and Noah had driven himself over to school.

"Good morning."

"Hey, *Jaime*, it's Chuy. How are you boys doing?"

"We're doing well. What can I do for you?"

He replied, "We wanted to let you know that Elma passed away. She calls Lupe every morning, as Elma puts it, to be sure we lived through the night. When she didn't call this morning Lupe went to check on her. She was sitting peacefully in her chair with her rosary in her hand—her body still warm. She must have died praying her morning Rosary."

"She certainly passed exactly as she prayed she would."

Chuy responded, "Yes she did, and you probably don't know this since you're not Catholic, but today is the feast of Our Lady of the Rosary."

I was rather stunned and didn't say anything right away. Chuy asked, "Are you there?"

I replied, "Yes, I'm here. I just lost any ability to talk for a second there."

He continued, "Lupe says Betsy has some instructions and a prayer for the graveside. Do you know about all that?"

"I do. Did you want to know that now or are you just confirming?"

Chuy replied, "I'm just confirming. I know Lupe plans to talk to Betsy after she's talked to her brothers and sisters and the priest. Right now, she's on her cell still calling that first round. She wanted you to know right away and to ask you to let Betsy know."

"Of course, I will do that," I assured him.

He said, "I guess that's it. I'm going to call Ernesto now."

"Take care, Chuy," I said.

Chuy added, "Elma really loved you boys—especially you. I guess you know that. Good bye, *Jaime*."

"We all loved her dearly. She was a saint. Goodbye, friend."

Billy had wandered in soon after I answered the phone. "I heard some of that," he said.

I asked, "Did you hear what day he said it was?"

Billy said, "I wasn't catching that. Something about a Catholic feast day."

"Today is the feast day of Our Lady of the Rosary. Elma died sitting in a chair, holding the rosary in her hands."

Billy put his arm around my shoulder, saying, "She died as she had lived—praying."

I said, "I'd rather not call. Let's go next door and tell them, and we'll stop at *Cielo Lindo* on the way back and tell them as well."

When we got there, we knew Noah and at least one of his teachers would be in Bill's office-schoolroom. At this time of day, I expected it to be Noah and Betsy, which it was. Billy went in the house to tell whoever was there.

I relayed the news exactly as Chuy had given it to me. I expected Betsy to cry, but she didn't. She state matter-of-factly, "Think of the praying we are all going to have to do now that the world is short her prayers. She always asked Mary for intercession. I may start asking for Saint Elma's intercession."

I confirmed, "I know I will."

Then she said, "I showed Bill the prayer *Padre Jesús* wrote that day. We decided since she asked that either he or I read it that we could actually both read parts of it. It lends itself to that pretty well."

"That's a beautiful idea." I looked at Noah who was sitting quietly but attentive to all we were saying. "Are you okay, Noah?"

He replied, "I'm okay. I knew I loved her. Now, I know just how much. It feels like a hole in me. I never felt that before even when my mom was murdered. The holes are only going to get bigger, aren't they?"

I held out my arms inviting him to come to me. He stood, walked over to me, and I hugged him and his grandmother hugged us both.

I said, "Yes, Noah. The holes are only going to get bigger."

Then Noah said, "Grandma, I didn't mean to make you cry."

She responded, "Noah, I think Elma has gifted you with something special. She's given you that hole as a place to store your memories of her, just as you will fill the other holes that come with death with other memories."

"You're right, Grandma. I can already fill in a little bit of it as I remember standing next to her on my tenth birthday—when she told Rosalinda, 'He's such a nice boy.'"

Billy appeared with Bill and Sallie following. He said, "I thought y'all would be coming into the house. We decided we'd have to come to you."

Betsy said, "Noah has been reminding us just how much we loved Elma and how much we love each other."

Billy observed, "I can see there was a hug involved and I wasn't included. We're going to have to have our hug now, Noah."

That took no coaxing. Noah went and embraced Billy with all the love he had in him, and Sallie and Bill hugged the two of them.

Billy finally said to Noah, "You can let go now. We're not going anywhere."

Noah whispered, "I just needed to remember this moment."

I explained to Billy just how meaningful a statement that was when we drove back to the house. And I was sure Betsy would do the same for Bill and Sallie once Noah came home in the afternoon to do his chores.

The next morning, Lupe called Betsy to lay out the plans for the Mass and burial. There would be a Rosary the evening before with a family visitation following. Lupe made it clear, we didn't need to feel any obligation to come in that evening. She said, "The important thing to *Mamá* was to have you all at the graveside. She even told me, 'The priest can do whatever he wants at the church, but don't you let him change anything for the burial.'"

Betsy told her, "I think she would appreciate it more if our family met in the chapel here on that evening and remembered her in that way."

Lupe laughed, "I'd join you if I thought I could get away with it, but I guess I'll be in the church with the rest. Betsy, I think that's a lovely idea."

Noah took the prayer that *Padre Jesús* had written and transcribed it in a beautiful script with a colored sketch he did of Elma, from her 90th birthday party with a watercolor wash as the background. We had it printed off to hand out at the burial. Underneath the drawing, he included her name and dates of birth and death.

Elma Maria Salinas Rodriquez
June 10, 1916 - October 7, 2012

The dawn of peace has come for your faithful servant, Elma Maria, who has held the love of Christ in her heart and shared that love through her smile, her touch, her food and her prayers.

Her small body was filled with a large heart for others. With her daughter, Lupita, and with her own mother since she was six years old, she celebrated the Easter feast with her meticulous care in decorating eggs with homemade dyes and sprigs from the garden, as the dozens of eggs would soon be turned into nourishing treats for family, friends and neighbors. Ninety Easter seasons of her simple devotion to this act of love and generosity—easily dismissed by the less generous as not worth the effort.

Her small body carried with it a loving touch as she would reach to touch the cheek of so many who brought her delight through their own kindness and generosity. Her smile beamed from ear to ear as eyes sparkled from the Spirit within she so willingly poured out for others.

Her hands in tune with her heart as she prayed every day the Rosary. She said, "I never liked to kneel. It hurt my knees. I hope Jesús and the Blessed Virgin don't mind that I sit comfortably in a chair while I pray." It was Elma's prayers that turned skeptics into believers as her faithfulness never faltered—her prayers so often answered.

We commend our sister, Elma, to your eternal love and care. May light perpetual shine upon her as the light of her life shined brightly on all who knew her. Grant that we who remain may partake of the inheritance of Elma and all the saints in light. Amen.

When Lupe saw it, she smiled brightly and said, "Oh, *Mamá* would love this and say, 'Oh, he's such a nice boy!' Thank you, Noah. I shall always keep this and cherish it."

Then she said to all of us, "*Mamá* laughed on her way home from the party in June and said, 'I got a preview of my own *elogio*. I'm sure the priest will come up with his own, but Chuy's, that I've asked Bill or Betsy to read at the graveside, you'll know is the officially approved one!' She was most tickled by her approval of it. She said, 'I sound like such a nice person. I guess he never heard me fuss at my other daughters.'"

I smiled, saying, "That is so Elma! I will always smile just at the thought of her."

Billy said, "As will we all."

At the graveside, Ernesto sang a cappella all the verses of "How Great Thou Art" followed by Noah, Billy and I singing "Abide with Me." Bill and Betsy then read the prayer by *Padre Jesús,* and Billy played *"Ave Maria."* The priest concluded with the traditional commendation rite. We stood for a moment as most wandered back to their vehicles. I looked at the metal coffin now lowered in the grave with its bit of dirt and flowers on top of it now, and I made my first sign of the cross.

"Rest well, good and faithful friend. Rest well."

Lupe had asked Noah, Billy and I to stop by their house after we left the cemetery. When we arrived she invited us in, saying she had something for us.

She began, "When *Mamá* told us that she'd had her last birthday, she said, 'I want you to do something for my three boys. I'd like each of them to have one of my quilts that you made.'

"I'd made one each for her and *Papá's* fortieth, fiftieth and sixtieth wedding anniversaries. She always made it clear to my brothers and sisters that she'd decide where they would go after she was gone. I'm only too glad to fulfill one of her last requests."

Lupe had all three quilts folded on the dining room table ready to hand to us—each inside a clear dry cleaner's bag.

Three gen-u-ine cowboys—one helpless mess. All we could do was stand there and cry.

Chapter Fifteen

Brett called us the Saturday before Thanksgiving to say he would not be out to spend the night per his now normal routine. His only daughter, Quinn, who had started college in the fall, called her dad asking him to come pick her up in San Antonio where she was enrolled. She was crying when she called and said she had first called her mother in Odessa, who'd hung up on her.

Between her sobs, she cried, "Daddy, I'm pregnant."

I was glad Noah was outside brushing the dogs as my first response was not very charitable. "How, in this day and age, do these young people not know the risks and take precautions? And I don't mean against just pregnancy, but all manner of nastiness you can catch."

Billy said, "He didn't say anything about calling Mom and Dad. I guess we'd better break the news to them in case he hasn't. She certainly didn't waste any time once away from home. And to your question, it beats the *hell* out of me!"

I replied, "I guess Noah will be a thirteen-year-old uncle."

"If she keeps it," Billy said.

"I suppose she's not processed that one way or the other. I'd just as soon we not take on an infant to raise, in case you were wondering."

Billy commented, "I don't guess we can make an argument out of that. Once again, we agree. You stay here with Noah, and I'll go over and break the news, if it is news."

He was only gone about fifteen minutes.

"Well?" I asked.

"It was news," Billy replied. "Dad said, 'Brett may finally have to get out of that apartment and buy a house if she comes to live with him and raise that baby.' Mom said, 'She will probably marry the man.' And Sallie added, 'If she does, I hope it's out of some semblance of love and not desperation.'"

"Lord have mercy," I responded. "Things were almost feeling settled for a change. You'd better call or email your sister while you're at it."

Billy said, "Oh yeah, I'll call her so I can hear her reaction when I tell her Quinn hopes she and Mary-Alice will adopt her kid."

I quipped, "I know they'll jump at the chance."

When Brett was back in Alpine with Quinn, he emailed all of us to shed some more light on the subject without her having to face any of us just yet. He'd stay with her in Alpine until she was ready to see us.

Her story was not a pretty one, and I suppose—of a kind—why the mother hung up on her only daughter. She had too much to drink and came onto a couple of frat boys who were only too glad to take advantage of the situation. She didn't know which one was the father and, as Brett put it, she doesn't seem too sure it was only two boys.

As Billy and I read it together he said, "At that line, I can hear Dad say, 'Good lord,' but not like he says it to me."

I replied, "Yeah, a good lord followed by long sigh saying, 'Ah shit!'"

Billy added, "There goes Mom's notion that some responsible man is going to marry Quinn."

I said, "Hormones and alcohol—a dangerous combination. I do have to say, her telling of it was an honest one. She didn't try to blame someone else for her behavior—which is in no way justifying the frat boys taking advantage of her inebriation."

When we went over for Sunday chapel service, both Bill and Betsy had the expression best described as the "Now what?" look. They didn't expect Brett to show up with Quinn that soon and were correct in their assumption.

At lunch, with Noah present, none of this was discussed, though he clearly sensed something was up. While he was never shielded from bad news, sharing his half sister's situation without knowing what she was going to do just yet, seemed too hard to talk about in front of him.

Privately, Bill had said to Billy, "Surely she sobered up enough the next day to realize what she'd done. Somehow, she needed to get a hold of the morning-after pill. I'm sure there are plenty on campus." Then he added, "It was always hard not to show my disappointment in all Brett's choices over the years. It looks like I'll have to relive that feeling again when I see Quinn."

When I filled in Zoey and Mark on what we knew, she responded, "If I were ten years younger I might offer to raise the child, but I can't imagine starting a family in my forties."

Mark said, "As Billy would say, 'If it ain't broke, don't fix it.' We've just settled into our new life here. I'd like to enjoy it unencumbered."

I added, "In the unlikely event any should ask, I'll say it's a 'no' from the Mendozas just like the Cruz-Schlatter household."

Zoey said, "The Cruz-Schlatter household. Did you two run off to Massachusetts and get married when no one was watching?"

"Cute," I replied, "though the piece of paper might be worth it for legal reasons, it must be said. Maybe we will tie the knot if it ever becomes legal in Texas."

Mark suggested, "I wouldn't hold my breath."

Brett knew he owed Noah some explanation for what would be his second Saturday evening to not come to the ranch. He called Noah midweek to tell him that Quinn was with him in Alpine and had left school. He told Noah that his sister was pregnant and had a falling out with her mother. He didn't offer any details beyond that.

When Noah was off the phone, he turned to Billy and me, "It's kinda weird how we're all coming into my dad's life now that he's close to his own folks. Me, because of my mom's murder, Jaxon to go to school in Alpine, and now Quinn because she's pregnant. Do you think she'll get married to whoever the father is?"

Billy felt he deserved the truth. "No, she's not even sure exactly who the father is without doing some DNA tests. There was no love involved. It was just sex."

Noah asked, "Is she keeping it?"

I answered, "We have no idea, and we aren't sure she does either."

He replied, "I guess she's gonna have to grow up pretty quick now."

Bill and Betsy made arrangements to go down to Alpine on Saturday and meet with Brett and Quinn. Then they hoped they could all meet Jaxon for lunch.

Betsy shared her thoughts with us. "All we can do is go and be sure she knows some sense of mercy over judgment. We certainly don't want to drive her into doing something like taking her own life over this."

They came over to the house on their way back from town and wanted to talk to all three of us—Noah included.

Bill said, "Noah, your half sister plans to keep the baby and is going to live with your dad for now. I'm sure her mother will come around at some point, but right now Quinn feels like she'd rather be in Alpine than try to work things out and go back to Odessa.

"Boys, as you know, Brett is still paying on his bankruptcy debts though he has paid off the investment money we put in to open the office. We've told him he should go ahead and find a house and we'll cover the mortgage. He needs to get something bigger if he's going to have a mother and child living with him."

Betsy added, "I hope all of them come to chapel tomorrow—Brett, Quinn and Jaxon. The sooner Quinn can face others, the sooner she can do what's right for herself and that baby."

Billy felt genuine compassion for Quinn—who we all barely knew. "It doesn't have to ruin her life, but it certainly is going to make for a different life than she probably imagined when she left for San Antonio in August."

Bill sighed, "That's for sure."

I suggested, "Being a single mother is at least accepted now more than it used to be. She could make a life in a small town like Alpine with the support of the family she has here—better than if she goes back to Odessa or San Antonio."

Bill said, "I think that's right, Jaime, and we said as much to her."

Noah offered, "I guess if she doesn't decide to give it up for adoption, I'll be Uncle Noah. Makes me feel all grownup."

"And Jaime and I will be great-uncles, Billy added. "I'm feelin' older by the minute."

Betsy lamented, "How do think Great-grandma and Great-grandpa feel? I feel like I've gained ten years in the last week."

Bill noted, "I've gained more gray hair in the last week—I know that!"

What we knew of Quinn and Jaxon's mother and her family had always been filtered through Brett. And given his poor communication skills during that marriage, Bill and Betsy felt like what they did know amounted to a hill of beans.

We were glad to see Brett, Jaxon and Quinn all show up for our Sunday gathering. They were there in plenty of time for chapel and stayed for lunch. I'd never heard either one say three complete sentences before. I still didn't hear Quinn do so, but over lunch Jaxon opened up, and he was as talkative as Brett had always been. In this case he was talking about his mother's family.

He related, "I'm not surprised Mom hung up on Quinn. There is no way she could face, in that moment, what she was going to tell our grandparents or our aunts and uncles. They all attend the same mega-church, and vote for any politician, no matter how goofy, so long as he—and it has to be a he—says he's against abortion and for capital punishment. I'm not sure what they'd do if the guy was for one and against the other, but that never seems to be a problem. I'm sure she thought Quinn would get an abortion and the news would somehow get back to the family."

Jaxon stopped long enough to look at his younger half brother and said, "I'm sorry. Maybe I shouldn't be saying all this in front of Noah."

Bill said, "That's not a problem. Noah gets the news unfiltered in this family like everyone else."

Sallie asked, "Have you talked to your mother about it?"

Jaxon replied, "I haven't called her, and she hasn't called me. I guess I've got enough Schlatter in me—I never liked going to that mega-church, which she knew. We started to go there after Mom and Dad divorced. I guess she thought she needed to get on her family's good side.

"I've been going to the Cowboy Church in Alpine, and I like it a lot better. I can't exactly describe it as progressive, but I like the smaller size and the guitar music. Now that I've been to the chapel here, I might come out on Sundays if that's all right."

Betsy exclaimed, "All right? Of course, it's all right. It would be wonderful!"

Bill added, "I'll second that, and you too, Quinn. You're welcome here, too. I hope you know that."

She didn't speak but just gave a smile in acknowledgement.

Back at the house, Billy asked Noah, "So what'd you make of all that?"

Noah replied, "I don't know why, but I thought about Jaime and his sayin' his letters are like casting seeds to the desert wind. I thought on the next Quiet Day, I might cast my seed and see if it takes root."

I asked, "Who you gonna write to?"

He answered, "Pamela. I always liked her, and if the family is comin' back together, I'd like her to be part of it. She was real nice to me, and is a lot better mom to her kids than my mom ever was to me. I know she said she'd never marry again, but I'm wondering if undoing a divorce and getting back together with Dad might fall in a different category."

Billy said, "She told Jean that Brett couldn't win her back no matter what change of heart he might have, but she might not have factored into the equation getting a letter from you."

I encouraged him. "Noah, I think you should do it, but as you know from my experience, it doesn't have much of a chance. She's also got custody issues to deal with which might make leaving El Paso next to impossible. As long as you know all this going in, then you'll be doing it for all the right reasons and not trying meddle in someone else's life."

Billy noted, "That'll put your letter writin' next Saturday. December 1st is Quiet Day, and the anniversary from when your grandma started it. Those anniversaries are when Jaime seems to like to write his letters. No better time, I guess."

Noah said, "I figure Pamela's at least better ground than Jaime had to work with when he cast his seeds, and he still had good luck with Zoey."

Billy asked, "Zoey's pretty wonderful, isn't she?"

Noah replied, "Just like her brother."

I laughed, "That's nice of you to say, but you might need to narrow that down if you ever say it to her. I don't know that either one of us wants to be compared to our brother, Mason."

Noah stated flatly as his grandfather would, "I don't know him. I only know you, and she already knows what I think of you."

Chapter Sixteen

Quiet Day not only brought with it the anniversary and Noah's first letter writing, but also a surprise guest. There, promptly at 7:30 when all the Geermann-Schlatter family including me, Mark and Zoey were quietly seated in the chapel already, came in a woman I did not know but who Sallie, Bill and Betsy clearly did. Betsy stood, went to her, and without saying a word, embraced her and pointed to an open chair for the woman to be seated.

As eager as Billy, Noah and I were to know the identity of the woman, we all respected the quiet of the day, as we would wait until afterwards to discover her identity. The woman stayed for the entire day and spoke only briefly with Betsy when it ended after the 2:30 service in the chapel.

As it turned out, she was from Betsy's old church and was one of the other ranch wives who was part of the old Bible study group. She said to Betsy, "I don't know why it's taken me so many years to get up the courage to leave after you showed me the way, but it has. I've had my fill of their constant judgment, and last Sunday, when one of them started to gossip about your granddaughter, I stood up and said, 'Y'all are good at casting stones when you have no business casting stones, and I'm done with you!' I walked out of that women's Sunday School class, went to my husband's men's Sunday School class, grabbed his arm and said, 'We're leaving now.' That really didn't take any persuading. We only went there because I insisted on it for so long."

Bill was most amused by the telling of this, and Betsy asked, "Why are you so pleased?"

"Because when you left they lost their biggest contributor, and now they just lost their second place holder in that category unless they've picked up some new support along the way."

Then Betsy was rather amused by it, too. "If we see that electric sign out front go off, we'll know they can't pay the electric bill."

She added, "If there was one redeeming thing from my time with that bunch it was the fact I was never a gossip. I can guess exactly which ones Ava was talking about. Not to give myself much credit though, it must be said, I'd have felt sorry for the parents and not the young girl for the shame she brought on the family." Looking at Billy she the added, "The same shame I felt about you leaving even though I knew I was the one who drove you away."

Betsy continued, "Ava said she liked Quiet Day and said she'd be back next month. Since she saw all the Schlatter men attending, she thought maybe her husband might come, too. I guess, we'll see if they show up in January."

Back home, Noah wanted to show us his letter before he sealed it up to mail to Pamela. Billy said, "I wasn't sure if you'd want us to read it or not, but Jaime always wanted me to read his letters before sending them."

Noah said, "You can tell me if you think it's worth sending, or if I should make another run at it sometime. Uncle Jaime, maybe you can read it aloud and then I can hear what it sounds like at the same time Uncle Billy hears it."

"Okay, I'll do that."

Dear Pamela,

This is Noah. I hope you're doing all right. I'm doing real good. I love living out on the ranch, and we've got two dogs, Koala and Kola, that sleep with me and are real good cattle dogs, too. Uncle Billy says Koala looks like Uncle Jaime. She does a little bit. I sure don't miss El Paso.

Mostly, I want to thank you for being so nice to me when there was nothing good going on between you and my dad and the mess with my mom and her boyfriend. I'm not sure what I would have done without you in those days. Gone crazy, I guess. I might have even committed suicide, though I'm not sure I was old enough then to know how to go about it. It never crossed my mind as something I might try to do, but that was all to your being so nice to me.

Since the crash finally taught Dad what he needed to learn, and since he's moved to Alpine, he's become a good dad. I don't live with him, but that's because he knows how much I love the ranch and Uncle Billy and Uncle Jaime. Grandma, Grandpa and Aunt Sallie homeschool me, and I'm learning a lot more than I ever did in public school.

You're the only wife Dad had he ever actually loved. I've heard him say that. And he doesn't know I'm writing this letter. I think it would be real nice to see you again, and would like to invite you to the ranch. You can bring your kids. We've still got the bunkhouse, and Dad has his own room here at Uncle Billy and Uncle Jaime's, where he comes to stay sometimes. Now that Quinn is living with him, he's been staying in town, but we see them on Sundays for chapel. Jaxon is living in Alpine and going to Sul Ross. He said he's gonna come on Sundays, too. We're finally becoming a family.

Aiden is the only one we don't hear from much. Maybe I'll write him a letter, too. I don't really know him. I feel like I know you better, and so I wanted to write you first.

I guess that's all for now.

Love,

Noah

I offered my two cents. "I wouldn't change a word."

Billy exclaimed, "Cast your seeds to wind, boy, and let's see if they take root!"

Then I added, "From our experience, instant results aren't a thing, but I'm pretty sure Pamela will be nice enough to write back to you, even if she doesn't want to come visit."

"I kinda figured that too," Noah said. "Aunt Sallie would say I've done my due diligence."

Billy noted, "I don't think at your age, I would have known what due diligence was, but you clearly do. And yes, I think that's what your aunt Sallie would say, and I'd say to you now, too."

Noah said, "If we go in for food pantry next Saturday, we can get it in the mail. I know Dad'll be here tomorrow, but I don't really want to give it to him to mail."

"Jean and Mary-Alice are still here," I pointed out. "Why don't you run it over to them, and they can mail for you when they get back to Marfa."

That was all it took. He said, "Come on dogs." He hopped in my pickup with the dogs and took off for the bunkhouse. I said to Billy, "I haven't had those truck keys in my own pocket for at least six months. He drives that thing like he owns it."

Billy laughed, "Pretty cute, huh?"

I said, "I guess when he's actually legal to drive it on the road, I'll title it to him. Since we always take your truck, I never did put any mileage on it. It ought to last a while yet."

Billy added, "Built Ford tough, I guess, just like the rest of us."

I said, "Ah, we're tougher than any old pickup."

Billy returned to the letter's contents. "That was something, that Noah said he might have considered suicide if it weren't for Pamela."

I said, "He couldn't have put in any stronger terms how important she was in his life back then. I don't know how she could read that with a dry eye. I barely could, and it wasn't written to me."

"Same here," Billy agreed. "I thought him putting the dogs in at the start was pretty funny, but it sounded so much like him, I was glad he did."

"Me too. I'd have never thought to tell him to write it the way he did, but I sure liked how he went about it from start to finish—even mentioning that he might write to Aiden."

Billy reflected, "It's kinda like he's the boy you and I wish we could have been, but never got to be. And it took murder to make it happen for him. Life is just weird."

"Never was a truer word spoken," I concurred.

Noah was back and came in to announce, "Mission accomplished."

Billy asked, "Did you let them read the letter?"

Noah replied, "No. I sealed it up before I went in. I decided I wanted to keep it between the three of us and the dogs, of course. I told them they had to stay in the truck. I didn't want them spillin' the beans. Jean just said she'd mail it and that they hadn't heard from Pamela in a long time. She thought it was real nice that I was sending her a letter, and she never did ask what I said in it."

"Indeed, mission accomplished." Then I asked, "Are you going to tell those three over at *Vista Grande* that you wrote Pamela?"

Noah replied, "Grandma knew I was writing her. I don't think she'll ask me what I wrote if I don't volunteer it. I figure she told Grandpa and Aunt Sallie."

"Probably so," I agreed.

Billy added, "Even Mom liked Pamela. I'm sure she'd be welcomed out here by everyone. I know she sends her a Christmas and birthday card every year. She's never said anything, but I've seen 'em in the outgoing mail bin."

"I never knew that," I said.

Billy replied, "I just never thought of mentioning it. I didn't think much about it until now."

Chapter Seventeen

Betsy said if we didn't mind, she'd come along to the last food pantry distribution of the year. She knew this was always an "all-hands-on-deck" day with extra food for the families as well as gifts for all the kids and special things for the parents. Ever since Betsy's changing attitude towards the pantry, she had contributed many gifts for the day, but had never joined us on the actual holiday distribution Saturday. Our new Quiet Day guest showed up at the pantry as well.

Afterwards, we had lunch at the Slo Poke Cafe with Ernesto and Rosalinda. Rosalinda said, "I was surprised to see Ava there this morning. Has she left the old church crowd finally?"

Betsy said, "Indeed she has. She came to Quiet Day this month, which is when I found out about it. This morning she said to me, 'I recall showing up here is like a coming out party to the town. Everyone will know I've parted company with the old crowd now!' I told her, 'I think you'll find the entire experience liberating. I can't say enough about what my leaving has done for my own family. I thought I was in the "family values" crowd, while I was really only alienating my own. Never again!'"

Billy asked, "When's the next trip to El Salvador?"

Ernesto declared, "It's official. I've retired."

Rosalinda interjected, "Of a kind. He'll still piddle on smaller jobs, and probably a big job, if it is for the Geermann-Schlatters."

Ernesto agreed, "I guess 'of a kind' is about right. I'm not out lookin' for any work but won't turn down small jobs to keep me in shape."

Rosalinda continued, "To answer your question, Billy, we are going to see Chuy in January and are going to stay two months this trip."

Ernesto laughed, "We wouldn't want to miss those winds we get in March and April!"

Betsy wanted to address what she was sure was front and center in their minds. "I'm sure you've heard some version of our granddaughter's story by now. She is in fact pregnant, won't be marrying anyone because of it, and is living with Brett, who is house-shopping as we speak. Quinn and Jaxon both come out with Brett to the chapel on Sundays now, and they have lunch with us. We just hope they continue doing that for as long as they stay in Alpine."

Just as she'd said this some man our age went by the table and said, clearly directed to Billy and me, "Well, well, if it isn't Jack Twist and Ennis Del Mar," and went walking right on by, stopping long enough to pay before leaving."

I asked, "Who was that?"

Billy said, "Pardon me, Mother. That's a *cabrón* I was in school with. I thought he'd moved away. I have no idea what that was supposed to mean, but I'm sure it was meant to be demeaning. He was a bully then and probably still is."

Rosalinda said, "He did move away. I think he's just here visiting what's left of his relatives."

I asked, "Do you know who those two names are he called us?"

She replied, "I don't know. Do you, Ernesto?"

"I don't know either," he said.

We all figured Sara heard it as she hears everything. When she brought our food out, Billy asked her, "Did you hear those two names he called us, and if you did, do you know who he's talking about?"

She shook her head in general disgust. "He's such an ass. Yes, I know what those names are from. They were cowboys in a movie —years ago now—called *Brokeback Mountain*. If you want to be depressed, it's a good movie. Those two guys were in love and both lived miserable lives trying to deny it. They were the opposite of you two. They got married and lived their lives pretending to love wives rather than admit they loved each other. People talked about the movie being so good. It won awards. Mateo and I went to see it when we were in El Paso. One of the actors even killed himself just a few years after the film was made. I guess his real life was as depressing as the one he portrayed in the movie."

Betsy added, "Your classmate's mother is the gossip in that group Ava walked out on when she started in on Quinn."

Ernesto growled, "The jackass."

Rosalinda asked her husband, "Is that directed towards the mother or the son?"

100

"Take your pick. I never called a woman a jackass before, but if she is, she is."

As we were getting ready to leave, we all wished Sara a "Merry Christmas," which prompted Betsy to say, "We've been so distracted the last couple weeks, we haven't even put up our tree! My tree committee needs to get on that Monday while Noah's in school. We can all decorate it as soon as his teachers let him loose from class."

Billy noted, "Noah, I would take you with us, but then I'd have to either leave Jaime or Sallie home. My grand entrance each year requires only three queens."

Noah said, "I know, Uncle Billy. I like to be there to see the show with Grandma and Grandpa anyway. Grandpa always sees you drivin' up and says, 'Prepare yourself. Here they come!'"

As we headed back to the ranch, we stopped to get the mail. Betsy rode up front with me and Billy and Noah were in the back. I saw in the rearview mirror Billy holding up a card-sized envelope for me to see. He handed it to Noah, but didn't say anything. Neither did Noah. I thought I might hear it tear open, but I never did. I was sure it was a note from Pamela.

When we dropped Betsy off, and ranch-west mail along with her, Noah confirmed, "It's from Pamela, but I didn't want to read it while Grandma was in the car. I thought we'd better read it first."

He tore it open.

Dear Noah,

How kind it was of you to write to me. I think of you often, and I am so glad to hear you love the ranch, as I knew you would. You've got a good family there, and I'm glad your dad is becoming a bigger part of it. He always had the potential for being a better man. It took life's hard knocks to make it happen.

You won't be surprised to learn that I have not remarried. I vowed I wouldn't—and that vow I have kept. When my kids are out of school for the summer, perhaps we'll take you up on your invitation to visit the ranch. It would be nice to see you and the rest of the family.

I know from Jean that Jaime's sister is living there now, and I've seen the GS Ranches brand in our grocery store here. You'll be pleased to hear I am a fan of the coffee and summer sausage. I wish I could get some of the beef as well. I seem to recognize the handiwork of the artist, if I'm not mistaken, and of all the models. That one on the morning blend Kick-butt coffee looks an awful lot like a sweet boy I know—well, young man now.

Noah, when I think about how a boy's life can go from terrible to wonderful, you're the face I always see. You are my symbol of hope for all that is good in this world. I'm so glad you reached out—it means so much to me.

Much love,

Pamela

PS My three kids remember you as their "big brother." I thought you'd get a kick out of that knowing how your own siblings treated you when you were the "baby of the family."

Billy asked, "How about that, young man? A sprout with the first toss."

Noah's pleasure was so evident. "It's real nice. I think maybe I'll show it to Grandma and Grandpa, but probably not my dad. What do you think?"

Billy replied, "I think that's a good plan."

On Monday, Billy, Sallie and I went on assigned duty to get the now long-overdue *piñon* for *Vista Grande*. Mark and Zoey followed us to where we go every year to cut a tree, and cut one for themselves as well. This would be their first Christmas on the ranch, and the end of an eventful year. Thanks to Zoey and Bill's processors, the GS Ranches brand rollout had gone quickly and smoothly.

When we arrived with the tree, Billy made his now customary grand entrance singing "We Three Queens." If it was growing tiresome for his parents, they were enjoying it now for the entertainment it provided for Noah. In fact, he said for the first time, "I don't see why it couldn't be 'We Four Kings' and next year I could go along."

Sallie was open to tending her resignation. "I could just pass the torch onto you. I'm no help to the boys. They'd put you to better use than they can me. Plus, Billy might get confused if he has to change up those lyrics."

Betsy asked, "Noah, would you like to play carols on your piano while we decorate the tree, or would you rather just decorate?"

To please his grandmother, I'm sure, he said, "I'll get my keyboard. Uncle Jaime, come help me carry it all in here."

I did as requested, and he was set up and playing through the half dozen carols he'd learned.

Sallie walked over to Noah, saying, "You sure are coming along on that piano. Why aren't you playing with the men's band when they sing for their supper instead of just singin' along?"

Noah replied, "I guess 'cause they never asked me, and I wasn't sure I was good enough yet."

Bill confirmed, "Consider yourself the official keyboard player. You're more than good enough for our band."

Betsy suggested, "You could leave that in here until after the holidays so you all can provide some regular holiday cheer."

"Then you'd better be thinkin' about what you're gonna make us for dinner," Billy suggested. "When we get our evenin' chores done, we can come back and sing for our supper."

"How's meatloaf sound?" Betsy asked.

"I wouldn't turn it down," Billy replied.

I said, "I'll never turn down your meatloaf. You make it better than any I've ever had."

She offered, "It's not a secret. If you want the recipe, all you have to do is ask."

Noah said, "I think it's more a treat this way though we ought to have it someday."

Betsy continued, "I guess you don't want me taking the recipe with me to the grave. You needn't worry about that. It's right there in my recipe box, though I haven't looked at it for years. I don't think I've added anything to it. I guess I should check."

Billy said, "It tastes like I remember as a kid."

Sallie concurred, "Sis, I'm with Billy. It's not Momma's recipe, which was pretty good, but yours is just that little bit better."

Betsy responded, "The only difference between the two is chorizo. I cook it first and drain it well so the fat doesn't overpower the hamburger. There—the secret's out."

Bill added, "I believe I recognize it in those meatballs you make every Christmas Eve. The only difference is the sauce those simmer in."

Betsy said, "All my secrets are out. You are correct."

And Billy added his usual, "If ain't broke, don't fix it."

Speaking of that," I said, "I saw in an article online some business guru saying, 'If it ain't broke, break it.' He was advocating for change in an organization, of course."

Bill replied, "I'm more of the mind, 'If it ain't broke, it could well be soon enough—be prepared.' I guess that's too long a title for a book."

Noah reflected, "Grandpa, I guess that's why you made the changes on the ranch these past couple years. Getting prepared for how ranching is changing even though it don't seem broke."

Bill answered, "That's right. I'm trying to prepare so you have something that ain't broke when your time comes along to run this place.

"Sometimes it may 'get broke' or you may 'go broke' no matter what you do. Still, I see too much in the merger and acquisition world where they take what ain't really broke and break it for the sole purpose of quick profits. That's the greed-driven economy that drives most of the world—how to get more in a few people's pockets no matter who it hurts. The prophets called that sin.

"Noah, it'd be better to lose the ranch than throw in with the unholy doctrine that everything bigger is better."

Chapter Eighteen

By Christmas Eve, Brett had a contract on a home but had not yet taken possession. Jean and Mary-Alice were booked in at the bunkhouse for the week between Christmas and New Year's. Aiden was going to be visiting his dad Christmas Eve and through "the third day of Christmas." We offered to let him stay in what had been "Brett's room" at our place. There certainly wasn't room for him in Brett's apartment. We also made it clear that Jaxon could get out of the residence hall at Sul Ross over the holidays and stay with us as well.

Noah replied, "I always felt weird around my brothers. Now, I guess Aiden will feel more like the odd man out."

I said, "It could be you need to make sure he doesn't."

Billy added, "I think he knows Jaxon better than he ever knew you. At least he'll be out here, too. I know we don't have to worry about you trying to make him feel like the odd man out like some boys would."

"I think the best thing for us to do is carry on with our normal routine," I said. "He'll see us working together mucking the stalls, brushing down the horses, feeding the cattle, you brushing the dogs —we'll let him tag along if he will and help or not as he sees fit. That'll leave it to him to try to fit in or not."

Brett and Aiden's mother agreed that he was old enough to ride on Amtrak by himself, and they booked a coach seat for his ride from El Paso to Alpine and back—saving twelve hours of drive time. Brett picked him up at the station, and delivered him and Jaxon to our door. We had suggested Quinn come along, and we'd have a chili supper ready and waiting.

Sitting around the kitchen table, I looked at this peculiar bunch from three different ex-wives of Brett's and saw a family for the first time. It had always looked to me like a bunch of misfits, forced together—of a kind—which it was. Now, even Aiden seemed to be sitting there a part of the whole. Quinn, who couldn't face anyone those first days in Alpine, knew that her careless behavior was forgiven, and the family had embraced her and the child she would bear in the spring—embraced by the church of mercy over judgment that defines this family now.

I sat there staring at Brett for whom I had had no respect for so long, and now I saw a man doing his best to be his best for his children. My meandering thoughts were abruptly ended when Jaxon shared with us that he'd finally talked to his and Quinn's mother.

"Mom finally called me to see what I knew about Quinn. She acted like I might not know what was going on. When I made it clear I did, she wanted to know if Quinn had an abortion or was getting one. When I told her she was having the baby, she seem relieved. I'm sure she was. She wouldn't have to worry about that getting back to the family somehow. Then she asked, 'When is she getting married?' When I told her she wasn't, she got real quiet. She finally asked, 'Is she going to get DNA tests to confirm who the father is?' And when I said she wasn't, she asked, 'What am I supposed to tell my family?' I said, 'Tell them you're about to be a grandmother. While you're at it, you can tell them I'm gay. 'Oh, my God!' she said. 'Deal with it, Mother!' I said. 'It's not the end of the world.' She pretty much just hung up after that."

It was clear Quinn was hearing this for the first time. When her brother finished she responded simply, "Thank you. I don't really want to talk to her right now, and I certainly don't want the moral lecture I'm sure to get from Grandma. I'm not going to punish this baby for my mistakes or let them put their shame on him or her, whichever it happens to be."

Brett assured her, "Quinn, the only way they can inflict their shame on you is if you allow it."

"I know, Dad. The shame I had left me when Grandma and Grandpa Schlatter came to Alpine to see me. I know my baby is already loved by them and by you."

Billy added, "By all of us, Quinn—the baby and you."

Brett asked, "Jaxon, to that last revelation you sprung on your mother and us just now, is that true or for dramatic effect?"

He smiled, "Only in theory—not in practice."

Aiden, who hadn't spoken since he arrived, said to his roommate for the next few nights, "I'm not gay, so don't think about putting your theory into practice while we're sharing a room here."

He looked serious but not in a mean way.

Billy poked Aiden in the arm, saying, "You're supposed to tell him that if he does, you'd better enjoy it."

I shook my head. "I'm sure that's the advice Aiden was looking for."

Jaxon replied, "He doesn't need to worry. He's not my type."

Billy asked, "You have a type, huh. Care to share?"

Jaxon replied, "I think I've probably said too much already. I do have my dad's ability to talk a little too much from time to time."

Billy wasn't quite ready to drop it just yet. "Are there good prospects that are your type at Sul Ross? It's a pretty small school. I suspect it's slim pickin's."

Jaxon answered, "All I can say at this point is there's one guy I hope might be a prospect, but I don't know for sure. He's friendly to me. That's as far as it's gone."

Then Billy added, "Jaime, we may have to take these boys to the gay bar in Marfa while they're here. Jaxon could invite his friend."

Aiden said, "I didn't think I wanted to go to a gay bar, and besides I'm underage."

I clarified, "Age isn't a problem, and it might be too cold this time of year, anyway. The gay bar in Marfa is the bar stools in your Aunt Jean and Aunt Mary-Alice's, back patio."

Aiden's comfort level returned. "I have to admit, that's pretty funny. I might tag along just to say I've been to a gay bar."

I said, "Even your Grandma gets tickled by the fact that she's been to a gay bar."

Noah added, "Grandpa just says, 'Good lord.'"

"Noah, these two dogs are lookin' at you wondering where their chili is," I pointed out. "Here, put this leftover cheese and hot-pan bread with it. It's plenty cool enough now to give 'em some."

Aiden suggested, "These dogs have it a lot better than half the kids in El Paso."

Noah replied, "I've lived there. Being on this ranch is better than any kid in El Paso has it."

He hesitated a minute and added, "It sounds like I'm rubbin' it in. I didn't mean to do that, Aiden."

"I know you didn't," he said. "I don't know if I'd want to live out here in the boondocks or not. I kinda like city life."

Billy commented, "Noah, Jaime and I know you can be lonely in the city or in the boondocks. If you can keep from bein' lonely, I don't guess it matters if you live in the city a small town or a ranch."

"Amen to that," I said.

When we all went over the next morning to decorate the chapel, to our shock, we learned Sallie had invited Norman to attend the family celebration on Christmas Eve. She had two things to say about it beforehand. "I thought we might as well have our own Santa Claus, and no, he will not be spending the night. Since he no longer has any family around, I thought it was overdue for me to include him in a family Christmas."

Billy said, "This year certainly sets a new standard for a family Christmas. I'm glad you thought of Norman."

She noted, "He is too. His exact words were, 'Sallie Faye, this sure means a lot to me.'"

Billy asked, "Is he coming in his Santa outfit?"

Sallie replied, "I hope not. He did offer. I said there weren't any children little enough to appreciate it except possibly my oldest nephew."

Billy jested, "I could sit on Santa's lap if it makes him feel more welcome."

"Good lord," Bill said shaking his head.

Jaxon asked, "Who's Norman, and what's all this Santa Claus talk?"

Betsy replied, "Norman was your great aunt's high school sweetheart. He moved away from Fort Davis right after graduation, and he has only come back to her in the last couple years. When you see him, you'll see why we call him Santa Claus."

Sallie concluded, "And that's a sufficient summary of my life history with Norman. Jaxon, he was not my long-lost love in case you were wondering, which everyone seems to always assume. He amused me then and still amuses me to some degree."

Billy asked, "Jaxon, are you going to share with your grandparents and great aunt your call with your mom?"

He had a momentary look of panic, but when he saw his dad nod as though he should proceed, he told them the full extent of the call just as he had told it to us the evening before.

Bill walked over to Jaxon prompting him to stand. He hugged Jaxon and said, "That was a very nice thing to do for your sister."

Both sat back down. Bill continued, "As for your own news to your mother, sometimes it's best just to shock people into reality. You gave her a healthy dose of that. Your news doesn't change anything in this family, but I'd hope you know that already."

"Thank you, Grandpa," Jaxon said.

Billy added, "He told us his news was still theoretical and hasn't been put into practice yet."

Bill said to Jaxon, "Theoretical or not, it will be interesting to see how your mother deals with it in that family of hers."

Quinn noted, "They will either blame her or say the Schlatters have been a bad influence on their grandchildren."

Betsy said, "They will probably do both. I can live with them blaming us. It won't change anything in this family."

Aiden added, "My mom wants to know where the dad I have now was while she was married to him."

Brett bluntly responded, "With his head up his ass. And, of my four marriages, your mother got the worst of it. I married her for all the wrong reasons after my first marriage failed. And while I'm confessing, I had an affair with Noah's mother which is why I left that marriage as soon as I did after you were born. I'm sorry about that. I'm not sorry I had you four kids, even if I've been a shitty dad all your lives. I'm trying to turn it around now."

Billy looked at the five rather pitiful faces of Brett and his offspring. "If it were me, I'd be calling for a big group hug right now. You all need it."

I guess they agreed. They all stood and hugged with Bill and Betsy hugging the group.

Billy whispered to me, "I don't think they need me in the huddle this time."

I whispered back, "I agree. They need this family moment."

I'd enjoyed every Christmas Eve since our first in the chapel those years ago, but none so much as this year—with Brett's children coming together in a new and accepting way and even

Norman, with his bright, blue eyes and wide smile at being included. I looked at him with a recollection of my own life when I first was becoming part of the family. I was even more the odd man out in those days, but it didn't keep them from embracing me and folding me into their lives. I imagined how, if he hadn't left for those fifty years, he too probably would have been folded in long ago with some life with Sallie, even if it included the "living in sin" arrangement without "the sin" as Billy and I have done all these years.

I had real hope for everyone, and a sadness for the alienation Jaxon and Quinn's mother seemed willing to self-inflict for the sake of her judgmental parents. As Betsy had said, if there isn't a story of a prodigal mother in the Bible, there ought to be. At the time, she had asked if perhaps I might know of one. I did not, and it put me to searching for one. I came up empty even though my own mother, Billy's, Jaxon and Quinn's and Noah's—all had some semblance of rejecting love for their own pursuits.

In my mother's case, I've never figured out what she was pursuing. In Betsy's, it was exchanging love for someone else's idea of moral certitude. For Jaxon and Quinn's mother, it seemed to be an unwillingness to lose her family's approval for a second time, as she'd done when she divorced. And for Noah's mother, whose dependence on a *terrible* man put her only, already-alienated son at risk, it brought no apparent happiness to her and led to her own death.

I set the peculiar history of our mothers aside and returned to the calm of the mystical night of Christmas Eve. I was filled with an overwhelming sense of joy. As I walked towards the chapel to sing and light candles with my adopted and growing family, I looked up at the cloudless, star-filled sky and said to myself, and any gentle spirit listening, "Oh, gentle spirit, bless this peace."

Chapter Nineteen

Ernesto was true to his promise or threat—I guess it could have been interpreted either way—to include Mark in his New Year's Eve act—*Nine to Five*. Ernesto was, of course, Dolly Parton as Doralee. Mark had his choice between Lily Tomlin as Violet or Jane Fonda as Judy. He opted for Violet and was instructed to be there early enough to greet the guests as they arrived.

Aiden was back on the train for home by then, but we had Rosalinda's okay if Jaxon wanted to come along with Billy, Noah and me. Brett still had not gotten on the invitation list, and it would have been too much for Quinn at that point, anyway. They spent their New Year's Eve in Alpine. Jaxon planned to stay with us at the ranch until the semester started. Zoey rode in with Mark. We rode in with two boys and two dogs.

Both Doralee and Violet were at the door to greet us. The first thing Billy asked was, "Do we all get to recreate the pot-smoking scene?"

Rosalinda was right behind Mark and said, "Dream on, Billy. What would Elma say to such a suggestion?"

I imitated Elma's quiet voice. "Oh, Noah and *Jaime* are such nice boys. I don't know about that Billy, though."

Ernesto said, "Billy, have I got a surprise for you? As soon as everybody's here, I'll reveal it."

"Hot damn!" Billy exclaimed.

I suggested, "You might want to withhold your enthusiasm until you see what the surprise is."

Billy said, "It'll be good. We know that."

"If you say so," I said.

I could only think of one thing related to the night's act that Ernesto might pull, but I wasn't about to suggest to Billy what it was. It was revealed soon enough, and my notion of the trick he was going to play on Billy was correct.

Ernesto pronounced, "Billy, come over here." He pulled a sheet off a contraption he'd rigged up and quickly had Billy in a leather sling and hoisted a few feet off the ground with his big hind end up in the air. "We're just going to leave you hanging there for the rest of the evening."

Not surprisingly, it didn't faze Billy. He just responded, "I can still drink a beer in this contraption. Zoey, bring me a beer!"

Rosalinda shook her head and leaned into to me. "I told Ernesto, after ten minutes he needs to let him down. He's *not* going to hang there until midnight!"

Jaxon asked, "Is this normal?"

I answered with Rosalinda still standing there, "Where normality is concerned, Ernesto and Billy aren't even close. They are kindred spirits in two parallel universes."

Rosalinda smiled, "But we love them, don't we, *Jaime*?"

"Yes, we do," I replied.

Jaxon said, "I had no idea Fort Davis was such a free-spirited place."

"Live-and-let-live is the motto, as best I can tell," I said. "Especially in the group we run with. It has its uptight crowd, which your grandma used to be tight with, but they are the minority. If you're friends with Ernesto or Billy, there's no way you're going to take life too seriously."

It was more like twenty minutes before Billy was finally set free. Back on his feet he said, "I'm a lot cuter than Dabney Coleman, and I would've never treated Doralee and Violet the way their boss did. I'm real good to my hands. Ain't that right, *Jaime* and Noah?"

Noah cracked up the crowd when he stuttered saying in a very subservient tone, "Oh, oh, ye-yess sir. You-you's a re-real nice bo-boss man. You-you say jump, and-and we-we say h-how high?"

Rosalinda said to me. "I see the next generation is coming on strong."

"I had no idea how strong until just now. Confident little bugger, isn't he?"

Zoey commented, "How could he not be, living with you two?"

"I'll take that as the compliment it was intended to be, but I'm inclined to say the credit belongs to Billy and the elder Schlatters. What a year! Your move here, Noah and Elma's birthday party, Elma's death, Quinn's pregnancy, Noah's letter to Pamela, Jaxon's coming out, Mark's drag initiation, and now Billy hanging in the sling with Noah gettin' the best of him. I guess that's as good an end to the year as any."

She responded, "It will be remembered for a long time, that's for sure."

Chuy and Lupe arrived late. When I saw them come in, I went immediately to greet them. "I wondered where you two were. This crowd is getting so big, I figured you were here somewhere, and I just missed you."

Lupe explained, "No, the old man required a trip to the emergency room. He thought he was having a heart attack. They said he wasn't, and once his heart was in a normal rhythm they sent us on our way. I didn't even call over here to tell them. I thought I'd wait until I had news, and then when we had some, I decided we'd just show up."

I said, "I'm glad to hear it wasn't a heart attack."

Chuy joked, "They said it was atrial fibrillation, most commonly brought on by a wife naggin' at her husband about his grocery shopping."

Lupe chimed in, "He still can't follow the list I give him, but he didn't go to the store today so he can't blame me. *Mamá* always said with my sisters, 'Orneriness has to come out somewhere.' That's what she'd say to them any time they griped about some ache or pain."

"I sure miss her, even though I didn't see her that often," I said. "I can't imagine how much you do."

She responded, "I might have to draft you, Billy and Noah to help me make Easter eggs. That's when I'll miss her most."

"As artistic as Noah is, he'd be good at it. I'm not too sure about Billy and me, but you know I'm a good water dumper."

Chuy pulled Lupe close to him, smiling brightly. "She reminds me every year how much better you were, rather than having to round me up every time she and Elma were ready to take a pot to the stove or back to the sink."

She pushed him back. "Crazy old man!"

"Still no tenant in the casita?" I asked.

Lupe said, "We do have someone staying there right now. A young girl at church is expecting a baby, and her mother threw her out. The girl's father is long gone. I don't see how she can live in that tiny place once the baby's here, but she's welcome as long as she can make do."

I replied, "I'm guessing her rent is even lower than what you charged me—maybe zero even."

Lupe continued, "You guess correctly. She's working part-time now, but she isn't going to have two nickels to rub together when that baby comes."

"No husband in sight?" I asked.

Chuy said, "We'll see when he comes back from deployment in Iraq. She hasn't told him yet, for reasons we don't really understand. I guess she just wants to see if he comes back to her of his own accord."

Lupe added, "Or maybe she's written to tell him, and we just don't know it. So far as we know, she's on her own at this point."

"On her own plus Cardona support," I said. "You missed Billy hanging in the sling. It was quite a sight."

Lupe laughed, "We knew Ernesto was going to do that. I told Chuy on the way back from Alpine, 'Your hospital visit forced us to miss the first feature.'"

I responded, "But you made it for the countdown to midnight."

Chuy joked, "I told the ER doc, I had to be back to Fort Davis by midnight, heart attack or not!"

Lupe added, "He's new to the area. When he asked why, I said, 'If you stay around here long, you'll hear about the Cardona New Year's Eve party. Let's just say, it's a family tradition unlike any other.'"

I smiled. "I'm sure that will have him asking around."

Between being hours past our bedtime and the contemplative side that Billy, Noah and I all have, we're used to driving home in silence after the party. Jaxon was not contemplative (at least not yet) and was wound up after his first Cardona New Year's Eve party, which was certainly understandable. He chattered the whole way back to the ranch and wanted to know more about all the people there. He'd met Tanya and Mando, so Billy filled him in on Tanya's lotto winnings and the dump truck she'd bought with the proceeds.

I explained how the whole drag thing came about with Ernesto's mother telling him she might as well have had a daughter rather than a dirty-mouthed boy after he'd made it clear he wasn't going to ever become a priest. And, how she would hit him with her purse every year, even though everyone knew she was amused by her son as much as everyone else. I also told him how their youngest was such a fine priest doing good work in El Salvador, though sadly the Cardona matriarch didn't live to see her youngest grandson become a priest.

Then he asked, "Were there any gay people there? In that crowd, it would be hard to tell."

Billy replied, "One nice boy from Alpine in theory."

I confessed, "I really don't know. Half the town thinks we are, and the great non-labler, your Uncle Billy, is only too happy to have them think so. But no one has ever approached us thinking we are, to open up that they are, too."

Billy said, "I think most either keep it very private or move away. But that was our generation and the ones before that. I'd hope you could stay around here and live openly just like Jean and Mary-Alice. No one bothers them, that's for sure. If we got out more, I'd suspect we'd know more couples. We just don't get out."

I stated the obvious. "We're real swingers, Jaxon."

Noah asked his brother, "Do you worry about it?"

"About what?" Jaxon asked.

"About others judgin' you?" Noah replied.

"I did in Odessa, and my first year at Sul Ross. Once Quinn came home, and I saw what this family is really like, I didn't worry any more. I felt like a weight had been lifted from the secret I was carrying. I knew there was no way to ever talk to my mom about it."

Billy said, "Blurting it out on the phone the way you did must have felt pretty good."

Jaxon admitted, "I was feelin' a little guilty about feeling so good about it, until Grandpa said giving someone a reality shock can be the best thing for them." Then he added, "I think my dad thought you two were lovers for a long time."

Billy said, "We are lovers. We just don't fit the mold people make for two men who happen to have committed to living their

115

life together. Jaime, you should tell him what Sallie says about love."

"Jaxon, your great aunt says she doesn't believe in one kind of love prescribed by someone else."

Jaxon replied, "That's a real good way of puttin' it. I don't know how I landed in this family when I did."

All I could say to that was, "You have that in common with everyone in this truck. I'd guess even Kola and Koala would agree. We've all healed together."

Noah confirmed, "Kola and Koala do agree. They just wish you and Uncle Billy could have adopted their momma before someone else spoke for her."

Billy turned his attention to the dogs. "Kola and Koala, we do apologize for that. Chuy told us your momma was a real good dog."

I asked, "Any reaction from them on that?"

Noah said, "They say she was a *real* good momma, but they understand. Kola says at least you gave 'em a real nice boy as a substitute."

Jaxon confessed to his little brother, "I was never nice to you growin' up. We were all really strangers, and I hated when we all had to get together. I'm sorry about that now. You're pretty special."

Noah reassured him, "I had no life before I moved to the ranch. There wasn't anything to be nice to back then. I was just a mess hidin' under the bed."

Once again, we let his truth sink in.

Billy said, "But you're doing all right now."

"But I'm doing all right now," Noah responded.

Billy asked, "Jaxon, you doing all right now?"

"Yes, sir. I'm doing all right now."

Chapter Twenty

With classes at Sul Ross not starting until after the MLK holiday, Jaxon was out on the ranch for a few weeks. Billy and I got a break from mucking stables as Jaxon and Noah told us they'd take that on while Jaxon was there. We didn't argue. It must be said, we didn't just leave them to it. We enjoyed standing there watching them as they'd fill their wheelbarrows and take the loads out to the compost heap.

Billy would say, "Good work, boys. We'll make horsemen out of you both yet."

Jaxon said, "I haven't been around a lot of animals, but I have to say, horse shit stinks bad!"

I added, "I would say you get used to it, but I never have. They are beautiful animals but dump a lot of shit."

I asked Jaxon, "The few times you've gone riding out here, was that something you enjoyed or just something you felt like you had to do?"

He replied, "I liked it all right. It beat sittin' in the bunkhouse all day not knowing what to do."

Billy offered, "When the weather is good, we'll take a ride or two while you're here. It might be more fun now that we all know each other better."

Jaxon said, "I'd like that."

Billy, pleased with himself, added, "I'll take you to where I proposed to Jaime."

"You proposed to Jaime?" Jaxon asked.

I replied, "That's what he likes to call it. And I guess it was a proposal of a kind. Bill, Betsy and Sallie hoped I would make a life with the family on the ranch, and Billy was given the directive to decide if two men could work and live together to make a life together, or was one of us going to get the itch to get married."

Billy said, "Dad thought Jaime to be the more likely to have luck in the romance and marriage department. Dad had a pretty good idea from my years in Van Horn that I wouldn't leave the ranch long enough to find a wife."

Noah laughed. "I guess he was right about that last part."

I added, "And I assured Billy, and the family, that I wasn't going anywhere either if they'd have me."

Billy continued, "Jaime's chick cruisin' days were over by then. They'd worn him out by the time I came along. I think that's why he never cuddles up with me at night."

"The only place we ever cuddle up is at the Slo Poke Cafe," I said.

Jaxon stated, "I'd like to see that sometime."

Noah replied, "You probably will if any of Grandma's old church group is in there. That's what gets Uncle Billy going."

Billy said, "They need to loosen up, and I'm there to remind them. It could be I'll do a special show just for you whether they are there or not. The first time I grabbed Jaime was pure inspiration. There weren't any church ladies to perform for."

I noted, "It was Ernesto-inspired, which should explain it well enough now that you've met him."

And so we took that ride on a sunny January day. We had a big breakfast and set out for the day. Even the dogs trotted along, though they thought we ought to be movin' cattle at some point. They'd look to us every time we passed through a section with steers, waiting for the whistles that never came. When we got to the rock outcropping we recreated the hug.

Jaxon said, "We've been up to this outcropping before. I just didn't know it had such significance."

Billy joked, "You might want to break in your friend to horse ridin' if he isn't already, and bring him here when you're ready to pop the question."

I noted, "Could be, Billy, you're gettin' just a little ahead of things."

Billy responded, "Some nice boy will come along. I can see Jaxon's got some of that Geermann-Schlatter charm that makes people want to like us."

"The Geermann magnetism is real enough," I said. "Sallie's got it, Billy's got it and Noah's got it. Jaxon, I'd say Billy's probably right that you've got it too. It was just hidden in insecurity for a long time. Noah can relate to that and maybe Billy, too, but not by the time I knew him."

118

Billy added, "I certainly suppressed it, if it is a gift. Though, as I've told Jaime, there were guests to the ranch up by Van Horn who wanted me as their cowboy conquest, but I never allowed them the satisfaction."

I asked Jaxon, "Did your dad ever tell you much about your great-grandparents—the Geermann ones, I mean, who owned this ranch?"

"I don't know anything about them," he replied.

I said, "Billy you owe the boy the story of how special they both were. Noah might even learn a thing or two, though he knows most of it already."

Billy laid out everything—from his identical looks and mother's surprise at seeing him after twenty years to the old man's head for numbers, his ability to craft a plan in an instant and his crazy-good humor. He shared the river road drive where he recalled the quietness of his grandmother and the great influence she'd had on his life, and how Sallie had told him she had no idea anyone understood their mother as she and Betsy had known her.

Jaxon asked, "Why don't you think Dad ever talks about them?"

Billy answered, "Mostly, I suppose, because growing up he almost never came to the ranch. I came every chance I got. Your dad and Jean never really got to know them like I did."

Jaxon reckoned, "I guess that's why you and Sallie are so close."

I replied, "Billy is the son Sallie never had. She loves that boy."

Jaxon asked, "So who do you think I look like? Noah certainly favors Grandpa Schlatter—I can see that."

Billy said, "Height-wise and build-wise you're somewhere between the short and stocky Geermann and the tall and lanky Schlatter. Of course, I don't know your mom's side of the family. Could be, you've got a lot of their characteristics, but your dark hair and eyes certainly could be Geermann. Both grandparents had dark features which Grandma said was from their Swiss ancestors."

Jaxon asked, "The Geermanns were Swiss?"

Billy replied, "The Geermanns and the Schlatters. The families knew each other back in the old country and came over at the same time—same boat and everything. Grandpa Schlatter's mother was from Alsace. I don't know much more about her than that. She was dead by the time I came along, and Great-grandpa Schlatter remarried. Dad never was too close to him, and certainly not close at all with his brother, who still lives in San Angelo."

Jaxon said, "I don't know where my mom's family is from. I think they were English or Scottish or Irish or something."

I noted, "They could certainly be all of the above and then some."

Noah added, "My mom's family was Scandinavian. I guess my lighter colored hair mostly comes from there."

Billy rightly noted, "Where they are all from really doesn't matter. What matters is to honor the good parts you learn from them and leave behind the baggage. Jaime says we shouldn't forget the bad. It's there to remind us how far we've come."

I added, "You just don't ever want to give the bad parts power over your life like so many people do—reliving a hurt over and over or bearing a grudge for your whole life."

The days went quickly by. We told Brett we'd deliver Jaxon back to campus. When we drove into Alpine, we finally had lunch at John and James's bistro. We enjoyed it, but we didn't see either of them, which disappointed Billy. We all thought none of the servers were up to Sara's high standard. What little sophistication they tried to pull off was offset by their overall low-grade level of competence.

When we dropped Jaxon off, he stood looking into the pickup for a few seconds. "This has been the best three weeks of my life."

Billy put out his hand to hold Jaxon's. "You know our place is a safe place for you anytime you need it. We hope you'll spend more of your breaks with us. Jaime likes having someone to shovel horse shit for him."

I said, "Jaxon, when he says such things, we just tell him he's a mess."

Noah added, "He's our mess and now he's yours, too."

Billy smiled, "Good thing I've got a lot of mess to share the way I keep gettin' passed around! For a long time, I was just Jaime's mess."

Jaxon laughed, and just as he was ready to slam the truck door, his eye caught someone from across the way. "Over there—see that guy going up the walk?"

Billy asked, "That's him, huh? Pretty cute! You'd have beautiful children."

Jaxon shook his head. "Uncle Billy, you *are* a mess!"

Billy chuckled, "But apparently, I'm your mess, too, now."

I was in the driver's seat since leaving the restaurant, and I gave two quick toots of the horn as we pulled away with Jaxon waving goodbye.

Noah said, "I went from not feelin' like I had any kind of brother to having a brother and a real good friend."

Billy added, "Who knew? What a great kid."

I said, "I think 'young man' is the better-suited term."

Billy looked back at Noah. "Great young men seem to be in abundance these days."

Then he said, "Jaime, let's take the long way home. We can drop in unannounced at Jean and Mary-Alice's if they're home. We won't bother them long. I just need to tell 'em what a bad influence they were on Jaxon."

I smiled, "I'm sure they will be real worried about that."

They were home and shocked to see us. Jean said, "This is a first. Since when do you drive all the way to Marfa for an unannounced visit?"

Billy responded, "We just dropped Jaxon off, and figured we'd take the long way home."

"Oh," she replied. "That halfway explains it."

Billy said, "I told Jaime and Noah I had to get on you for corrupting Jaxon with your deviant lifestyle."

Jean replied, "We are wild things, but nothing compared to you and Jaime."

"Touché," I said.

Then Billy added, "We finally ate at your client's bistro. It was pretty good, but we didn't see them. The help was kinda surly."

Mary-Alice interjected, "They were over here this morning telling us all the latest restaurant drama. I think they are about to say to hell with it."

Jean said, "TV reality shows have nothing on them. They've had three chefs named Joseph, who came and left in short order. The first one they really liked, but his wife wanted to leave Alpine and move back to her family in Austin. The second was a drug addict who just quit coming to work. The third arrived as a husband and wife team who moved from across the country, were there for two days and left. They couldn't live in a small town after all, it seemed."

Mary-Alice continued, "And that is just the start of it. The line cook is having an affair with one of the waitresses, using the couch in their office as their love shack; and hundreds of dollars and pounds of food go missing every time they are gone for even half an hour from the place. Of course, the employees play real innocent when John and James confront them. They never know who to believe."

Jean said, "They even had one employee tell them that her drug dealer told her to tell another employee that he needed cash from then on. His freezer was filled with all the Bistro shrimp and steaks he could use."

Mary-Alice added, "They have also had sewer problems in the old building and equipment breaking down constantly. John said he told James last evening, "What the 'F' are we ruining our retirement for? I don't care if we lose every cent we've put in the place. This nightmare has to end!'"

I questioned, "That was all from your visit this morning?"

"Every word of it," Jean replied.

Billy asked, "Won't they try to sell it?"

Jean said, "We had the distinct impression they will just shut it down and sell off the equipment for whatever they can get and pay off the lease."

Mary-Alice noted, "You may have eaten the last meal they'll be serving. Unless they changed their mind between here and there, they were going to close it down."

"Holy shit!" Billy exclaimed. "I'm glad Jaime and I didn't give up our day jobs to tend bar for 'em."

I said, "And Sara was right about not getting into restaurant drama. I had no idea a small town restaurant could compete with big urban drama on that scale!"

Jean replied, "As John put it, 'This may sound like a lot, but it's only the tip of the iceberg.'"

Noah used Bill's line. "Good lord."

Jean added, "And something else we learned recently. Billy, they are not the gay guys from Dallas after all. They are half brothers who owned a successful business together—both divorced with grown kids. They both wanted to retire out here."

I said, "I guess Rosalinda was right all along. We are gayer than they are."

Chapter Twenty-one

Billy's curiosity was getting the best of him. When we were back home, he emailed Brett, filling him in on the restaurant drama, along with the directive for Brett to see if the half brothers had closed it down.

When Brett got home from work, he emailed back.

I can confirm the sign on the door says—closed permanently.

Brett

Billy said, "I would say they just needed a good foreman like me, but after hearing the mess those guys have put up with, I'll just say, I'm glad I'm a cowboy!"

I replied, "A gen-u-ine cowboy's life may be tough, but at least the only real shit we have to deal with is coming out the backside of a horse."

Billy shifted gears, saying, "Speaking of shit, when is Zoey gonna get her chicken enterprise going? I thought we'd have fresh eggs long ago."

"Well, at first she was waiting on getting the GS Ranches ventures up and running, and then she decided with winter coming, she should wait for spring."

He acknowledged, "I suppose that is the better plan."

I added, "I think she even has a bunch of chicks ordered and is just waiting until sometime late March to pick them up at the feed store in Alpine. She told me she's watched dozens of *YouTube* videos on raising chickens including letting them run around the yard. There are dogs that will protect them from raccoons and such, though with our fencing that should not really be a problem— but I have warned her about checking for snakes when gathering eggs. Apparently turkeys are good to mix in with them, too, for protection."

Billy noted, "Raccoons can climb fences when they want to. She might want a guard dog if she's going to let them run in the yard."

I said, "I'll let her know. She told me, 'I've gone from city girl to someone ready to gather eggs around rattlesnakes, and it doesn't even intimidate me.'"

Billy joked, "You Cruzes adapt quickly."

"Yes, I guess we do."

Mark and Zoey were also getting their first visitors. His parents were coming in on Amtrak for a two-week visit in the latter half of February.

Billy had noted, "I'm not sure why they picked February, but I guess it's better than the crazy winds of March and April and hot, dry May."

Betsy hosted a welcome dinner, and the Schlatter band provided the pre-meal entertainment. Mark's parents weren't interested in riding, so we let them be for the remainder of their stay, assuring Zoey that if they wanted to interact more they could just say the word.

After they were gone, Mark said, "They told us they were glad we liked it here, but it was just a bit too remote for them."

Zoey added, "They are used to eating out practically every meal and going to a movie every week. They are both in a bowling league on top of that. I'm glad for them, but I'm just as glad for us."

"Hear, hear!" Mark exclaimed.

Billy asked, "Did they try to talk you into moving back to California?"

Mark replied, "They knew that would be as futile as me trying to persuade them to move here."

Zoey said, "We did take them to the Cowboy Poetry gathering in Alpine, which they really enjoyed."

"I never have gone," I said. "I'm not sure why. Certainly, I would enjoy it."

"You would," she continued, "and Bill really ought to sign up sometime to recite some of his poetry. They have several sessions where there are two or three different poets in the hour-long program, so it's not like he'd have to carry the whole show."

Billy added, "I've never been either. I think Mom and Dad have gone a couple times. I'll tell him you say he could knock their socks off."

I said, "You might take a more subtle approach if you really want him to do it. I don't think appealing to his ego is going to get you very far. Urging him to share his gifts would be appropriate."

He agreed, "I suppose that's right. It would be a good field trip for Noah, too."

The next Saturday, we went in for food pantry distribution though our motive was as much to see if John and James would be at the Slo Poke Cafe. We knew we wouldn't be having lunch with Rosalinda and Ernesto—they were in El Salvador. Lupe had said she'd help out at the pantry in their absence, and we looked forward to seeing her and hoped she and Chuy might join us for lunch.

Lupe was hard at it when we arrived, and seemed to have sufficient help even if we had not shown up. The first thing she said was, "I'm really glad to see you, and as you can see, I couldn't get the old man to join me."

I asked, "How is he feeling after his trip to the ER?"

She replied, "He's fine—playing it for all it's worth. He has me waiting on him hand and foot. I told him, 'You're not sick in bed. You could at least get up and get the remote yourself.' He says, 'I don't want to strain my heart.' I would refuse, but then he really would have a heart attack, and I'd feel guilty. He's still a Cardona, 'Honey, get me beer while you're up.' I may ship him out to the ranch for rehab."

Billy joked, "Jaxon thought shoveling horse shit was real therapeutic. We could have him work a little on that every afternoon."

Lupe laughed, "That would be a good job for him. When can he start? I guess, I need to quit chatting and get this thing opened up. Are we going to lunch afterwards?"

I replied, "We hope so."

"Good," she said, "I told the old man to be on standby."

She called him when things were winding down, and he was at the Slo Poke by the time the four of us arrived.

Sara was quickly there with our iced teas. Billy asked, "Sara, did you know the guys from Dallas closed their restaurant?"

"Oh, yeah, and they were here the next day. That's the first time I've heard you say the guys from Dallas and not the gay guys from Dallas."

126

Billy added, "It turns out they are half brothers. At least that's the story they told my sister."

Sara smiled, "They are. I've always just wanted to see how long it was before you found out. News travels slow to that ranch."

I replied, "That's an understatement, though I can't believe Rosalinda and Ernesto never said anything."

Lupe said, "I don't think they knew either. They call them the gay guys from Dallas same as you. Chuy and I assumed they were, too."

Sara said, "I told them once that y'all thought they were gay, and John's reaction was, 'We figured Billy thought we were, but it seemed to amuse him so, that we never corrected him. He isn't the first one to assume we're a couple of lovers and not brothers.'"

"Billy noted, "It was the different last names that threw me off. Modern families—you never know who's related." Then to Chuy he said, "I hear you're going to come muck the horse stalls as part of your rehab."

Chuy instantly dismissed such a notion. "I've got a good thing goin'. I'm not about to mess it up."

Lupe added, "I told 'em what a good thing you had going."

Just as she said it, John and James came in and sat in their old booth—the booth that had been Claude's preferred spot before them.

Billy poked me. *"Jaime*, let's go offer our condolences."

I said, "I'm not sure they are going to want to be reminded this soon. And we were never patrons, so I feel kind of bad even bringing it up."

Billy offered an alternative strategy. "We can at least say how we know they've missed seeing me."

I stood to go over to them. "That you can probably get away with. They'd almost be expecting it—almost."

Billy noted, "They don't look depressed."

I said, "If as described by the girls, I'm sure they are relieved to be out from under it."

We went over to their booth, and Billy reached out to shake each one's hand. "It's nice to see you. It's been a long a time."

James replied, "I'm sure you've probably heard that we closed the hellhole down."

Billy said, "My brother reported seeing the sign on the door."

"You have a brother in Alpine?" John asked.

Billy replied, "My brother, Brett, is a realtor there."

"Duh," James said. "I don't know why we didn't put that together. He would eat in the restaurant sometimes."

I said, "So back to retired life, I guess."

John answered, "Why did we ever leave retired life in the first place? We're just glad it's over. Any romantic notion of it being fulfilling was shattered before we ever opened the doors. That was the longest nightmare we've ever had."

James exclaimed, "Ex-wives included!"

"I used to call you the gay guys from Dallas, Billy commented. "I guess I'm going to have to adopt a new name."

"Sorry to disappoint you, Billy," John said. "We understand your own carrying on with Jaime is for the benefit of the good church ladies in town. We're glad to contribute what we can in that regard."

Billy smiled, "I always knew I liked you guys. Maybe now that you have your freedom, you can come out for Quiet Day. We still do them the first Saturday of every month."

James said, "We might just take you up on that. We could use some balm in our life right now."

John added, "We enjoyed it the one time we came, but we got so wrapped up in our enterprise it consumed us ever since."

I shifted gears. "Jean told us you had your own business in Dallas. I take it, it wasn't a restaurant."

John replied, "No, we leased floors in office buildings and then leased offices out to small businesses where we provided secretarial support, office equipment, conference rooms and even billing services—though an accountant handled that part of the business for us. We sold all the leases and goodwill to a competitor and moved out here."

Billy said, "So playing office is a lot better than playing restaurateur."

"Much better!" James exclaimed.

I saw Sara back at our table. "Billy, Sara just set down our plates. We haven't even let these guys order. I hope we see you at Quiet Day soon."

John replied, "You will."

"I still miss that black Jag," Billy lamented.

John said, "Now you sound like James. He says we now drive dull and dependable."

Billy laughed, "Too true. Too true."

As we were just about to head back, James asked, "I guess that boy with you is the one whose mother was murdered?"

I answered, "Yes, that's Noah, and he's a fantastic young man. We're so glad to him have living with us."

Billy joked, "Jaime just likes Noah's help shoveling horse shit. You guys take care."

"That's quite a way to leave it," I said.

Billy replied, "I thought you'd work in 'of a kind,' but you left it alone."

"I didn't know what to say after that," I added.

When we rejoined the others, Noah asked, "What y'all talk about?"

"For that, your uncle will have to tell you."

As we were leaving, Noah stopped at John and James's table.

"Hi, I'm Noah. I already know your names. It's nice to meet you. My uncle Billy is a mess, but he's my mess and Uncle Jaime's mess, too. Uncle Billy says it's a good thing he's got plenty of mess to go round. I hope we see you at Quiet day."

James responded, "You take care, Noah. We'll see you real soon."

As we walked to the truck Noah said, "I hope that makes 'em feel real welcome."

I assured him, "I'm sure of it."

As the Marfa crowd seemed to continue to diminish, slowly but surely, the Fort Davis attendance at the next Quiet Day seemed to be on an uptick. Indeed, John and James were at Quiet Day along with Ava's return, and with Ava was her husband, Dew. Billy wasn't sure what his real name was. All he'd ever heard anyone call him was Dew.

Billy said, "I know their last name ain't Dewey, and I've never heard that as a first name."

I asked, "Did you ever ask your folks or Sallie?"

He replied, "No, I never thought to as a boy. I never knew who he was married to. Dad would talk to Dew if he ran into him at the feed store or hardware."

I said, "I guess we'll ask them this afternoon. We're supposed to be quiet until then."

Billy made a gesture with his hand zipping his lips shut.

Another woman arrived at the same time as Ava and Dew, and we had no idea who she was. We'd just have to wait until Quiet Day was dismissed to find out. Betsy clearly knew her. Perhaps another fundamentalist was being corrupted before our very eyes.

As people were leaving mid-afternoon, Bill visited for several minutes with Dew saying later, "Dew ought to like this kind of thing. He rarely has more than ten words to say at any given time. Quiet comes as naturally to him as anyone I've ever known."

Billy asked, "Who was that other woman who was here?"

Bill replied, "I don't know her. Your mother told me she was from the church group—a newer arrival. She knew who she was, but didn't know her well."

We had to leave before having a chance to talk to Betsy, who was still visiting with Ava and the new woman. We'd invited John and James to come by *Casa Vieja* to visit for a bit, and they followed us over.

Kola and Koala do not like Quiet Day. According to Noah and Billy, it starts too early and ends too late. The only saving grace is it's only one Saturday a month. They were both at the door ready to launch into the backyard. When they saw the two men getting out of the car, they started barking their heads off.

I said, "Oh, yeah. You're both real mean. Go tear 'em up."

Billy added, "We've upset their routine even further. They don't expect any company when we return from Quiet Day."

Neither man looked too comfortable with barking dogs. Billy issued the whistle to stand down and both did—with a couple little, lip-muffled "woof-woofs" for good measure.

John said, "You have good guard dogs, and you obviously have them well trained."

Noah replied, "They're trained to help us move cattle." Pointing at each, he said, "The one that looks like Jaime is Koala and the other one is Kola. Kola used to sleep with Uncle Jaime and Koala with Uncle Billy. Now they both sleep with me."

We went into the warm house—it was too chilly even for us tough cowboys to sit outside. Billy lit a fire, and figuring they'd had their fill of coffee for the day, I offered them a drink.

"We don't have much of a bar, but we do have beer, and in the winter we like a Grand Marnier every once in a while. Can I get you anything?"

John seemed to answer for them both. "We wouldn't turn down a Grand Marnier."

We visited about their restaurant horror stories, acting surprised by most of it, as we didn't want to betray a confidence with Jean and Mary-Alice in case such would have bothered the brothers.

Billy said, "Memo to Jaime and Noah—shoot me if I ever suggest we open a GS Ranches steak house."

James raised his eyebrows, saying, "For Noah's sake our account was the 'G' rated version. It would be generous to say the real account would be rated, at a minimum, of 'R.'"

John added, "Male or female, the language in that kitchen was enough to make a sailor blush, like their extracurricular activity wasn't bad enough."

I noticed they'd left out the sex on the couch, presumably for Noah's sake, who'd already heard about it, of course. I thought Noah might bring it up, but he didn't. He could see we were acting surprised, and thought he should keep mum on knowing more.

Billy asked, "So what do lapsed Baptists think about Quiet Day? We know it's not everyone's cup of tea."

James replied, "Driving over here, we agreed, it's something we will probably attend with more frequency. It helps you get out of your head for a few hours and just contemplate the world around you, and the ranch setting is the perfect place to do that."

John added, "We also decided we'd get more involved with the food panty. If we'd stuck to Quiet Day and volunteering, we'd have saved tens of thousands of dollars of our retirement and untold hours of frustration."

James said, "I never will forget, the second day on the job with the last Joseph, when I came in all excited and asked John how it was going. He stood by the bar and started to cry. It took him a good two minutes before he could get the words out to tell me the couple had left."

John continued, "Then we found out he'd ordered a bunch of Axis venison he was going to add to the menu. Our temperamental line cook didn't know squat about cooking venison and ruined most of it."

James stressed, "It was delicious if you like eating dried shoe leather."

Billy looked at Koala and asked, "You hear that, girl? You love dried shoe leather, don't you?"

I explained, "Billy lost his best pair of cowboy boots to a puppy who wasn't too happy about being left home alone with only her sister for company."

John smiled, "She could have had an all-you-can-eat venison buffet had we known."

I said, "I know from my own observation over the years that the likes of Sara is a rare thing in the restaurant world."

John added, "And she had sense enough to warn us and steer clear herself but, somehow, we thought as long as we treated our employees well and paid more than the going rate, we'd be just fine."

James concluded, "Eating at home has never sounded better."

Lupe called on Sunday afternoon, "*Jaime*, I'm soon going to be decorating Easter eggs. Is Noah going to help and are you going to carry and dump the water?"

I replied, "We are ready and standing by. What time do you want us there? I recall you and your *mamá* getting an early start."

She asked, "Is 7:00 too early?"

"Not at all. You know we get up early."

She replied, "I'll have some breakfast tacos ready and waiting."

I said, "Noah has been gathering things for months from around the ranch that he will be bringing along. He says to make it clear, if you don't need them or don't think they will work, not to use them just because he brought them."

Lupe laughed. "*Mamá* always figured out how to use whatever I'd bring in as a little girl. I even had dead flies and spiders."

I said, "I guess you weren't afraid of spiders then."

Lupe laughed again. "I don't remember ever being afraid of anything. The first time Chuy and I argued he asked me after, 'Did I frighten you?' I laughed at him and asked, 'Did I look frightened?' He said, 'No, but I was.' I kissed him on the lips and said, 'That's all you need to remember, dear!'"

"You two are quite a hoot," I said. "How is the old man?"

"He really is getting old. I might have to cut him some slack, though he needs to think I'm still giving him a hard time. That keeps him entertained."

On Holy Saturday we arrived at 7:00 as requested and got right to work while enjoying our tacos.

Noah said, "You must have been up since 5:00 with all you've gotten done including making tortillas."

Lupe confessed, "I'll be worn out by tomorrow night. Easter always wears me out, but I look forward to it all the same. It was such a big day for *Mamá*."

Noah said sympathetically, "We all miss our *abuela*. I'd like to do three eggs with her name on them—one for you, one for my grandma and one to take home with us."

Lupe smiled, "I think that would be real nice."

The two artists got to work. Billy even got in on the act.

Lupe said, "Billy, you're pretty good at this. *Mamá* would have invited you to help years ago if she'd known."

"I'm surprised myself," Billy noted. "I didn't think I'd have the patience, but this is quite therapeutic."

Lupe asked, "*Jaime*, you going to try your hand at it?"

"I'm happy doing the heavy lifting and dying. Keep up the good work, team."

We looked at the small mountain of eggs all ready for Easter. "Now, are you all coming back tomorrow?" Lupe asked.

Billy assured her, "We'll be here. Do we have to make deviled eggs?"

Lupe gave a negative nod, "No, that's my sisters' job. I tell them, 'I decorate 'em. You peel em.' That's our bargain."

We left after the long day of steady work, got the mail and headed to the ranch. I asked, "Noah, do you think you could make that an annual tradition?"

Noah replied, "As long as Lupe wants my help, I'll help. And after she's gone, I'll do some every year just to remember her and Elma."

I said, "I think we'll keep you."

Noah feigned a super-serious tone. "That little suitcase of mine still sits up in the closet. Uncle Billy, I guess you figured out I ain't gonna pack up and leave."

"I forgot all about that suitcase! I meant to take it to Goodwill years ago," Billy exclaimed.

Chapter Twenty-two

It was shoeing day, which is always on a Saturday so that Noah can benefit from his apprenticeship with Sallie. On these days, she arrives early and has breakfast with us and a leisurely third or fourth cup of coffee before we all get serious. Once Billy is done shoeing his own horse, he's off to fill feeders. Once Sallie is done with Nellie, she and Noah help me "of a kind" as I am chief shoer for the remaining four horses. Mostly Noah, Sallie and two red heelers sit there watching me work. I enjoy their company. I like to throw little hoof clippings to the dogs who enjoy chewing on them.

One day, Sallie asked, "Are you boys going to officially designate one of these horses for Jaxon? It seems like he might want to spend more time out here on the ranch."

I replied, "We hadn't talked about it, but that's a good idea. If this family keeps getting closer, we might even have to up the inventory."

She continued, "I suggested to Bill that the ranch ought to hire Jaxon over the summer break—*if* he wanted to come out here and work some."

Noah jumped in, "Hire? Since when does anybody get paid to work around here? I sure don't!"

Sallie chuckled, "They still got you tricked into workin' for free, huh?"

Noah replied, "Uncle Billy says Uncle Jaime can pay me, and then Uncle Billy can charge me rent."

I added, "And then there is all the tuition you'd have to pay for that private school you attend. That would have to come out of your wages, too."

Sallie exclaimed, "Noah, they've got you boxed in good!"

I asked Sallie, "Does Billy know about your idea? He hasn't said anything about it."

She replied, "No, I just thought of it myself, and I asked Bill last evening. He's all for it."

I said, "I'd be all for it, too. I'm sure Billy would like to have another hand to boss around for a few months."

Sallie said, "You boys should talk it over and let Jaxon know before he and his dad come up with some other idea. Maybe he'll just go to summer school. If he does, that'll shoot down workin' out here."

I added, "The motivation for summer school might depend on whether he's had any luck in the romance department, and if he has, on whether that boy is going to be enrolled in summer school or not."

Sallie asked, "Does that boy have a name?"

I joked, "You know this family doesn't like to use the name unless they think there's some prospect for a longer-term relationship."

She gave her head-bobbing chuckle. "Too true. Too true."

"To your question," I replied, "No, we don't know his name. Jaxon just pointed to him when we dropped him off. He didn't say his name." Then I added, "Jaxon didn't get to spend much time with you when he was out here over the holidays, and I think he'd really like to get to know you better."

She said, "I'll make it a point to take him under my wing. He won't get the full benefit Noah gets with me being one of his school teachers, but I'll do my best for him."

Noah suggested, "You could take him on a ride, just you and him, like you do with me sometimes."

"I'll do that, Noah, assuming he's not too scared of such an old, tough cowgirl."

Then she said, "Last time I ran into Alpine to have lunch with Norman, I spent the good part of the afternoon with Quinn. She still hasn't talked to her momma. I asked her if she tried to call her or email, and she said she dreaded getting the shaming she was sure she would get, if not from her mother, then from her grandparents. I think she's right. If her mother was ready to get on with it, she'd have called by now."

I added, "The ex-husband, unmarried pregnant daughter and a gay son—her life is not going according to plan!"

Sallie chuckled, "If you want a plan to fail, try to run your children's lives. I don't have to be a parent to see how many try and then seem shocked when it all goes to hell in a handbasket."

I laughed, "Too true. Too true."

"How is Quinn doing otherwise?" I asked.

Sallie replied, "She and Brett are gettin' along, and she's hangin' in there. She's lucky to have the grandparents she has, and it's a good thing it wasn't back in the days when my sister was with that church bunch. I'm not sure what we expect these girls to do once the deed is done, but if you want anything approaching a happy outcome, all you can do is get on with life. Shaming a girl isn't helping anyone."

"Amen to that," I said. "Amen to both her luck in having the grandparents she has, and amen to getting on with life shame-free."

Sallie observed, "Young girls getting pregnant has only been happening for as long as there have been young girls. We really learn quick. I hope I never hear anyone say to Quinn, 'You'll pay for this mistake the rest of your life.' She can't look at that child like it's a mistake, or she'll resent it for what might have been. The best thing Quinn can do is celebrate what is about to be."

I said, "You're a wise woman, Sallie Geermann."

She responded, "I don't know about that, but I'm old and have observed a lot of unnecessary heartache."

Noah echoed, "You're a wise woman, Aunt Sallie."

Then something tickled her. "Care to share?" I asked.

She said, "I was just thinking about people sayin' that baby will be born out of 'wedlock.' I don't know where that word comes from, but it sounds like you've been incarcerated. No one ever got me locked up in a bad marriage. Of course, once you're married, having babies is just hunky-dory no matter what's really going on in the house."

Sallie looked at Noah, "I'm not sure if you get class credit for your sex-ed lesson this morning or not."

Noah replied, "Some of the best lessons are taught outside the schoolyard."

She gave a good chuckle, exclaiming, "Too true! Too true!"

When I told Billy about Sallie's idea of having Jaxon work on the ranch, he made a quick call to his dad to confirm he could extend an offer and was then immediately on the phone to Jaxon's cell.

"Jaxon. It's Billy. Dad and Sallie wanted to know if you were going to summer school."

Jaxon replied, "I wasn't planning on it. Are they wanting me to? I guess it might save Grandpa some money in the long run if I did."

Billy said, "No. We're all hoping you might take a job as a ranch hand this summer."

Jaxon noted, "I'd have to think you aren't getting much in the bargain. I'm far from being a cowboy and only starting to learn to be a little handy, thanks to some of my hands-on courses."

Billy replied, "Jaime will tell you, you're not as green as he was, and look how he turned out—a gen-u-ine cowboy! I like working with a new ranch hand while he doesn't know shit. That way he doesn't have to unlearn a bunch of bad habits."

Jaxon said, "After Christmas break, shit's the one thing I thought I knew something about."

Billy laughed, "You'll fit right in. Is it 'yea' or 'nay' or do you have to think about it?"

"It's a yea."

"Hot damn!" Billy exclaimed. "By the way, how's your love life? You ready to introduce him to the family?"

Jaxon replied, "You don't even know if he might like boys or girls or happens to like both."

Billy asked, "Did you ever work it out, which it might be?"

Jaxon said, "I'm in luck in that regard."

"Then we ought to at least get a name," Billy said.

Jaxon said, "His name is Caleb, but he's not at all sure how his family is going to take the news. He hasn't blurted it out like I have. I told him what Grandpa said about the value of a good shock, but he's not gotten the courage to try it out."

Billy, all too satisfied with himself, added, "You can't rush him. I'm still waiting on Jaime to come out to his parents."

I could hear the conversation as I sat in the kitchen, and I said loud enough for Jaxon to hear, "Yeah. You know that's the holdup to my sleeping with your uncle."

Billy said, "There you go, Jaxon. Jaime just confirmed it. Tell Caleb he doesn't want to be an old man like Jaime still waiting on the courage to open up."

Jaxon asked, "Isn't Jaime younger than you?"

Billy answered, "By a sliver, but I've never denied being an old man. I've known that ever since the first camping trip we took together down in Big Bend. That's been a bunch o' years ago now. We may have to all go down there over the summer. We're due for a quick vacation before our substitutes get any older than they already are."

"Grandpa and Aunt Sallie, I presume," Jaxon said.

"That's right," Billy replied. "Your grandma says they moan and groan the whole time we're gone, but your grandpa says they're good for a few more vacations, so long as we don't get carried away."

Jaxon said, "If we do, we should try to take Aiden."

Billy liked the idea. "I'll see what your dad has worked out, if anything, as far as gettin' him out here over the summer. Hopefully, he can stay a while. What's Caleb doing for the summer?"

Jaxon replied, "He's going home to Junction, but I might try to coax him into coming back a week or two early and coming out to the ranch if that would be okay."

Billy said, "You don't even have to ask. He'll be wantin' to meet me, I'm sure."

Jaxon laughed, "He already said so."

"Well, there you go! What you waitin' on, boy? You just let us know when you're done this spring, and we'll come pick you up. If Caleb is still there, maybe we can take him to lunch, or he could even spend a few nights before he heads home. Does he have his own wheels?"

Jaxon answered, "He has a car. I'll let him know of your offer."

"Okay, behave," Billy said.

When he hung up I said, "That's a first."

"What?" Billy asked.

I replied, "You telling someone to behave. I was expecting you to ask if he and Caleb were still theoretical or if they'd put things into practice."

He said, "I thought about it, but it's his to amuse us with if he wants to, and none of our business if he doesn't."

139

I noted, "We can't even make an argument out of that. Once again, we agree."

Billy said, "I thought we would. This summer will give us a good chance for Noah and Jaxon to become the kind of brothers who are friends, too. I think you and I are pretty good at raisin' boys and cattle dogs. I think we could even raise a cowgirl given Aunt Sallie's good example. Quinn is all girl. I'm glad Brett's become a good dad to her. I don't think we'd know what to do with her."

"Once again, we can't make an argument out of that—I agree."

Billy added, "It won't be long now. She'll be having that baby about the time Jaxon is out of school and on his way here. Maybe it will be born on your birthday."

I joked, "You'd like that just so you don't have to remember some other date. It is about the time the baby is due from what I recall. I guess, we'll see."

On Sunday, when Brett brought Quinn and Jaxon out for chapel, Jaxon had a guest in tow.

Jaxon said, "Caleb had already told his mom and dad he'd be home as soon as the semester was out, but I said he might as well come to chapel just to meet everyone. He might see if he can work out comin' back early like we talked about, Uncle Billy."

Billy shook Caleb's hand, smiled and said in jest, "I don't remember extending that invitation. It must be Jaxon wants you to muck the horse stalls for him. Jaime and I will let you stay whether you do any chores or not."

Jaxon said to Caleb, "I've never seen the foreman go easy on anyone before."

Caleb was carrying an instrument case. I asked, "So what's in the case? Are you playing something for chapel this morning?"

"Yes, sir," Caleb responded, "Jaxon called his grandmother to ask if it was okay for me to come this morning, and he told her I played the trumpet. I guess I'm playing for my lunch, according to Jaxon."

I noted, "That's how it works around here—of a kind. Do you sing, too?"

He replied, "I sing some. Ms. Schlatter wanted us to start the service with 'Guide Me, O Thou Great Jehovah.' She said the

140

trumpet with that hymn would really make for a rousing start to the service. Jaxon is going to sing the second verse as solo."

Afterwards, Brett said, "Jaxon, I didn't even know you sang. I don't recall you ever singing at home or wanting to be in a choir."

Jaxon smiled, "I was too insecure back then. But I'm doin' all right now."

I repeated, "But you're doin' all right now."

As we walked towards the house, Brett put one hand on his son's back and the other on Quinn's. "We're all doin' all right now."

Chapter Twenty-three

We knew by the afternoon of May 10 that Quinn had gone into labor. When the phone rang that evening I said, "Noah, you get that. It's probably your dad."

He was soon back, "Dad said, 'Uncle Noah, it's a girl. Mother and baby are well.' That was the extent of the conversation. I guess he's making other calls or was just too excited to talk. I couldn't tell which."

Billy asked, "Not even a name? They've been holding out on if it was going to be a boy or girl, and they never did say what names they had in mind."

I replied, "Not to put too fine a point on it, but I think they were afraid to do so in case things went wrong."

Noah said, "Uncle Billy, you could suggest they call her Billie with an 'ie.'"

Billy rejected the suggestion. "Betsy, Bill, Billy, Brett—we've got enough 'B' names in this family. I never knew how Jean got her name. I called her Bean when we were growin' up, so she'd feel like she fit in better."

I said, "I'm sure that made all the difference."

Billy laughed. "Truth is, I'd forgotten I'd given her that nickname. I haven't used it since I left home all those years ago. I may have to put it back in use."

"She'll be thrilled, I'm sure," I said.

We all drove in to see the new mother, now long settled in the home Brett had bought with his folks' help. We were introduced to Anna Catherine Schlatter.

Billy smiled, "Well, I'll be damned. You named her after Grandma Geermann."

Quinn said, "When I asked Dad about family names, he said that was his grandma's name, and I thought it was beautiful."

Sallie was delighted with their decision as well. "She was as beautiful in spirit as that name sounds. That little girl has a good start in life with that name. You've done good!"

Betsy said, "As usual, my sister is right. How sweet that you settled on naming her after our mother." She chuckled, "That's a lot better than the names our daddy picked for us, isn't it, Sallie Faye?"

"Yes it is, Betsy-Mae. We never did like our middle names, and I never got the impression my sister liked her first name much more. I never minded Sallie, but mostly because it was spelled a little different, and I always felt a little different, so me and the name got along just fine."

Betsy clarified, "I didn't so much dislike my name as I thought it ought to be short for something else more proper, like Elisabeth."

Sallie said, "Daddy would say too many of his Swiss ancestors had too long o' names so he kept to 'economy models' as he called them. Of course, his full name was Johannes Konrad Geermann, but he told us all he wanted on his marker was John Geermann. I don't know if you kids knew his full name or not."

Billy confirmed, "All I knew was John."

Sallie chuckled, "He had a brother, Huldreich Rudolph, and thought in that regard, he'd gotten lucky."

Bill said, "You think those are bad—my Grandpa's name was Heironymus Siblingen Schlatter, although he said that middle name came from the town in Switzerland where he was born. I suppose it was a family name in there somehow."

Betsy said, "I didn't know that. No wonder I never heard you call him anything but Grandpa Schlatter."

Bill laughed, "We had to take a vow of silence we'd never reveal his full name. I guess I'm gettin' a little senile. I just broke that vow for the first time!"

Billy asked, "What'd he go by?"

"He just signed everything HS Schlatter and even introduced himself that way, 'HS.' He said if he'd been in this country a little sooner, the boys in school would have picked on him and said it stood for horse shit. He was strong as an ox and built like one. I don't think he'd have ever had to worry about someone bullying him. I get my slim figure from my mother's side of the family. It would take at least two of me to make one HS Schlatter."

Jaxon said, "I've just learned more family history than I ever knew."

Noah added, "I knew the Swiss part but none of those names! Noah and Jaxon sounded pretty good, huh, Jaxon?"

Quinn smiled, "Thankfully the women seemed to have fared better in the name department." Then looking at her baby she said, "Isn't that right, Anna Catherine?"

Noah took his niece in his arms. "Anna Catherine. I can see she likes that name. Anna Catherine, I'm your Uncle Noah. I've never been anyone's uncle before, but I'll try to be a good one for you. You're lucky to come into this family so early on. I had to wait a few years, but it was worth the wait."

I looked at Billy and he at me. I noticed how Bill and Betsy did the same, as did Jaxon and Quinn. Without saying a word, we knew the wound that brought on that thought. It was, of course, Noah's truth. On some level, it was also Jaxon and Quinn's truth, though not as dire as having lived through a mother's murder and before that a fearful life with a drug trafficker in the house.

Even so, I had a tinge of pity for Brett as he stood there having to realize that his own years of alienation by his own decisions had contributed heavily to what Noah had been through. Now, he was here for his children. I hoped that was enough for him. He's certainly in the right family to not wallow in regret and shame—a lesson one look at Quinn confirmed was true for her.

Jaxon said, "I emailed the woman in Odessa who used to claim us as her children to tell her she had a granddaughter. She hasn't responded yet. I even left off the part about me dating a nice boy, so she might not scream when she read it. I guess we'll hear from her sometime."

Betsy suggested, "Quinn, it might be nice if Jaxon sent her a picture of Anna Catherine. Putting a name and an innocent face together might soften her heart."

Quinn agreed, "That's a nice idea, Grandma."

Jaxon took a picture with his cell phone, typed what must have been no more than the name and maybe the date of birth and sent it on its way. "Done," he reported.

Sallie was quite amused. "Momma used to take nearly a year to use up a roll of film, another month to get to town to get it processed, and another two weeks, at least, before we'd get back in town to pick it up. Now everything is instantaneous!"

Bill added, "From what I hear circulates with those instant pictures, I think it's safe to say it's not all to the good, though it certainly was in this instance, unless Jaxon typed something he shouldn't have. He typed so fast, I'm not sure he knows what he sent."

Jaxon looked at his sent message, "One typo, Grandpa, but nothing bad. I seemed to have spelled May as Msy. My finger was off a key there. She'll probably figure that out."

As we prepared to leave, Jaxon said, "I'm done with school. If you're ready to have me, I'll ride home with you guys."

Billy answered, "Let's go! We got horse shit waiting!"

Brett added, "Oh, by the way, Aiden is going to come the second week of June and stay for six weeks. He can stay here as much as you want, but I know he'd like to spend time out on the ranch with his brothers shoveling horse shit."

Billy said, "We'll take any time he wants to be out there. It's not like us to deprive anyone the honor of mucking out stables."

I joked, "With all this labor coming in, maybe we need to get some pigs, too."

After I said it, I regretted it. I had the sudden feeling Billy would think pigs were a good idea.

He immediately said, "GS Ranches brand smoked bacon. I wonder if we can outsource that to Ernesto now that he's retired of a kind."

Bill shook his head, "I'm glad you've got the barn over there. I don't want to wake up to hogs squeelin' in the night. I grew up with that in San Angelo. I like pork, but I'd just as soon not raise 'em."

Noah asked, "They're real smart, aren't they Grandpa?"

Bill answered, "They're smart enough, but if you never heard a pig squeal up close you can't quite imagine it. And it don't take much to get 'em going. I'm not saying you can't raise hogs if you want to. Just don't expect Arnold from *Green Acres*."

Billy noted, "Noah, *Green Acres* was a tad before your time— almost before mine."

Bill looked at Billy. "You like making me feel old, don't you? You best remember, you need the old man and the old cowgirl to cover for your summer camping trip down south.

"Jaxon, you keep these boys in line this summer, and you call me if the foreman starts putting all his chores onto you. That foreman title is only a part-time job. The other job title is ranch hand, and we've only got one rank in that department—everyone's the same no matter how green or seasoned."

Billy exclaimed, "Dad, you've ruined it! Even Jaime didn't know about that part-time title of foreman. All these years he's assumed he was lower on the totem pole."

"I happen to know better than that," Bill said. "We've all had you fooled into thinking you were the only one that knew you had two titles. Jaime and Noah have known it all along."

Billy feigned disgust, "Come on crew! I've suffered enough abuse for one day."

Noah asked, "Uncle Jaime, do you think that was an order from the foreman or the ranch hand gettin' bossy?"

"Noah, to be honest, I've never been able to tell the difference. Out of generosity, I've always leaned toward the foreman just keepin' things runnin' smooth."

"There," Billy said. "Something almost resembling respect. Thank you, Jaime."

I snapped to attention. *"Jawohl, herr kommandant!"*

Billy smiled, "Boys, that's from another TV show before your time."

Jaxon said, "That one I know. They still play reruns on Saturday. Jaime does a good Sergeant Schultz."

Billy offered, "A cheap imitation, isn't that right, Mother?"

"No comment," she replied.

Billy said, "If we don't get back home, we're going to have dogs walkin' back into Fort Davis at the first sniff of freedom to go to the shelter and report us for animal abuse."

Noah said in a super-serious tone, "Too true. Too true."

Chapter Twenty-four

Billy and I heard Noah call from the office-study room — "Hey, come back here!"

We did as ordered. "What?" Billy asked.

"Jean and I just got an email from Pamela."

Noah and Jean,

If Noah's offer to visit the ranch is still an option, I'd like to come out with all three of my children the third week of June and stay for the full week. I can move the dates around a bit if it's more convenient for you. Let me know if Bill and Betsy are okay with this, and if we can stay in the bunkhouse while there.

Love,

Pamela

I asked, to no one in particular, "Did we ever tell Jean about inviting Pamela? I can't remember."

Billy replied, "Neither can I. I'll call her right now. Then I'll call Mom and let her know so we can get right back to Pamela."

We both followed Billy to the kitchen and sat at the kitchen table while he made his calls.

He was already talking to Jean. "We don't remember if we told you Noah wrote to Pamela … Let me relay that. They'll get a kick out it … Jean says we're more senile than Dad. She reminded me that Noah took the letter to her to mail it."

Noah recalled, "Oh, that's right. They were over at the bunkhouse."

Billy said, "… She says Jaime and I are old, what's your excuse, Noah?"

He replied, "Tell her, I reckon I don't have one."

"… She heard you say it. Hey, Bean, I'll call Mom and then we'll email Pamela … I thought you liked that name. Bye, Bean.

She told me she'd just as soon I not remember my old nickname. I'll have to use it a lot now."

He was dialing while he was talking. His mom answered.

"Hey, Mom, any problem with Pamela and her three kids staying in the bunkhouse for a full week the third week of June? She's taken Noah up on his invitation to visit. We never have told Brett, at least not that we can remember, but then all three of us forgot we'd told Jean and she mailed the letter for us." … He looked at us and said, "Mom confirms we all decided not to tell Brett" … Then to Betsy he said, "Okay, we'll let her know the light is green. Are you tellin' Brett or are we? … All right. Bye. She'll tell him. Go email Pamela, Noah, and say we're all set on this end. The bunkhouse is confirmed. I can't remember hardly anything about her kids. What do you remember, Noah?"

"Remember, Pamela said I was their big brother. Her oldest daughter is only a year younger than me. Then the other two are twins."

Billy asked, "How did I not know they were twins?"

Noah replied, "'Cause they don't look alike, but they're both boys. I remember Pamela saying those kinds of twins are rare— when they aren't identical but are both boys."

I said, "I'll take her word for it. It must be true. I can't think of any. Billy, as to how you didn't know they were twins, I'll remind you that you didn't even know Pamela's name for some time."

Billy confessed, "My interest in my brother's marriage saga was less than acute in those days. I certainly didn't pay attention to children not in the Schlatter bloodline, as I figured they'd be out of our lives sooner rather than later."

Noah added, "I confess to feeling the same about Pamela's kids."

I said, "Well, now we need to pay attention. Surely, you remember their names, Noah?"

Noah replied, "The girl is Alina. The boys are Josiah and Colton. I'm not sure what last name they use. Remember, Pamela never used Schlatter. She had gone back to her maiden name after her first divorce."

I said, "That I remember. Her last name is Hartman."

Noah added, "And don't ask me which twin is which. I haven't seen them in five years."

Billy joked, "It could be Alina's a tomboy and we can't tell any of them apart."

I said, "I'm just guessing we'll probably be able to discern one as female—though these days, I suppose either she or one of the boys might be transitioning."

Billy asked, "Noah, did you ever think you should have been born a girl? Are you a girl stuck in a boy's body?"

"No, I'm happy being a boy, but that might explain a lot about you, Uncle Billy."

I said in all seriousness, "I've known some who I'm convinced were trapped in the wrong body, and everybody knew it. I never could understand why people had to be so cruel about it."

Billy added, "Before I even knew what I was asking, I'd asked Aunt Sallie if she was supposed to be a boy. I was just asking if her dad wanted a boy instead of a girl, but she thought I meant did she want to *be* a boy. She told me she was all cowgirl and didn't want to trade that for anything. To your question, Noah, I'm all cowboy and glad to be that way. Like Jaime said, though, it ain't so clear-cut for a lot of kids, and I feel real sorry for them—for the bullying they have to put up with, and the the parents who disown them all too often. It just ain't right."

Noah said, "Judgment over mercy. The opposite of what we live by."

Billy smiled, "I think we'll keep you."

Noah, pleased with what came to him in response, added, "You're both gettin' old. I'll be keepin' you before you know it. I just hope there's a Mrs. Noah, or Jaxon and a Mr. Jaxon living here to help out. I don't think I can run the ranch and carry you two to the toilet when you can't get to it on your own anymore."

Billy asked, "You thinkin' you might be wantin' a Mrs. Noah, or you gonna follow in your great aunt and your uncle's footsteps and stay single?"

Noah replied, "Don't know yet. I'd say Aunt Sallie is single. I'd say you are only 'of a kind.'"

I said, "I'd say you're right about that last part, and there's no rush on you deciding what you're gonna do."

Billy added, "I only asked because Jaime and I might need you to prod us when it's time to let you out of the stable long enough to go prospecting for companionship. We forget about such things being important to a young man."

I clarified, "I didn't think I was that far gone, but your uncle's point is sound enough. We might need a reminder that you're only on loan here. You'll have your own life to sort out when you're ready to start sorting."

Noah said, "I've done a little sortin'. I want to go for my GED the same time I get my driver's license."

I asked, "And, are you planning on getting your license at sixteen?"

"Yup."

Billy asked, "You going to college then?"

He answered, "I thought I'd take a year off, and then start something online and maybe take some Ag classes at Sul Ross."

I replied, "You have been doing some sortin'. Do the folks at your private school know of your ambition to graduate early?"

"They do. My history and social studies teacher says I'm already nearly up to college level."

I agreed, "I don't doubt that. You're way ahead of Billy and me. The way we all talk, I'm not sure we're helping with your grammar and vocabulary."

Noah replied, "Grandma cuts me *no* slack in class, but she says how I talk on the ranch is up to me. She said being prim and proper is only gonna make people in town look at me funny."

"It would make us look at you funny," Billy said.

Then Billy asked, "Where's Jaxon been all this time?"

Noah said, "He was in his room texting back and forth with Caleb."

I responded, "If Caleb's parents see those texts, he won't have to come out to them. That's pretty risky."

Noah noted, "I sorta said the same thing, and he said not as risky as talkin' to another boy on the phone. They delete their texts when they're done chattin'."

Billy exclaimed, "Enough chit and enough chat, the foreman says it's time to do chores. Jaxon! Get off that cell, and let's get these chores done!"

He came out, fingers still at it, hit "Send" one last time and laid the phone on the kitchen table. *"Jawohl, herr kommandant!"* he responded.

Billy shouted, *"Mach schnell!* Noah, that means make it quick."

High season in the desert mountains was upon us. Not only did we have Aiden's extended visit plus Pamela and her three kids for a week-long visit, but Mark's brother and his wife were coming for two weeks in June as well.

Billy said, "I can't think of a time in my life when the ranch was this hoppin'."

Bill agreed, "It certainly never was in all my years working out here. Jaime, if the congregation keeps growing we may have to build on to that chapel."

Billy replied, "We'll just do two services. One Protestant and one Catholic."

"Exactly what are you going to do differently with no priest here?" Bill asked.

Billy stated matter-of-factly, "We'll make the sign of the cross when we pray at the Catholic service."

"I guess I could attend either one then," Bill replied. "I have a good idea how to do that even though I never have. I like that better than building on."

We gave Pamela one evening to settle in before we had a huge barbecue party complete with brisket, pork and chicken from Ernesto's pit, Lupe's deviled eggs, and Betsy's wonderful hospitality skills in managing the diverse crowd of all that defined the Geermann-Schlatter ranch family, the Cardonas, the Mendoza guests and Pamela and her children.

Anna Catherine was the center of attention all afternoon. Betsy sent an invitation to Quinn and Jaxon's mother but had not heard back. Betsy even made it clear that if she decided to come at the last minute, that would be just fine. Jaxon and the rest of us knew of the invitation. Quinn did not. We were halfway through the afternoon and there was no sign of her yet. Jaxon sent her another picture of a beaming mother with her beautiful child surrounded by people caring dearly for them.

He showed me the picture. I said, "I don't know how she can separate herself so absolutely from her own children. I can't even leave the dogs for half a day."

Jaxon replied, "I would say you don't have parents like she does, but I know yours were on a whole other level of terrible."

"Toxic was the word Zoey and I used to describe them. I use the past tense hoping such is not the case these days, but we have no idea. Years of estrangement turn into decades before you know it. Let's hope your mother doesn't come to such a fate. You're right to throw your seeds to the wind and see what might take root. Your pictures of her grandchild are your seeds."

I couldn't help but notice that it was Pamela who went up to speak to Brett, and not the other way around, which Billy and I had predicted would be the case. They talked a while, then Pamela held Anna Catherine for several minutes. Finally, she settled into a long conversation with Jean and Mary-Alice. Noah did what he could to include her children into whatever he could think of—introducing them to people, showing them his school room and letting them play his keyboard if they wanted.

I knew Chuy had finally had that heart attack, and he was rolling around in a wheelchair. He explained, "Lupe says I have to roll myself around for the exercise. I told the doc about it on my last checkup and he said, 'Good advice.' I can't win."

I looked at Lupe while addressing Chuy, "You won when you married this one. There aren't many like her."

Chuy confessed, "Okay, I'll admit when it comes to the Rodriquez women, I got the only one worth anything."

Lupe laughed, "For what was available at the time, you got the only one worth anything in three counties."

Chuy shook his head. "She gets that line from my *papá*. That's what he told me when he said I needed to get off the stick and get this woman married. Lucky for her and unlucky for me, he said it right in front of her."

Lupe pulled in Rosalinda who was walking by, "I was the favorite daughter-in-law until this one came along."

Rosalinda smiled, "Old man Cardona used to say, 'Anyone that can handle Ernesto moves to the top of my list,' but I know he really liked Lupe best. I didn't mind coming in second to her."

The party slowly wound down. No grandmother from Odessa in sight. No message back to Jaxon after he sent the picture of Anna Catherine. The invasive seeds of estrangement were slowly taking root—choking out of her life these three lives now closely bound with ours in the good soil of compassion.

Chapter Twenty-five

As Pamela was preparing to head back to El Paso, she told us what a good time they'd had. I wasn't too sure about the children, but Pamela did indeed seem refreshed by her stay. She gave us all a hug—but none bigger than for Noah. We would always be grateful for the support she had provided for Noah in his darkest days.

They were no sooner on the road, than we were all packing up for our trip down to Big Bend. We even had to invest in a second tent, as we figured with three young men, two old men and two red heelers, it would be way too cozy in our one big tent. And as both dogs rode in the cab with the five of us, it was already plenty cozy.

We knew beforehand that rough camping was not on the agenda. Five men sharing a Porta Potti just didn't have any appeal —and while a few years ago, Billy and I would have found it amusing to try, we opted for public restrooms in the campgrounds. We would only stay four nights, and then spend the last few days of Aiden's visit riding around the ranch and doing our daily chores.

I stayed behind in the camp while Billy and the boys hiked into the canyons and went back into Cattail Falls. We were both concerned that it could get too hot for the dogs in the truck in late June, even with the windows cracked open, and just decided the best course of action was for one of us to stay at the campground. I certainly didn't mind. Solitude, even with dogs present, was far more rare to me than in my early years. I knew that I would find the time compelling in its own way. I had brought paper and pen along in case something inspired me to write anything or to anyone.

I knew who I would not be writing to. Just days earlier, Zoey and I got a letter from California. It was from a lawyer's office so we didn't know what to expect. While Billy and I had picked up the mail, we waited to open it with Zoey.

Dear Mr. Cruz and Ms. Mendoza,

I am the court assigned executor for the estate of your brother, Mason, who died of health complications related to alcoholism on April 15, 2013.

He died intestate. In clearing out his apartment, I found the kind letter you had sent to him. As it was clear you had reached out some time ago, I wanted you to be aware of his untimely death.

Per California law, what little he has in his estate after expenses will be divided between your parents as the nearest living relatives. This amounts to $1,976.53 to each of them.

Please accept my sincere condolences, and feel free to contact me with any questions you may have.

Yours sincerely,

Mia Harvey-Smith

Zoey and I both thought the only odd thing about the letter was it seemed to presume our parents would not have informed us of his death, despite the fact that Ms. Harvey-Smith had apparently already been in contact with them. We had to guess that they informed her that they had no contact with us, and she felt the compassionate thing to do was send the letter. Zoey sent her a simple thank you card for letting us know—and that was that. A miserable life and a miserable death, it would seem.

As I sat quietly at the campsite, I had the thought—what would I write if I scribbled across the top, "What My Life Might Have Been," by Mason Cruz? The only context I could create in my mind was his life falling into love somehow as mine had and as Zoey's had. When I tried to apply it to Mason, I realized I couldn't imagine such a life for him. Because he was so alien to me, I couldn't imagine his life at all. It was that realization that had me say out loud—I guess to Kola and Koala as they were the only ones within earshot—"My parents' lives are as distant and empty as my thoughts are for whatever defined Mason's life." I sat staring out at the Chisos window for several minutes when my pen began moving across the blank page.

Elegy to a Lost Brother

A death perhaps no one mourned.
A life so vapid, will anyone know you're gone?

Am I harsh thinking such thoughts as these
now that your body has failed you in the same
way your heart had failed to ever know love?
Brother, did you love?
If so, why didn't you reach out?
We were here—waiting for a word from you.
A word that never came.
The executor's letter stated you were dead.
Your meager estate divided—given
to the other strangers in our lives
for whom we ask,
Mother, Father, do you love?
If so, why don't you reach out?
We are here—waiting for a word from you.

I showed it to Billy when they got back from Santa Elena. He asked, "Are you okay?"

"Absolutely. I'm going to give it to Zoey."

Billy instructed, "All right, boys, huddle up. Jaime needs a big group hug, and we're the only ones that'll do!"

That evening would be our last in the park before heading back to the ranch. We watched as a small cloud over Emery peak built up until it decided to move our way.

Billy said, "I haven't seen any lightning. I think it just wants to dump a little shower to settle the dust."

Aiden asked, "Are we just gonna sit here and let it wash the dust off us, too?"

Billy answered, "I don't see why not. The rain'll feel good, and we leave tomorrow. We can always chuck our wet clothes in a trash bag if we get wet enough."

I suggested, "Maybe one of us should sit in the tent with the dogs so the boys don't have to smell wet dog all night."

Billy exclaimed, "A little wet dog smell never killed anybody!"

Noah said, "That's convenient for you, Uncle Billy, since the dogs sleep with Jaxon and me in the tent and not with you, Uncle Jaime and Aiden."

Billy asked, "Does it look to you like those dogs wanna go in?"

We were about to find out. The rain started to drop on us quickly and heavily. The dogs didn't move, and neither did we. It was over in about two minutes.

Jaxon said, "I am wet, but maybe I'll dry out some before we call it a night."

Billy stated flatly, "We'll be sittin' out here for several hours yet. Those dogs will dry out unless that cloud turns around. They do that sometimes."

I observed, "That cloud is done for the day. It's still moving and about rained out."

Aiden asked, "Are we ever gonna eat? I'm gettin' hungry. That peanut butter and pickle sandwich we had up in the canyon has long worn off."

I replied, "I guess Jaxon and I can get to it, now that he's the official head camp-cook."

Aiden said, "Let me guess—Mendoza scrambled eggs and Owen's Country sausage."

Jaxon answered, "Might be or it might not be."

We had eaten that for three nights in a row, but we were now out of both. The only thing left was hot dogs and canned chili.

When Billy saw what we were putting together he said, "I hope you still got cheese. Those dogs are gonna want cheese with that chili—especially comin' out of a can."

Noah added, "Koala is already wondering why she doesn't smell any of Jaime's hot pan bread."

I replied, "There ain't even any cold pan bread tonight, boys. Just hot dogs, chili and cheese."

Jaxon said, "We do have one onion left that I'll chop for whoever wants some."

When we'd finished, we sat drip drying as Billy decided the boys should know the unvarnished truth of his departure from home at age sixteen, complete with the dramatic expletive that sent his mother over the edge, telling her firstborn to get out. He also shared his account of how guests—male and female—came onto him for their "cowboy conquest" at the ranch outside Van Horn, and how he never gave them the satisfaction. He even shared how it looked to him like the ranch hands who had to drink before and after their nights trolling for sex just seemed to be men hollowing out their lives slowly but surely.

He looked to me to see if I might open up to the boys about my dark years in California. I did, and I didn't gloss over the toxicity of my parents' hatred for each other, or the hollowed-out life I had become.

Jaxon, Aiden and Noah all three opened up about the alienation from their own dad over the years, and how he seemed like a completely different person now.

I said, "Boys, I'm a completely different person, and so is your dad. Billy is the only one who never really had to change. He just had to come home."

Billy responded, "I owe a lot of who I am and how I held it together all those damn lonely years to Aunt Sallie. No one taught me more as a boy than she did. She treated me much more as a man than a boy."

Noah said, "That's the same way you and Uncle Jaime treat me —even back when I was a mess after the murder."

Billy smiled, "You were a little shaver then. Everybody said, 'The boy's an angel.' I guess only an angel could come out the other side the way you did."

I said, "We need to get to bed. Y'all gave me your group hug earlier. I think y'all need your own right now."

Billy exclaimed, "All right, boys, huddle up. We need a big group hug, and we're the only ones that'll do!"

Chapter Twenty-six

Annie approved of Brett's idea to let Quinn cover the phones in the office in Alpine. She could bring Anna Catherine to work with her and, while it couldn't pay much, it was something to get her out of the house and seeing and talking to people. With few exceptions, people were either oblivious to her being a single parent or didn't judge her for it.

Annie stated, "If I have anyone try to lecture me on who I hire, I'll tell them to take their business elsewhere."

Jaxon continued to send "progress shots" to their mother every couple weeks—still no word from her.

Jaxon was a good hand on the ranch. He loved to work on anything that needed some repair. He would have been a really good hand for Ernesto, and I wondered if he shouldn't start his own construction business somewhere down the road after college.

When I asked him about it one evening, he said, "I'm taking drafting and all the hands-on courses I can get worked into my schedule, so I could maybe do something like that."

Billy said, "J & C Construction."

Noah asked, "What's that name mean?"

Billy replied, "Jaxon and Caleb construction."

"That might be getting the cart before the horse," I suggested. Then I asked, "By the way, what is Caleb's major? Is he in Industrial Technology as well?"

Jaxon said, "No, he's a business major."

Billy exclaimed, "Well, there you go! He can run the business side and you can run the crew. You wouldn't even have to pay Bean to keep your books."

Jaxon noted, "Somehow, when they pass out degrees, they don't come with start-up capital. I don't see how we could get that going even if we wanted to."

Billy, ever willing to volunteer others, continued, "Between Ernesto and your grandpa, I don't think you'd have to worry too much about that. You'd just have to decide if you wanted to work that hard because bein' slackers won't cut it."

Jaxon replied, "I ain't afraid to work. I don't know about Caleb, and as Jaime said, where he's concerned, that's gettin' the cart before the horse."

Billy asked, "Is he comin' back early or not this fall? And has he told those parents of his that he's got a boy waiting for him out west?"

"I think 'yes' to the first question and a definite 'no' to the second."

I added, to offer some consolation, if you can call it that, "We know well enough how hard it can be in some families. Sometimes you just have to make a life, and let the people around you draw their own conclusions."

Jaxon pondered by response. "You're sayin' maybe he can't come out to his parents, but that doesn't mean he can't find some way to be with someone?"

"Yes, that's what I'm saying. It might not be as open as you'd like, but if you care enough for him and he for you, you'd find a way."

Noah gave a disconcerting look in my direction. "That don't seem too honest as we've come to know it in this family."

I explained, "I'm not advocating for dishonesty. I'm just saying some things are no one else's business, and people see what they want to see. Look at how the church ladies look at Billy and me. We put on a show, and their minds judge us, as they habitually judge everyone. Is it dishonest on our part? I don't think so. We're living our lives as we see fit. The fact that they've confined their minds to one way of how things must be is about them—not about us."

Noah seem to understand, saying, "So it could be Caleb's parents might not even judge him, but they just want to pretend they have the perfect family."

Jaxon said, "Now you've perfectly described my mother and her family."

Billy added, "That's what sent Mom over the edge all those years ago. I crushed her perfect family image."

I noted, "And, to her credit, she finally saw her image of perfection was far from it, and was so narrow it had forced out love itself."

Jaxon sighed, "I wish Caleb was here to talk about this."

I assured him, "When he is, we can talk about it again."

Noah laughed, "We couldn't even remember Jean mailed the letter I wrote to Pamela. It could be we won't remember what we talked about tonight!"

Billy chuckled and added, "But we'll remember we talked about somethin' important."

I said, "We'll be wonderin' if it was something we maybe could argue about, if we could only remember."

Billy continued, "I'm pretty sure we'll remember it had something to do with Caleb that we wanted to talk about while we have him."

Noah added, "Uncle Billy, you'll be wantin' me or Jaxon to remember sayin' you and Jaime are too old to remember such things."

I replied, "We are too old; that's why you boys need to remember."

Billy said, "I'm already forgettin' what it was we are supposed to remember."

Jaxon shook his head. "I've gotta work on how your minds go off on these tangents so I can join in."

Billy offered, "You just gotta start in and let the spirit move ya."

Caleb arrived at the ranch a week before he and Jaxon were due to move back into the residence hall for the start of their junior year. He was mostly prepared for Jaxon's three peculiar housemates—as much as one can be without first-hand experience.

The evening Caleb arrived we sat out on the patio, and we had a serious chat with him about his family.

He began, "I really was planning to tell them, but then they started talking about this family they knew at church whose daughter said she was a lesbian. Mom and Dad had a fit. Mom said, 'We've known that girl all her life. How do these kids get so easily corrupted?' I said, 'Maybe it's not that easy to blame someone else.' I don't think she knew what to make of that, but at least I didn't hear any more about corruptive influences all summer."

When I shared the conversation we'd had those few weeks earlier, Jaxon said, "Your memory isn't as bad as you let on. I think you recalled all that word for word."

Billy answered, "There are some things that stick in our minds when our hearts know we're gonna need 'em later."

"Too true. Too true," I said. "Speakin' of what the heart needs, Sallie wants to take you three young men on a long ride while Caleb is here. Caleb, she may amuse you more than inspire you when you first see her, but she is a wise soul, and we cherish every hour we spend with her."

"Amen to that!" Billy exclaimed.

"Too true. Too true." Noah responded.

Caleb asked, "So what's this 'Too true, too true,' all about?"

Jaxon said, "That comes from Aunt Sallie. She likes those comments where she repeats it a second time. 'Too true, too true' is her favorite."

Noah added, "She can add that to about anything we're talkin' about. Jaime has his own he adds when he thinks whatever is being described or named doesn't fit just right. He adds 'of a kind.' He said Jaxon and I were brothers of a kind because we didn't have the same mother and never lived together."

Caleb said, "I guess that makes me gay 'of a kind.'"

Billy said, "You've got the hang of it. If you understand Sallie's expressions and Jaime's 'of a kind,' you're pretty well clued in on the family communication peculiarities. Now, let's get down to serious business."

Caleb interjected, "I thought this was pretty serious. I've never opened up like this to anyone before."

Billy said, "I'm talkin' about your future! Now about J & C Construction or C & J Construction, I think we ought to start thinking about launching that as soon as you two graduate."

I reminded him. "Didn't we talk about gettin' the cart before the horse?"

Billy said, "All you gotta do is look at these two, and you can see they're in love as much as you are with me. It's only a matter of when and not if that these two make a life together."

Noah added, "Caleb, you might as well know that when Billy or Sallie see into the future it always comes true."

Billy corrected, "I wouldn't say always, but often enough the family takes our premonitions seriously."

Noah said, "That included me living here on the ranch long before my dad moved to Phoenix and my mom was murdered."

Caleb responded, "You have my attention."

"While you're here we need to get Ernesto to show you boys his yard and equipment," Billy began. "It's quite a setup, and I don't think he's done anything with it since he mostly retired."

I interjected, "He told me he was waiting for the spirit to move."

Jaxon said, "You're probably catching on that there is a lot of waiting on the spirit to move around here."

Caleb smiled, "Apparently, you don't wait in vain."

Billy laughed. "Too true. Too true. I'm gonna go call Sallie and see when she wants to ride. Then Jaime can call Ernesto about meetin' him at the yard."

"Do you and I have the funds needed to help them buy out Ernesto's business?" I asked. "I don't have that much under my mattress. I guess we could garnish Noah's wages except we never got around to paying him any."

Billy state matter-of-factly, "Dad and Sallie both said not to worry about that part."

I shook my head. "The great planner has everything falling into place once again."

Noah added, "That's another thing, Caleb. Great-grandpa Geermann and Uncle Billy can put together a plan like it was all filed away ready to go in their mind long before it was needed, Uncle Jaime says, with no apparent flaws."

I confirmed, "Noah is exactly right and describes the gift well."

Billy said, "And I know it is a gift. I claim no credit for it. It just comes up from somewhere."

Caleb said, "That spirit moving again."

"I'd say so," I confirmed.

Billy and I went in the house to make our calls. When he hung up, he handed me the receiver. "I'll go tell 'em the ride is on for tomorrow."

When I shared Billy's latest idea for the construction company, Ernesto remarked, "You know, I'll have to throw in that tractor as part of the deal. I can't hardly sell the Schlatters the tractor they gave me … hang on, *Jaime*, Rosalinda's trying to tell me something … She says I need to be part of the deal. She wants me out of her hair some. I guess I could show them the ropes as long as they don't work me like I worked you *chicas* back in the day."

I said, "I'm pretty sure they'll need your talents to hone their own skills."

He replied, "Meet me at the yard day after tomorrow then, and we'll talk turkey."

"Deep fried, I presume."

Ernesto laughed, "No gunnysack turkey deals from me."

"That I know," I said.

He ended, *"Hasta luego, amigo."*

Part III

Chapter Twenty-seven

I would observe, over the course of the next two years, how Noah's intent to "graduate" would indeed coincide with his sixteenth birthday. We decided we'd have a joint graduation and birthday party for him. He hadn't had a party since his last one with Elma, for his 13th and her 96th. Aiden also graduated from high school, and it would be a college graduation celebration for Jaxon and Caleb as well. And since the "old man's" 80th birthday was on July 1st, Lupe liked the idea of giving him an early birthday party. So we lumped the events into one big bash. Because of Chuy's inclusion, all the Cardona family was invited.

Chuy's response to our idea was, "I guess you're not sure I'll make it another month."

Lupe reckoned, "When you're our age, rounding up or down to the nearest month is close enough."

Sallie suggested, "I guess while we're roundin', we could celebrate my 80th now, in case I don't make it two more years."

Billy said, "We'll risk it. You still got boys you're raisin'. You'll have to hang on a while longer. Besides, you wouldn't want to beat Nellie to the finish."

Sallie signed, "That old gal can't be good for much more. She's the oldest horse we've ever had on this ranch—too damn ornery to die at this point."

Noah said, "Aunt Sallie, I don't think you have to worry about her buckin' you off the way Great-granddad's horse did."

"Why do you say that?" she asked.

"Because Nellie can hardly get her feet off the ground anymore."

Sallie chuckled, "Too true! Too true!"

Then she added, "When the old gal saw those two new horses come into the stable, she wasn't any too happy about it, though she said it would take two to replace her. I told her she was gettin' a little full of herself and assured her the two new ones were for Jaxon and Caleb when they come to the ranch. That was okay with her, because she didn't want any young'uns to get any ideas about ridin' her."

I loved the conversations between Sallie and Nellie. Whether it was proof of Sallie's ability to communicate with creatures well known to her, or just proof that her imagination was still intact and active, really didn't matter to me. It was delightful, whichever it was. I am convinced, with a good imagination, all manner of possibilities are open to us—something passed on perhaps both genetically, and certainly through influence, to Billy and Noah.

Sallie said, "I guess we'll hold off for my 80th then. Maybe I should bring Nellie over for the party. She must be the equivalent of ninety or a hundred. Maybe we could get Ernesto to sing happy birthday to her."

Noah asked, "When's her birthday?"

Sallie answered, "I have no idea, but it doesn't matter. She doesn't remember her own. We'll just tell her it's June 10th—same as yours."

It was a crazy enough idea that Billy and Noah both saw to it. They even had Betsy make a little carrot cake to give to Nellie. Betsy had one rule for the party as pertained to the horse in attendance, "Son, you and Noah are both on pooper-scooper duty if that horse dumps anything. I don't want to smell it or step in it."

Billy jested, "We'll just dump it on your roses."

She instructed, "You'll put it in a bucket in your pickup and take it home with you."

But it would make the cycle back eventually. Betsy's roses, and every other plant around all three houses, benefited from the compost we produced from all the stable mucking and, now, the added chicken manure component from Zoey's coop. The old ranch house even had a modest greenhouse that old man Geermann had put up soon after Betsy and Bill married. It had long produced all the tomatoes and peppers eaten on the ranch, and we seemed to plant more each year just to keep up with the larger family that called the ranch home, or at least visited with great frequency. Mark and Zoey had taken care of the greenhouse on as their chore which Billy greatly appreciated.

When the day of the party was upon us, we led Nellie over to a small rope pen we'd set up on the north side of *Vista Grande* where we always held our parties. We did keep it well away from the ridge itself so that no one would be worried about the old gal falling ever the edge.

When Chuy and Lupe arrived I wasn't surprised to see her carrying in the deviled eggs, but I was surprised to see him in a wheelchair. "I thought you were back out of that thing. You haven't had another heart attack, have you?"

He replied, "No, but I thought it would be the best way to keep off my feet for the afternoon."

Lupe laughed, "I told him we might need to get another one so I can roll around with him. I'm not even quite two years younger than him, you know."

"I see Tanya and Mando rode out with you. Does she still like drivin' her dump truck?"

Lupe answered, "You'll have to ask her about her truck."

Chuy interjected, "Oh, she's mad as hell right now! Mando backed into it—right into the driver's side door where she has that can-do-it woman painted on it."

I asked, "When did this happen?"

Lupe replied, "Just yesterday, and she was carryin' on about it the whole way out here."

Chuy added, "She's got pictures on her phone of it—her door smashed and not a scratch on the back of Mando's dump truck."

Lupe clarified, "Well, no scratches the back of a dump truck might not have out of the ordinary. Tanya said there wasn't a scratch on it."

I laughed, "I won't argue with her about it!"

Chuy asked, "What's the horse doing over here? You gonna give rides around the house? She looks like she's got some years on her."

I said, "That's Nellie, Sallie's horse. We're celebrating her 90th or maybe 100th while we're at it. Sallie can't remember how old she is exactly, but she's over thirty years old. Sallie thought she'd get Ernesto to sing 'Happy Birthday' to her."

Chuy said, "Not this year, she won't. When he gets here, you'll see what I mean."

I replied, "That certainly has me curious."

Chuy ended it, saying, "That's all I'm gonna say."

I made my way to Billy to tell him about what Chuy had said about Ernesto. We both kept an eye out for him, and went to greet them when he and Rosalinda pulled in. Ernesto had a sign hanging around his neck that read, *Rosalinda's prayers finally answered—I have laryngitis.* He did indeed. He couldn't even eke out a half whisper.

Billy said, "*Jaime*, we should have hired entertainment. I had no idea we were going to need it until now."

Ernesto gave Billy a little fake, tooth-filled smile.

Rosalinda said, "It's gonna be up to you boys to carry all the singing today."

I added, "It will take the whole choir to make up for the big voice out of commission, but Noah, Jaxon and Caleb can help us out.

Billy smiled, "I know, Ernesto, you're dying to say it takes five to replace you."

Ernesto gave a big thumbs-up to Billy.

Rosalinda continued, "I thought the sign around his neck was a bit much, but I decided it was a good idea rather than him wearing out the little bit of voice he has trying to tell people he can't talk. Can you believe I am actually worried about him losing his voice? I thought I'd appreciate the quiet, but I miss the singing."

I agreed, "We all will miss that!"

Bill saw us all standing there by the truck and came to see what was going on. When he saw the sign he shook his head. "I can think of quite a few people who, if they couldn't talk, would be an answer to my prayers. Several talkin' about running for president right now. But for you, my friend, such is not the case. I hope you get better soon."

Ernesto gave him the same big thumbs-up he'd given Billy.

There was a time when Noah would have clung pretty tightly to Billy and me at a gathering like this. These days, he was just as likely to hang out with Jaxon and Caleb, and all three would be with Sallie. Aiden's mother was at the party, but he seemed to be spending most of his time with his brothers and Sallie. I saw the five of them keeping Nellie company. Betsy was making sure

Aiden's mother wasn't ignored. With Betsy's gift of hospitality, I wasn't concerned that she'd feel out of place.

Betsy had, of course, invited Quinn and Jaxon's mother to the big bash, who remained estranged from her own children. No response as usual.

Caleb's family had been invited, and his parents and sister came, though they had also had a graduation party for him in Junction a week earlier.

Pamela and her three children were included, and they were staying in the bunkhouse. Pamela and Brett were on very good terms, and we all wondered if some further reconciliation was in their future.

Norman, Annie, Ava and Dew, and John and James were invited as well and all of them came. Quinn and Jaxon's mother was the only one invited not to show up.

Anna Catherine was sailing through the "terrible twos" without the terrible. She had such a pleasant disposition that Billy was sure she must take after him. Betsy would neither confirm nor deny what Billy's disposition had been like as a child saying, "He doesn't need to know everything." Of course, we assumed that was confirmation enough that, despite the hard labor of his birth, she'd been spared the terrible twos by at least her firstborn.

As we all mingled with the crowd—now topping even the big barbecue from a couple years earlier—Billy leaned towards me, saying, "My quiet side is telling me it hopes these people don't stay around into the night. I never did like big crowds, but I like them even less these days."

"I can relate. I think we're part hermit."

He added, "You were a hermit for those first years here. Now we've got these boys who'll keep either one of us from becoming one altogether."

I said, "The boys are fine. I am glad we rolled so much into this one party, so we don't have to do another again anytime soon."

"Amen to that," he agreed.

"Now it's time to corral our men's chorus and start singing."

Billy agreed, "Good idea. The sooner we get that cake eaten, the sooner these people can go home."

After we had the singing all taken care of, including Nellie's, Noah said to Billy and me, "Can we go home yet?   Too many people."

Billy jested, "Jaime and I love big crowds.   What's the matter with you, boy?"

Sallie overheard the conversation and chuckled, "Then you two stay here, and I'll take Noah home.   Somehow, I doubt you'd be far behind us, despite your professed love of crowds."

I laughed, "Don't we need to go shoe some horses?"

Noah said, "Shoveling horse shit sounds pretty good to me right now."

Billy exclaimed, "Amen to that!"

Chapter Twenty-eight

Post party, C & J Construction commenced full-time operations. Already, Jaxon and Caleb had spent the summer of their junior year working with Ernesto to learn about making and building with adobe. During the school year, they spent what time they could away from school to work with him on small jobs.

It took Bill and Ernesto about the same five minutes it took to agree on the terms for the house building to settle on the sale of Ernesto's yard and equipment. The only point of contention, which required a minute to work out, was the tractor. Ernesto said the tractor was going back to its rightful owner, and Bill insisted he give him a fair price. Bill had already researched the depreciated value, and they finally struck on that number as part of the deal.

Bill and Ernesto are an odd pair. They don't have much in common, but the respect between the two runs deep. I think it's fair to call it love of a kind. I believe that if life's circumstance ever called on one to risk his life for the other, there would be no hesitation.

Caleb's parents seemed to be perfectly content to think their one son was going into business with "a fine young man" who the parents had met a few times during their junior and senior years. Of course, with each visit they would ask Caleb if he had a girlfriend and when he might settle down and give them grandchildren. Caleb simply skirted the question for a long time, until he finally said to them on a Sunday afternoon phone call, "You'll have to get your grandchildren from my sister. I have no intention of having children."

His dad asked, "Who is going to care for you in your old age?"

Caleb answered, "The people at the old folks home—same as the ones who are going to take care of you."

His dad responded, "That doesn't give me much comfort."

And Caleb said, "You asking me about my love life doesn't give me any either. In case you hadn't noticed, Jaxon and I are doing just fine as we are."

I asked how that went over, and Caleb said, "I've never heard another word about marriage."

They bought a hovel in Fort Davis that was, according to them, "almost habitable" to which the rest of us added "of a kind." It was more like rough camping, which they did, with some breaks staying with us when they'd have to have the plumbing or electricity out of commission altogether.

Jaxon had consulted with me on his design ideas for the place, and as I told him, "You don't really need my input. Your plan looks great!"

On June 26th, Billy was all excited and on the phone to Jaxon. "Y'all need to come out here for supper tonight."

He didn't disclose the urgency, and he hadn't told me what was on his mind either, though I was sure I knew what it was that got him wound up. I decided to just play dumb and see what was in store for the two of them when they arrived.

I asked, "Is there anything in particular I should be preparing for this supper of yours?"

"No, but make it nice," he said.

I considered what was on hand. "We don't have ribeyes thawed out. I guess I'll make our zucchini carbonara. I know all the boys like that."

"Sounds good," was all he said.

With that settled, he was off to the office to do something on the computer which he kept under tight wraps. When Jaxon and Caleb arrived, he acted as though it was just another typical evening together. He asked them about their day, and they also seemed to have nothing remarkable to share.

When we finished eating, Billy left the room momentarily to get what it was he'd worked on earlier. He handed them a colorful "announcement" he had created.

The Cruz-Schlatter family is pleased to announce the upcoming marriage of our beloved nephew, Jaxon William Schlatter, to Caleb Jeremiah Benton. Date to be determined, but sooner rather than later is preferred.

Then he asked them, "Did you hear the Supreme Court legalized gay marriage today?"

Jaxon answered for them. "No, we had not heard that. Quite frankly, we expected it to go the other way."

Caleb added, "I'm sure Texas will find some way to fight it, or at least pitch a fit about it for the next twenty years."

I suggested, "Billy, isn't your announcement, again, getting the cart a little ahead of the horse?"

Billy answered, "I don't want someone else getting in there to get a license before these two. They could be the first to get married in the county. We'll have the wedding out here at the ranch."

I turned to Jaxon and Caleb. "He planned your business. I guess you might as well let him plan your wedding, too."

Caleb said, "I'm not sure my parents would be too keen on hearing the news. Right now they operate by plausible deniability."

Noah's mind kicked in gear over the possibilities. "Uncle Jaime, we could not only make it a double wedding but a triple one. Jean and Mary-Alice can finally get married and Uncle Billy can finally make an honest man out of you."

"It might surprise you all to know, I'd actually consider it for legal reasons, though we've worked that out pretty well with a bunch of legal documents already—none of which a married couple needs."

Billy responded, "Jaxon and Caleb, that right there is a good reason to get married."

I added, "You have to weigh the pros against the people in town who will be disgusted by the very idea. You'd lose some business for sure, but maybe you'd get some in the process, too."

Billy made a sour face, saying, "You can bet that old-biddy gossip from Mom's old church who makes wedding cakes won't make one for you."

Noah exclaimed, "We don't want her cake! I'll get Elma's recipe from Lupe and make one for 'em."

Caleb asked, "Jaxon, is this what passes for proposals in this family—they just tell us when it's time to get married?"

Jaxon replied, "I think we're the test case. Since only Dad ever got married, and always without the family being consulted, I suppose we can say going off on your own to do it doesn't work too well according to precedent. This might work better."

Billy proclaimed, "That's right! You're marryin' the family, so we might was well weigh in early and often."

Jaxon said, "It might have to be a four-couple wedding. That man who came with Quinn and Brett to the party is getting pretty serious."

"Your dad has a boyfriend?" Billy jested. "I did not see that coming. No wonder he could never keep a wife."

I said, "I don't think I need to clarify for anyone the intent of Jaxon's observation. I did see the young man carried Anna Catherine around like she was his own. I hope it works out for Quinn."

Noah interjected, "It could be a five-couple marriage if Pamela gets back together with Dad."

I replied, "I think they are far more likely to 'live in sin' together. Pamela has never faltered from her 'never marry again' stand. Besides, I think this wedding circus would detract from the two main attractions. We can break all these into separate ceremonies."

Billy noted, "We can control crowd size better that way."

Noah said, "You're right, Uncle Billy. That last party got out of hand."

I said, "Seriously, boys, the things you think of in life as impossibilities—at least in one's own lifetime—can suddenly become reality. Whether you marry or not is up to you, of course. But like you, I thought the court would go the other way. It's a rather remarkable day, and one worth celebrating whether you marry or maintain 'plausible deniability' for the sake of those who'd just as soon not deal with it."

Caleb responded, "The truth is, we already took our vows. It may have been privately, but we certainly meant them. Whatever we do now would be for legal reasons as Jaime pointed out already, and to let those who follow have someone who has paved the way."

Jaxon sighed, "Huh—role models versus under-the-radar contractors in Fort Davis—I guess those are our options."

"I guess they are," I agreed.

Billy conceded, "I suppose I can live with some other couple being the first in the county, but I couldn't wait to celebrate the fact that you can get married if you want to."

Caleb said, "I think it's safe to say we want to. The only question is, will we?"

Jaxon wanted one of us to take a picture with his phone of the two of them. He then typed something and hit "Send."

"There," he said. "I sent Mom a picture of us and said, 'Thanks to SCOTUS, you're looking at your son and future son-in-law. I'm sure you'll want to wish us many happy returns.'"

To his shock, he got a text right back. "Holy-hell!" he exclaimed. "She texted back, 'He looks like a real nice young man. Maybe I can meet him sometime, soon.'"

Then another text came right after that, "The boy at the party with Quinn looked like a nice young man as well. I'm glad my children are happy."

Jaxon exclaimed, "I gotta call Quinn!"

He went outside while we all sat around the kitchen table as surprised as he was.

Noah observed, "Uncle Jaime, it took Jaxon a lot of seeds tossed to the wind before one finally took root."

"Yes, it did, Noah. Jaxon had the faith to keep trying."

Caleb echoed softly, "The faith to keep trying."

Chapter Twenty-nine

Jaxon's call to Quinn morphed into a three-way call with their mother. We were rather eager to all go sit on the patio on such a nice evening, but decided to stay in the house to give him privacy. It was only after he finally hung up that we realized their mother had been part of the conversation. When we saw he finally was off the phone, we went outside to join him.

He reported, "For the last half hour of that call, we were on with Mom. Can you believe it?"

Noah said, "We can believe it. You had the faith to keep casting seeds, and they finally took root."

Jaxon agreed, "They sure did. She said she finally told her parents she really didn't care what they thought—she was going to have a relationship with her children and not lecture us on family values. The only thing their family values had taught her was to value their approval over her own children."

"Damn straight!" Billy exclaimed.

Then Jaxon added, "She's going to drive down here this weekend. She wants to stay at a hotel in Alpine rather than with any of us, but at least she is finally going to meet her granddaughter."

Billy said, "And her son-in-law 'of a kind.'"

Caleb smiled, "I guess I'll have a mother-in-law 'of a kind.'"

I said, "It won't be 'of a kind' if and when you really do marry."

Noah offered assuredly, "Caleb, to me, you're already my brother-in-law."

Caleb replied, "Noah, I never had a brother before you, and when my sister marries, I doubt I'll ever be close to that brother-in-law. You'll always be number one in my book."

Jaxon said, "By the way, Quinn had heard the news about gay marriage, and suggested that maybe we *should* have a double ceremony. Jay *has* proposed to her. She said if she gets married, it could be our grandparents would show up for that so they could pretend it was all okay now, but if she got married with me and Caleb it would still be too much for them to face."

I replied, "I take it she isn't too keen on them attending her wedding then."

He said, "We agreed that unless Mom insisted, their invitation might not get mailed."

Billy offered flatly, "I could accidentally drop it in the compost heap."

"Jaxon, you and Caleb need to run over to *Vista Grande* before it gets any later," I suggested. "All three will be so pleased to hear that you finally heard from your mom. Whether you tell them how it came about this evening is up to you."

Jaxon responded, "We'll do that, and we'll tell them the whole story including showing them Uncle Billy's announcement."

"That will, no doubt, amuse them." Then I added, "Billy, call and tell them they are coming over."

"*Jawohl*," was all he said and was off to call on the kitchen phone.

As they got in their truck to leave, Caleb said, "We'll just head home from there. We've got a small concrete pour in the morning, or we'd stay out here tonight."

I gave each boy a hug as they left. "A momentous day."

"And not over yet," Jaxon said.

I stood in the drive watching their truck head down the ranch road. What would I do in their shoes? I certainly would not have had the courage at their age to even contemplate a marriage outside what passes for traditional. I could never even contemplate marriage to a woman just because of the toxic divorce Zoey, Mason and I lived with growing up. Now, they had to decide if a marriage between two men in a small, west Texas town was a wise thing to do or even a safe thing to do. I had no small degree of angst for them as they would weigh what they already held in their hearts, to put out there for all, destroying Caleb's well-chosen line—plausible deniability.

The only comfort I had was from Billy's enthusiasm for it. His goodwill toward most any notion always turned out well. I hoped it would be the same for Jaxon and Caleb. It was not something Billy and I had discussed, other than casually, since none of us seemed to think it was even a possibility until now.

I sat in my chaise on the patio, where Noah and Billy had already settled in.

Billy stared in. "Hell of a thing. I'm not taking any credit, even if it sounds like I might be, but Jaxon sending that message about his mom's son-in-law and her responding right then seemed close to a miracle."

I said, "Her heart was coming around. Whether that's a miracle or not, I can't say. We can certainly agree the day, that picture and his text seemed to finally give her some courage she'd lacked up until now."

Noah added, "Grandma Schlatter's prayers may take a little longer than Elma's seemed to take, but they get answered."

I clarified, "I think Elma would say hers sometimes took way too long, and I know she said some just never got answered. They never tied the faithfulness of their prayers to not getting the outcome they wanted."

Noah smiled, "They cast their seeds in their own way."

"That's right," I said.

Billy pondered, "I wonder if two men *can* get married in this town. It could be, there will be people protesting at the courthouse if two men or two women even try to get a license. I suspect they'll be worse towards two men doing it."

I asked, "Now, why do you think that?"

He said, "I don't know. Dumbasses abound, that's all I know."

I asked, "Did you have any of these thoughts before you shared your engagement announcement with the boys?"

Billy said, "Of a kind, but they are so already one, I just can't imagine them not married."

I asked, "What about us? You've always said we were one."

He answered, "Like you told them, if we didn't have all the legal stuff worked out, it would be a no-brainer for me."

I said jokingly, "Someone not wanting us to get joint benefits might want proof of our consummation of the marriage. Then what?"

Billy laughed, "Then we'd *both* better enjoy it!"

I laughed as well. "That works for me."

Noah, acting all serious, said, "I'm gonna have a lot to tell a therapist someday about my childhood."

Billy and I both cracked up at that, and said in unison, "Too true! Too true!"

A few days later Brett called to update us on the mother's visit, and to report that while she was in Alpine, Quinn and Jay announced their engagement. For whatever reason, they wanted to get married in the little chapel down in Lajitas, if they could get permission to do so. Jay seemed to have some connection with someone at the Episcopal Church that shared the use of the chapel with the Catholics. They saw no reason to dawdle. They set the date for mid-August, and proceeded to make the necessary arrangements.

Jay was a recent graduate of Sul Ross and was on a managerial track with the local Texas building supply store. He was fully bilingual which the store very much appreciated. Caleb had known who Jay was from some common coursework, but they had never spoken to each other. Brett's family was growing right around him —his healed-self no small part of what now held them all together.

When Billy, Noah and I finally got a chance to visit with Jay, Billy's first question was, "How does a Ramirez get a name like Jay?"

Jay answered, "I have two brothers and two sisters and none of us have Spanish names even though our parents are both hispanic. I've seen our baby pictures. It's not like we could pass for lily-white. I guess they just liked the names. They never would really say. They didn't seem to have a reason."

Then Billy inquired, "Anna Catherine is named after our great-grandmother whose ancestors were Swiss. You and Quinn gonna name your first child after one of your grandparents?"

I interjected, "He's been known to get the cart before the horse on more than one occasion."

Jay replied, "I always wished I would have been named after my great-grandfather. His name was Francisco Diego Rafael Ramirez. There's something about that name I like. I don't even really have a middle name. Just the initial C.—Jay C. Ramirez. I guess they were conserving the alphabet or something."

Noah said, "At least they spelled out Jay."

He smiled, "That's what I told my mom once when I asked why I didn't have a middle name. She didn't have a reason for that either."

Then Jay said, "I hope Quinn and I do have at least one child, but if we don't, that's okay, too. I think Anna Catherine is pretty wonderful. I just hope one of those frat boys don't decide to show up someday wanting to claim her."

I offered my thoughts on the subject. "I doubt very much any of those frat boys are off searching for any possible progeny."

It did confirm what we'd been wondering—did he know how the pregnancy came about in the first place. Clearly, he did and accepted Quinn and her baby without judgment.

Billy gave Jay a hug. "I have to initiate most hugs in this family. I just wanted to hug you for loving our niece and great-niece."

Jay said, "You all have certainly been on a journey together. I don't know many families that have dealt with things the way y'all have and come out the other side better for it."

I offered my perspective on it, saying, "Since you're landing in this family, let me just say as someone else from the outside, now part of it, I wouldn't trade it for anything."

There was not a double wedding let alone a triple or quadruple. Jean and Mary-Alice appeared in no hurry to embrace the new law even though they'd been together now for over twenty years. Jaxon and Caleb thought it prudent to see how things progressed with people's attitudes before risking the next step, which they'd already taken in pledge to each other. If not in the eyes of the law, they considered themselves married 'of a kind.'"

Brett would continue to come to the ranch for the chapel service and lunch, largely to maintain his strong ties, now so much a part of our lives. He was finally out from under all his bankruptcy debt and thought he might sell his house to Quinn and Jay and get something smaller for himself. Jay's apartment was a bit small for the family of three, so for the time being he had moved into Brett's house.

Jay and Quinn were married on a warm, sunny Saturday in the Lajitas Chapel by the Episcopal priest. The customary counseling had been provided ahead of time; the small family of three were attending services at the church in Alpine. The wedding was for immediate family only. Defining immediate family these days gets interesting. Mary-Alice and I were assured we were immediate family as was Caleb. It included Jaxon and Quinn's mother, but not their grandparents or aunts, uncles or cousins. It did, of course, include Bill, Betsy and Sallie and even extended to Pamela, who made the effort and came, leaving her children with their fathers for the weekend. Jay's parents and one brother and one sister attended. Jay's older siblings, who were married and lived out of state, didn't attend. Zoey and Mark opted to stay home and tend to things.

Jaxon, Caleb and Noah provided the music for the simple service, and Betsy read First Corinthians 13. Bill wrote a blessing, which he read as a kind of prayer.

The wedding was such a modest affair, Brett offered to pay for their honeymoon. They wanted to go to the River Walk in San Antonio for a few days.

Bill's reaction to both the wedding venue and San Antonio in August had been the same. "They must like heat lot a more than I do. Lajitas in August is gonna feel like an oven. And they get down on that river walk, where a breeze can't find its way in even if the remnants of a hurricane went through, and they'll be soaked with sweat. I guess it's easier when you're young."

Lajitas was hot, but not unbearable. We went to the nearby resort restaurant for a luncheon reception.

Billy saw that Pamela was sitting next to Jaxon and Quinn's mother. He asked, "What do you think—the ex-wives reliving the past or wondering where this Brett was when they were married to him?"

I smiled, "The latter almost certainly. I even saw Pamela take Brett's hand as they were walking in here just now."

Billy added, "Noah, you might get that seed to sprout yet."

Chapter Thirty

On the first day of fall, we got an early morning call from Rosalinda. "*Jaime*, the old man really did it this time. Lupe found him on the living room floor this morning—heart attack. He's gone."

"How is Lupe doing?" I inquired.

She replied, "Good as she can be, right now. She knew it could happen anytime. The doctor had told them as much, and Chuy and Lupe had told Ernesto and me as well."

I said, "I know she'll be well tended to. I'll let everyone out here know."

Rosalinda said, "Lupe wants to ask a favor."

"Anything."

"She would like you boys to provide the same music at the graveside you did for Elma."

"Of course," I agreed. "Is Ernesto going to sing as well?"

She lamented, "That laryngitis really knocked him for a loop. His voice is still weak and he said, 'No public singing.' He claims he can't get through a single verse of a song without it giving out on him."

"Wow!" I exclaimed. "Ernesto without that voice is hard to imagine."

"It's slowly getting better," she assured me. "He hopes by New Year's he'll be back to his old self. He said, 'If the voice doesn't come back, I'm retiring the drag act. It's no fun if I can't sing and carry on.'"

I said, "I'm sure that's true."

She laughed, "I told him he's gettin' old enough maybe he should retire the act, voice or no voice. He said he thought maybe the same thing."

I noted, "I guess we're veering off track. I don't suppose you know yet when the services will be?"

She responded, "No, but either Lupe, Ernesto or I will call and let you know. I think Lupe wants to be the one to call you about it."

"Okay. Take care, Rosalinda."

"Bye, *Jaime*," and she hung up.

I finished getting breakfast ready, and called Noah and Billy in from the barn and told them the news. I said, "After we're done with the dishes, I want to run over and tell the others, but I also just want to spend some time in the chapel. You two can come or not, as you see fit. Chuy was my first lifeline when I arrived. It will feel odd not to have 'the old man' around anymore. I just want to sit silently in the chapel and remember him."

Billy said, "You go. We have things to work on. You should have the solitude to just be for a while."

"Thanks, Billy."

I stopped at Mark and Zoey's on my way over, and told them the news. After telling Betsy, Bill and Sallie I went into the chapel. With no watch on, I don't know how long I was in there. It was a long time. I found I was grieving in a way I might have grieved a father, if I'd had a father who loved me and I loved in return. Maybe the grief was more acute than I had anticipated simply for that reason.

Zoey and I had both made one last attempt at connecting with our parents following Mason's death. Like the previous attempts, no word ever came. She and I were at peace with ourselves and happy to have each other. Their lives were theirs to wallow in. It would not burden us in any way. Our last attempt to communicate was certainly for their sakes and not ours.

Chuy was the oldest of the Cardona siblings, and, except for an infant daughter who died at birth, the first to be laid to rest. His grave was one row over from his *papá, mamá* and infant Maria, in the Catholic cemetery—the same cemetery where Elma was laid to rest. Lupe sat between Ernesto and Rosalinda at the graveside, and smiled as we offered our musical tributes to our fine friend. When it was over, she said to me and Billy, "You have to do this at least one more time when I go."

I told her, "When Elma died, Noah told us it left a hole in him, and he knew the holes were only going to get bigger. He was right, of course. Chuy leaves a big hole we can only fill with our memories of him. For me there are many. For you, a lifetime's worth. I'm none too eager to open up a hole for you, so stick around a while if you don't mind."

She said, "I probably have a couple good years in me yet. Plus, Noah and I are pretty good at decorating eggs together. I'll stick around for him."

I smiled, "He'll appreciate that."

We had no sooner laid Chuy to rest when Billy came in from the horse stables one morning, while I was still working on breakfast, and pronounced, "Call Sallie and tell her Nellie is down. I don't think she's gonna last long. She's breathin' real labored."

I turned off the skillet, and I did as instructed. Sallie was there within minutes. We all looked at the old gal lying there and debated on what was the kindest thing to do. Sallie knelt by her and stroked her head. "Old gal, don't you hang on for me. You let go. I'll be all right as long as these boys are here to tend to me."

Noah, Billy and I stepped back to leave the two of them alone—just waiting to see what she might want us to do. I couldn't imagine shooting Nellie, but I knew that Sallie or Billy would do it, if they decided it was the merciful thing to do. I figured Sallie would not put it on Billy to do, even though doing it herself would be even harder than it would be for one of us.

A few minutes passed in silence except for the morning birdsong filling the air and the occasional breath of the horse we could hear. I could see Sallie trying to feel Nellie's pulse in the artery running down her neck. Once she found it, she kept her hand there and didn't move or say a word. I could no longer hear the horse breathe.

At least fifteen minutes had passed when Sallie finally said—not taking her eyes off Nellie—"She's at rest."

She stayed there another minute or so, stood and said, "Jaime, it's time to see when Jaxon and Caleb can bring that backhoe out here. We need to get her in the ground."

I didn't say anything but went and made the call. Jaxon said they'd be out early afternoon.

I also called Bill and Betsy, Jean and Mary-Alice, and Mark and Zoey and let them know when the boys would be out. We used the small tractor to get Nellie onto a trailer which would carry her to the ridge that afternoon. Sallie stayed at our house all morning and would go have an occasional conversation with her departed companion of over thirty years. She also had her favorite birds coming round to keep her company and pay their respects. At least that's what Billy told us the birds were doing, and it did seem like there were more than usual that morning perching on anything nearby.

Sallie came in to have a light lunch with us. "I must be getting sentimental in my old age. We always just dug the hole, put the horse in and covered it up. Now I'm thinking I need to get some kind of marker for Nellie. Of course, I already had promised her a good Christian burial, so you boys are gonna have to sing something, and I'll have to have my sister come up with one of her good prayers."

When Jaxon and Caleb arrived, Billy and Sallie led them to the ridge and showed them exactly where Sallie wanted the hole. I knew I was to give them about thirty minutes and follow with my truck and the trailer carrying Nellie. Bill, Betsy, Mark, Zoey, Jean and Mary-Alice all followed Noah and me up the ranch road to the family burial ridge.

Sallie had brought along Nellie's horse blanket, and when we had her lowered into the hole, Sallie tossed the blanket over her as she'd done with each horse before. "Look there!" she pronounced, "I got it laid over real nice in the first toss." Then she tossed one her Swisher Sweets on top of the blanket. "She told me right before she died, I could throw one in as long as it wasn't lit."

We sang "Blest be the Tie That Binds," and Betsy recited the prayer of Saint Francis.

Lord, make me an instrument of your peace:
where there is hatred, let me sow love;
where there is injury, pardon;
where there is doubt, faith;
where there is error, truth;
where there is despair, hope;
where there is darkness, light;
where there is sadness, joy.

O divine Master, grant that I may not so much seek
to be consoled as to console,
to be understood as to understand,

to be loved as to love.
For it is in giving that we receive,
it is in pardoning that we are pardoned,
and it is in dying that we are born to eternal life.

Sallie said, "Y'all, that was real nice. I don't know if horses have an afterlife. I'm not even sure we do. No one I've ever known who died came back to tell me one way or the other. It doesn't really matter to me if we do or if we don't. I just know Noah's right—the holes we get are filled again with the memories." Then she added, "I'll not get a horse again. I vowed if Nellie went before me, I'd give up ridin'. I'm old enough now, I should anyway. Keepin' that vow won't be difficult."

She turned to Caleb. "Caleb, get on the tractor and cover her up." With that she turned to her nephew. "Billy, take me back to my truck."

Chapter Thirty-one

Billy had a hard time accepting the news that a new year would be rung in without Ernesto to do it. His voice was still mending ever so slowly, and he made it official, "From here on, someone else will need to host New Year's if they want a big party. No more drag nights in the Cardona household—no more big New Year's Eve bashes."

Billy asked, "Why's he givin' up the party?"

I replied, "Think about it. To him his act was the party."

He offered, "I guess we'll have to start some new tradition out here."

I said, "I'd like that. I never enjoyed driving home through the mountains after midnight on New Year's Eve, though I loved everything leading up to midnight."

Billy smiled, "We could adopt Dad's idea of going by the Swiss time zone so we can all turn in early."

I said, "Don't tease me. I'd gladly do that in a heartbeat. I might even compromise to some time zone in Greenland to shave off a couple hours at least."

Billy offered, "We never have been night owls."

"And Noah isn't one either," I said.

Billy laughed, "I think he'd go to bed at 8:00 if we let him."

"Yeah, but he'd be rousting us out of bed at 4:30 if we did."

With Quinn now married and Jaxon and Caleb living in Fort Davis, we, more times than not, had Friday-Saturday night guests. One weekend it would Brett and the next the boys.

Billy observed, "Everybody always used to call us the boys. Now we don't even use Jaxon's and Caleb's names—we just say 'the boys.'"

I had already resigned myself to reality. "We're at the point the boys probably call us what your dad made the mistake of calling himself, his wife and his sister-in-law."

Billy stated flatly, "We're the old farts. That's about right."

I suggested, "The next time 'the boys' are out here, we'll talk about what, if anything, we'll do for New Year's Eve. I know we don't want anyone on the roads late because of plans we set in motion."

Billy asked, "Do you think Mark will do drag?"

I replied, "That appeared to me to be a one-off. He enjoyed it, but not enough to repeat it."

Billy continued, "We also need to think about plans for the end of March."

I asked, "What's happening in March?

He said, "You have to ask? March is the anniversary of *Vista Grande* being done, and me coming into your life."

"Oh, so it is," I said. "We've never celebrated it before. Why now?"

He said, "I meant to on the tenth anniversary, but somehow I forgot all about it until now."

I noted, "Yeah, you're a little late for that milestone."

He said, "Still, we ought to mark it somehow. I'm sure Dad and Mom would like to mark the occasion themselves as much as Mom loves that Chapel and they both love that house."

"You'll have to work out how you can add your own flare to the event. I'm not too good in that department."

Billy seem to say out of the blue, "You hardly ever call me a mess anymore. Do you still love me?"

I assured him, "Now you're just askin' questions you already know the answer to. You can't get smarter that way. I suppose it's nice to hear all the same. Yes, I still love you, you old fart."

He replied, "I know I liked being a mess a lot better than an old fart."

I rubbed it in, "We've gotta play the hand we've been dealt."

"Too true. Too true." Then he hollered, "Noah!"

I said, "You could walk back there and tell him whatever it is you're fixin' to tell him instead of always making him come up here."

Billy stated, "We just said we're old farts. I've gotta conserve my energy."

Noah appeared in the kitchen where we were seated. "What?"

Billy asked, "There's no party at Ernesto's this year. What are we gonna do?"

Noah responded, "Oh, I understand the urgency now. It's only two months away. We couldn't have squeezed in talk of this over dinner or breakfast or while we're doing chores?"

Billy asked, "You busy back there?"

Noah replied, "I thought I was. I was in the middle of working on my assignments for my online college credit courses."

Billy said, "Oh that's right. You're a student again. I got used to the year you took off."

Noah asked, "You do remember I plan to drive into Alpine for the Ag courses I want to take, don't you?"

Billy interjected, "Speaking of drivin', when are you gettin' your own wheels? You drive Jaime's pickup like you own it."

"The title of that old pickup says I do own it," Noah said.

Billy asked, "You making payments to Jaime?"

I replied, "He paid cash."

Billy asked, "We never paid him any wages. Where'd he get cash?"

I clarified what Billy already knew. "I gifted him a dollar, and he gave it back to me for payment in full on the truck."

Billy shook his head in feigned disgust at both me and Noah. "You always did spoil this boy. No tellin' how good he'd a turned out with a little more discipline and havin' to do some work around here. Then, maybe I *could* have paid him some wages."

"I know it. I'll bear all the blame for how he turns out."

Billy said, "That wouldn't be right either. I've let you two get away with way too much all along. Being foreman, I'll have to bear some of the burden of where the boy went wrong."

Noah asked, "Is this a conversation I need to be here for? Or should I get back to studying before I fail, and Grandpa has to pay for the same courses twice?"

"You mean your grandpa is payin' for your college education?" Billy asked.

Noah replied, "Somebody'd have to. You just admitted you don't pay any wages."

Billy said, "Oh, I did say that, didn't I? I seem to keep working myself into my own quandary."

Noah replied, "Most people get themselves into their own quandary from what I've seen."

Billy barked, "I don't know why you came out here anyway. You should be back there studyin'. I always said you could find an argument where Jaime couldn't. Now you've pert-near put me in a disagreeable mood."

Noah started back to the office, muttering as he went, "Uncle Billy, you're a mess."

I offered, "Noah, keep a record of this for your therapist."

Billy waited until Noah was out of earshot. "Hey, he didn't call me an old fart. I'm still a mess in his eyes."

I asked, "We can live with that, can't we?"

"Damn straight," Billy said.

I suggested, "Before we get too carried away with our New Year's planning, you should talk to your mom and see what, if anything, she plans to do on New Year's Day. I'll bet she wants to have Quinn, Jay, Anna and Brett. The girls will be coming, too, I'd guess, and probably they will be staying in the bunkhouse."

Billy said, "If the weather isn't real cold, I'd like to take the boys riding."

"That," I said, "we will have to play by ear. I guess you've just put your order in for good weather so maybe you'll get it. We could make either New Year's Eve or New Year's Day a movie marathon, and show them young'uns some golden oldies."

He asked, "What'd ya have in mind?

"You could pick your theme, or we could let the boys pick the theme. We could go for crime family and watch all three *Godfather* movies."

Billy interjected, "Aren't those all double sets? That *would* be a marathon, but I bet they've never watched them."

"At most, probably one of them," I said. "Otherwise, I'd guess they've not seen them. Or we could go with an actor theme like James Dean and watch *Giant, Rebel without a Cause* and *East of Eden.*"

Billy interjected, "*Giant* was filmed around Marfa."

I said, "I figured that out somewhere along the line—I guess when that hotel in Marfa reopened. Back to the movie options. We could get some other theme going and include *Gone with the Wind, Ben Hur, The Ten Commandments, Lawrence of Arabia, Judgment at Nuremberg, A Man for All Seasons, The Sound of Music.* I can think of multiple themes we could tie together with other movies."

Billy said, "But they all have to be made in the 1900's—agreed?"

"Absolutely, they have to be well before their time."

Billy added, "There are several you just rattled off I've never seen or, if I did, they will all seem new to me."

I noted, "For most of them, they will seem new to me, too. It's been years since I watched any of them. I used to rent videos and sit in my apartment in California and watch them by myself."

"No chick-flicks?" Billy asked.

"Rarely."

Billy observed, "I think we could keep this running for the next ten years."

I offered, "The boys might not like our picks as well as us old farts do. We'd have to be open to them forcing us to watch their picks from the current century maybe every other year."

"I suppose that's fair," he acknowledged. "I doubt I'll like them."

I added, "Some of these old ones, like *Gone with the Wind*, we may not like as much as we think, either. I know that one is gonna look dated just from my vague memories of it."

Billy said, "I think the entire movie is now rated PI."

"PI?" I asked.

"Politically incorrect," Billy stated.

I said, "I would say it's that, and then some, but it would be interesting to hear their response to it. I certainly wouldn't sell it ahead of time as a great movie. Just one to watch, observe and discuss."

"Making it educational—I like that," Billy affirmed.

"I'll type up a list of various combinations on various themes, and we can present them to the boys. If they like the idea, we'll give it a shot this New Year's. I'll include a very brief synopsis for each movie since most of the ones on the list will probably be unfamiliar to them."

Billy agreed, "Sounds like a plan, and one not dependent on nice weather."

I emailed the boys my list, and the three coffered on the matter. Noah reported back on their decision. I was surprised both by the enthusiasm they had for the idea—and what they picked. The theme selected by Noah, Jaxon and Caleb was "conscience in time of war—WWI to Vietnam." The movies would be *Sergeant York, Judgment at Nuremberg* and *Platoon.*

Billy said, "Noah, you boys didn't go for light-weight movies."

I added, "I think it will inspire some interesting discussion, especially when they see the shift in perspective between the hero in the World War I movie and the other two."

Billy replied, "I never did see *Judgment at Nuremberg,* but I did see *Platoon.* That one will make you ask, 'What the *hell* were we doing?'"

Noah asked, "Aren't we still asking that? I know Grandpa is."

I concurred, "We sure are. One dumb unending war after another."

Noah continued, "We were in agreement that New Year's Eve should be just a gathering time. The movie marathon is for New Year's. That way we've got all day."

Billy added, "When Dad hears the list, he may be over here on New Year's. For some reason this takes me to something Dad said before I left home. He was talking about some news report that he thought was deliberately misleading. I know it was during Vietnam —that's all I remember. He said, 'Beware of those who tout facts devoid of context.' I didn't know what to make of it at the time, but I get it now."

I said, "He's a wise man, and all are welcome. I was going to be sure to invite Mark and Zoey as well. Noah makes a good point— these three are over seven hours of film time, and we'll want some breaks in between each."

Billy asserted, "The even better point is, I can turn in early on New Year's Eve, and these boys can stay up and ring in the new year if they want to."

I smiled, "That works for me, too. Good job, Noah."

Noah said, "I told 'em how you two come close to being grumpy on New Year's after being up so late at the Cardona party every year."

I laughed, "And your Uncle Billy used to say he wanted us to be hot-cowboy bartenders. I told him he'd last about two nights, and then he'd be crying to me saying, 'Take me home! Take me home!'"

Billy said matter-of-factly, "We would have gotten good tips, though, while it lasted."

Chapter Thirty-two

After launching the GS Ranches brands, Bill held an annual year-end review between Christmas and New Year's. It always included any and all involved in one way or the other. Mary-Alice didn't attend, but Jean did. It included both Mark and Zoey; Bill, Betsy and Sallie, of course; and Noah, Billy and me.

At the 2015 meeting, Bill started by saying, "I move we take all my ill-gotten gains from oil and the proceeds from selling this ranch and buy ranches in Wyoming and Colorado, farms in the midwest, at least one truck line, a couple tractor dealerships and two or three meat processing plants and take GS Ranches national, selling beef, pork, lamb, goat, chicken and a vegan certified line as well. We'll all live in Denver, so we can fly around in our private jet to inspect everything. Is there a second to the motion?"

Noah exclaimed, "Grandpa, you got a lot more oil money than I ever thought you had if you can do all that!"

Bill waited a second or two for a response. "Well, I guess that died for lack of a second. We'll just have to keep doing what we're doing. All in favor?"

"AYE!" we all shouted.

Then he continued, "Our 2014 results don't appear to have been a onetime fluke. We are clearly going to end this year well in the black for a second year. Sallie and I can't take much credit for any of this. We owe the ranch hands credit for the stewardship and care given to the land and the stock, to Noah for his label designs, and to Zoey with help from Mark, for making it all happen.

"I'd have to say the timing is good because, as you know, oil has been tumbling downward this past year, and I don't think it's bottomed out yet. It has to be gettin' close.

"I never allowed the boom years to blind me to the inevitable busts that seem to always happen in the oil and gas industry, so the ranch trust is as sound as ever. Still, it's nice to see the ranch with a life of its own after so many years of just hangin' on."

Sallie leaned forward towards Noah. "Noah, it looks like you might have a ranch to run one day after all—if you want a ranch to run."

Noah said, "I'm trying to learn all I can, because I can't imagine any other life for me than working out here."

"You aren't playin' the lottery so you can have the easy life?" Billy asked.

Noah replied, "I did better than winning the lottery years ago when I landed here."

Sallie added, "We all won when you landed here."

"Amen to that!" I said.

Noah said, "It was because of Grandma and Elma's prayers."

Sallie added, "And Billy's notion that you were gonna land high and dry."

"Jaime says that was my first prayer for you, Noah," Billy reflected.

Noah noted, "I still sing the Noah song whenever I shower."

"Billy and I can confirm that. We've suggested he expand his repertoire, but he never has."

Billy added, "We'd have to admit now that we like hearing it."

"Too True. Too true," I acknowledged.

Jean said, "As usual, we're sticking tightly to the agenda. I didn't see a recap of shower singing on it, but I guess I missed it."

Bill suggested, "I suppose that falls under old business."

Billy said, "There you go, Bean! It fits right in with old business."

"I'm so thrilled you have revived that stupid nickname," Jean lamented.

Billy stated, "That still falls under old business."

Bill always enjoyed wandering off-topic with Billy but now conceded, "I think we've exhausted old business. Is there any new business?"

We all looked at each other around the room waiting for someone to think of something.

Noah finally spoke. "Soon, I'll be going into Alpine for my Ag courses, and it could be while I'm there, I may meet someone I might get interested in enough to want to make a life with them. It could be then, we'd be needin' our own place out here. I know I don't get paid any wages, but it might be GS Ranches could throw in some housing."

Sallie smiled, "You got your great-granddad's notion for seeing well down the road. I guess you see Jaxon and Caleb gettin' goin' on this house buildin' sooner rather than later."

Noah said, "No rush, of course, but something we ought to keep out there as an option."

"What's the foreman think about this idea?" Bill asked.

Billy responded, "Maybe we should have been paying wages all along. Then he could build his own house. Now he's wantin' the ranch to build it."

Bill noted, "I think the net is the same."

"Probably the ranch still is getting the better part of the deal," Jean added.

Billy conceded, "I suppose that's right. I can't undo the boy being spoiled by Jaime and the rest of you. The foreman's always been on his own to work some discipline into the boy and try to teach him how to work."

"Maybe the old cowgirl needs to set him straight," Sallie offered.

Billy exclaimed, "The old cowgirl spoils him most of all! I always thought it would be Mom, but she's the only other one trying to help me out!"

Sallie suggested, "Jaime and Billy could move back over to my quarters when I join Nellie, Momma and Daddy up on the ridge, then, Noah, you could stay put."

"I could have grown kids by then," Noah said. "You're gonna 'get up' there where Elma was at least."

She replied, "I don't know about that. That's a lot of years yet."

Billy noted, "If he's got the Geermann instinct, I think you just got the word you'll be livin' a long time."

She acknowledged, "I had the same feelin', but it wasn't one I was fishin' for. I guess I'll have to find a new hobby or two to occupy the years."

Jean shook her head, adding, "Even new business takes on a life of its own with this bunch."

Bill said, "Since we don't live by who might kick the bucket first, I move Jaime and Jaxon get a house designed, and we get it built. I'll take it as a matter of faith that Noah won't get his head spun around when he heads into the big city of Alpine. Do we need a second to the motion, or are we just gonna do our usual acclamation?"

"AYE!" we all shouted.

Bill said, "I'd say that concludes new business. Noah, you'll have to work with the foreman on where to set it. Mother, I guess we'll adjourn and all have lunch now."

Betsy said, "I'll second that."

As the plans for 2016 New Year's came together, it was decided that we'd all spend an early evening at *Vista Grande*. The next day, Betsy would host all the non-movie goers, which seemed to divide solidly along gender lines—well, almost. Mary-Alice opted to join us for the movie marathon.

Betsy suggested we could have a theme next year that she'd be more interested in such as mission work. She even had her movie choices lined up—*Keys of the Kingdom, The Inn of the Sixth Happiness, The Mission* and she said she'd throw *Gandhi* in there to remind us that you don't have to be a Christian missionary to do the work of mission, adding, "There is that nice Christian missionary who works with him for a long time."

At movie marathon day, none were surprised by the patriotism celebrated in *Sergeant York*. We all still see that spirit alive and well. Equally, as disturbing as *Platoon* is, even the young among us were not surprised by what they saw, as they'd heard plenty about the failure of Vietnam. Noah, thanks only to his grandfather's history teaching, understood well what transpired in *Judgment at Nuremberg*, but it is no exaggeration to say that Jay, Jaxon, Caleb and Mary-Alice were all quite taken aback.

Caleb observed, "I thought we were the good guys in World War II, but in that movie, we don't come out looking nearly as moral and as just as I thought we were."

Bill stated, "You chose your words well. We were then, and still remain, quick to compromise what is truly just at the first sign of inconvenience to power and profit."

Noah added, "Lincoln would say, 'It's the same tyrannical principle.'"

Bill said, "The context may be slightly different, but Noah is correct. The World Wars were tyranny run amuck, and the tyranny continues to our day."

Mark added, "I lament greatly our country's role in the world's destruction. Zoey and I watch *Judgment at Nuremberg* once a year or so as a reminder of how shallow our 'moral superiority' really is."

Billy asked, "Dad, while we're over here contemplating our nation's role in war, what are the others next door doing today? Mom seemed to keep tight-lipped about it."

"It could be argued they are doing the better measure of things. Your mother invited Lupe out, and she was going to help them stitch a quilt to give to Anna Catherine."

That caught Billy off guard. He got immediately, glassy-eyed, which made me do the same. I knew, for me, it had as much to do with Lupe as it did the generosity of Betsy to think of a quilt for Anna. Whatever it was that moved Billy, his dad saw his tears, went over to him and patted him on the back. Then Bill added, "Sallie said, 'My ridin' days are done; I guess I'll see if I can't become domestic in my old age and join these ladies quilting.'"

That made us all smile. Billy noted, "Lupe will be inspecting her stitches and pulling them out if they're not up to snuff!"

I explained for the sake of the younger ones, "That is a fact. When she asked Chuy to try a few stitches, he was soon sent out to work in the yard. She has to have tiny perfect stitches in every quilt she's ever made."

Noah went and got his quilt to show the others. He said, "I know y'all have seen these quilts we have. Lupe quilted these for her mother, Elma, and Elma wanted us to have them when she died. Just look at these stitches."

I said, "She pours her love into those quilts and the Easter eggs that Noah helps her decorate these days. Noah, you should show them the pictures you have of those eggs."

He went to retrieve them. When Caleb saw them he remarked, "Mom always bought the plastic kind filled with candy. These are real eggs? I've never seen an egg decorated like that. What does she do with them?"

Noah explained, "They hide 'em for an Easter egg hunt, then they peel 'em all to make deviled eggs."

Jaxon said, "Short life for all that work."

I was glad Noah understood enough to explain it without me having to do so. He replied, "Lupe's mother, Elma, who had the same birthday as me, started doing eggs like that with her mother when she was a little girl. She did them for ninety years, and Lupe did them with her from the time she was a little girl. It's all about doing something for the love of it and not for the utility of it."

Bill smiled at his grandson. "That's a nice way of putting it, Noah."

Billy added, "Dad, your stewardship of this ranch has always been more about the love of it, and those who come after you, than the utility of it."

Bill said, "I hope that is true."

Brett asserted, "I know it's true!"

Chapter Thirty-three

When Billy and I talked about going site-spotting for where the new house would go up, Noah said, "Maybe my Geermann vision of lookin' down the road hadn't fully developed. Here, we steered Zoey and Mark onto that spot I might have had for an option now."

I said, "You could talk trade, but I doubt they'd jump at the offer."

"That's all right," he replied. "I really was picturing the site up closest to the family cemetery that we looked at that day."

Billy asked, "You want to look at that other site across the cattle guards?"

He answered, "I guess we can look, but I'm pretty sure I'd like to go with the one on this side of the ranch. It's handy to the stables, and I can keep an eye on you two better."

Billy asserted, "I thought we were supposed to keep an eye on you."

He jested, "You are for now. But when you get old, I'll have to start watchin' out for you two, and make sure one or both of you aren't lying in a heap somewhere."

I said, "There's that planning ahead workin' itself again. I'll take comfort from it, knowing it's you lookin' out for us and not some stranger."

Then Noah added, "I drew up a color rendering of what I think it might look like."

Billy asked, "Is this gonna be a ten bedroom house? We didn't think of putting a limit on you when we had that family meeting."

Noah replied, "I was thinking more like three bedrooms and an office. We still have the bunkhouse for overflow—and like we talked about a long time ago, I don't need to be too eager in my breeding program. Two kids would be plenty for me, or none if that happens to be the case. I do know I want to make a life with someone."

Billy asked, "What do you see that lookin' like?"

Noah replied, "I don't know. It might mean marriage. It might not. Certainly, you two have taught me whatever it looks like, it needs to be the best kind of friendship you can have. Dad's marriages taught me that if friendship isn't at the root, then it soon enough will wither and die."

Billy said, "Jaime, I guess we haven't been the worst role models. He might save money from needin' those therapy sessions after all."

I smiled, "I think that's probably right. We can add the money that might have gone for his therapy into the appliance budget."

Billy added, "Nowadays, Noah, you could adopt children if you end up making your life with a Jaime instead of a Janie."

I noted, "He could still choose to adopt with a Janie."

Billy responded, "Yeah, I wasn't meanin' to limit that in the way I did."

"Noah," I said, "Billy, Sallie and I know all about lonely, and you too had a run of that when you were a boy. I'm just glad you want to make a life with someone, somehow, because as I'm sure we've said before, if the heart is open, love finds a way in. It found me, and I know it will find you."

Billy sighed, "That's always been a beautiful thought."

I said, "Grab that rendering of yours, and let's take it with us when we look at these sites."

Noah offered, "Let's go to the ridge site first."

When we got there, he unrolled his drawing, and we noticed he'd drawn from memory the land around the home—so when he held it up you could see exactly how and where the new house would sit.

Billy exclaimed, "I'd say, you nailed it! I don't think we need to look at the other site."

Noah replied, "I'm glad you like it. Now, I need for Jaime and Jaxon to make it into a set of house plans."

I said, "I can already see it."

Billy, talking to himself as much as to me and Noah, said, "Dad was real involved with the other two houses. I wonder if he will be with this one?"

I replied, "I certainly would give him right of first refusal. Jaxon and Caleb are still new to contracting. Bill can certainly make sure everything flows along the way it should."

Billy asked, "Who's taking that on to talk to them about it?"

I said, "You talk to your dad, and if he wants to be involved, I'll talk to the boys. I know Ernesto would tell them to accept Bill's help, and I certainly would, too."

Billy added, "When we first talked about Jaxon and Caleb buying Ernesto's yard and equipment, Dad mentioned if he'd not been a rancher, or had to give up ranching, he'd have liked to have had a construction business with Ernesto."

"The odd couple," I remarked. "But I'm sure it would have worked, and it wouldn't have taken any persuading on Bill's part to get Ernesto to go along with it."

Noah said, "Grandpa told me once, the biggest difference between him and Ernesto was what came out of Ernesto's mouth—both that beautiful singing voice and the string of words he could use."

We laughed at that. Billy added, "Dad always says he never could sing. I'm not sure he ever really tried. I heard him halfway singin' 'Home on the Range' a bunch of times over the years, and it always sounded pretty good to me."

Noah said, "He sings along with the hymns in the chapel, too. He doesn't sing loud, but he sings in tune."

Billy replied, "I hadn't really thought about that. You can certainly pick out when someone can't carry a tune. There's that one woman who comes to Quiet Day who hits the right note only when we get to whatever note she's fixed on."

I said, "What she lacks in her singing ability, she makes up for in kindness."

Billy agreed, "I'll grant that."

I decided to share a bit of my history with Ernesto's language. "As to what comes out of Ernesto's mouth, the second part of that is sure true enough—though when he built *Vista Grande*, he began to clean up the language quite a bit. It's tame now to what it was when I first met him. I still remember him driving down the street past Chuy and Lupe's when we were sitting out. He had the truck window down, banging his hand on the door and hollering as loud as possible for the whole neighborhood to hear, 'Hey, *caca* head!'"

Noah asked, "What did y'all do?"

I laughed. "Well, Chuy hollered back, 'Hey, *pendejo*,' and Lupe said, 'You don't have encourage him." I said, 'Brotherly love.' Then Chuy said, 'You gotta love him.'"

Billy added, "When you move into that house of yours, I don't want you drivin' by our place banging on the pickup door hollering, 'Hey, *caca* head!' Do I make myself clear?"

Noah raised a stiff right arm. "*Jawohl!*"

"That's better," Billy responded. "That's more our family dynamic."

Bill was looking forward to "one last build," though he qualified it by saying that he had thought *Vista Grande* would be the one and only build, and here he was on number three.

"We're slowly raising up the GS Ranches subdivision," he said.

Billy added, "Our rate of growth won't impress any of those city-builders."

Bill noted, "What they call development, I'd call desecration more times than not. They certainly don't have Jaime's vision for what makes a house something special."

"Cheap but expensive," I said.

"Well stated," Bill agreed. "Expensive to the land, the watershed and its creatures—all else be damned so long as they have their hefty profit margin."

It was several weeks before Jaxon and Caleb could get to work on the new house, but we had the plans all done. Bill was off and running—getting all the subcontractors needed lined up and the materials ordered.

Once the boys were on it, it moved quickly. When the house was nearly finished, all the family went over one Sunday afternoon to take a look. As we were preparing to leave, Jaxon took Caleb's hand and announced, "While we're all assembled, we have some news. We've decided to get married."

Billy looked up and all around, getting as much attention as possible in the process.

Sallie said, "I guess he's seeing if either lightning is gonna strike or the roof caves in at such an announcement."

Billy replied, "No act of God to strike us all down for supporting such abominations. Congratulations! You'll have beautiful children."

I added, "I seem to recall you told them that once before. It's not original with him. That's what Rosalinda said to us the first time Billy 'loved on me' in the Slo Poke Cafe."

Billy said, "Tell 'em the rest of it—what you told me you thought Ernesto would say but didn't."

I feigned forgetfulness. "I might not remember what I said."

Noah rightly noted, "I don't think it is gonna shock any of us."

"All right, y'all asked for it. I said, 'Yeah, one with an ass and one without.'"

Bill said, "Good lord—though I am surprised Ernesto didn't say it. He must have still been recovering from seeing Billy carrying on for the first time."

Sallie chuckled even more than usual when humored. "I can't believe you never told me that!"

I said, "It's one of those things I forgot I ever actually said out loud to anyone. Of course, it would be Billy who I had to say it to, so we could all relive it at some point of convenience for his amusement. Think how many years he's been savin' it up."

Betsy asked, "When and where is this marriage going to take place?"

Jaxon replied, "We'd like it to be in the chapel and with one of you performing the ceremony."

Bill said, "Someone would have to get registered someway with the state to make it legal."

Caleb spoke up, "We were kinda hoping Jaime would."

I asked, "Why me, in particular?"

Jaxon replied, "You're more likely to stick to the script than Uncle Billy."

I said, "I see a lot of other people in the room you should probably consider before you decide for sure. I'm the one certifiable heathen in the bunch. I grew up heathen and still don't have the certitude that's needed for anyone getting ordained."

Betsy interjected, "If there's a family vote, I'm for the most spiritual heathen I've ever met. Jaime, you said long ago you were a professed member of the church of mercy over judgment."

"What I said out loud seems to keep coming around today."

Bill put the question, "All in favor?"

"Aye," they all responded.

"I guess I'd better get online and figure out what's required. It could be, you can't rush into this marriage if it takes a while to get me licensed—or whatever it is."

Jaxon said, "The date doesn't matter. You look into it and report back."

"*Jawohl!*" I responded in Geermann-Schlatter dutiful fashion.

Chapter Thirty-four

A little more than a month later, I was standing in the front of the chapel doing what was inconceivable to me not so long ago. Not only was I there witnessing the marriage of two men, but I was presiding over their sacred ceremony. As I looked at the humble gathering, I wondered why I had been elected when anyone in the Schlatter family would certainly have been a fitting celebrant. Perhaps being *in* the family but not *of* the family gave the boys the notion that I was the safe choice—not showing favoritism to some other family member. Whatever it was, I saw a family healed and whole.

Jaxon and Quinn's mother was there. Her parents and siblings were not. She was not estranged from them, but neither did she seek or need their approval any longer. She had become strong through her children's love for her, and learned to love herself for the first time. Accompanying her was a guest we all believed would become husband number two. Zoey observed, "He reminds me very much of Mark when we first met. I can see he brings himself to the relationship in a patient, gentle way that helped me heal and is helping her in the same way."

Pamela was sitting next to Brett. She would not marry again, but they had finally achieved that one thing that had eluded Brett for so many years—friends at the deepest level. They now held a deep bond of love for each other. He was traveling to see her in El Paso, and she was coming to Alpine. Perhaps, when her children are grown, which won't be long now, she will move to Alpine. Or perhaps, they will remain as they are, sharing everything, yet living separate lives.

Aiden had come with Pamela from El Paso. While they were no relation, other than Pamela being his stepmother for a short time, she maintained a connection with each of Brett's children and was a supportive friend to them. Of Brett's four children, however, none would be closer to her than Noah. Noah sat with Pamela on his one side and Billy on the other.

And there, next to Billy, was his mother, the woman from whom he was estranged for two decades—longer really—but for whom there had been complete separation from for so long. And next to her, the faithful husband and father who made sure the connection was never severed altogether.

Sitting with Jean and Mary-Alice was Sallie, who in her own right had sustained a relationship with the girls despite her own sister's estrangement from them. Sallie was dressed as formally as she ever gets, in her black slacks and deep-red blouse. I still had never seen her in a dress and don't expect I ever will. One could look at her now and forget that the old, tough cowgirl with her Swisher Sweets was still alive and well in her mind. In her singular strength, she had sustained Billy all those years he was away from home by the treasure of his memories of her.

We all thought Norman would be there with her, but he couldn't abide two men marrying and said so rather forcefully, which caught Sallie off guard. That was the end of that. Sallie forcefully announced to him, "Norman, you are no longer amusing and no more a part of my life. Don't call me!"

Caleb had seriously considered not telling his parents of the wedding, allowing them to continue their plausible deniability any time relatives, neighbors or people from church might ask about their only son—but in a moment of strength, he risked it. Now, they were there in the chapel, looking a bit uncomfortable, but there.

Caleb's father, young enough to be Bill's son, but perhaps feeling the old traditional rancher might be as troubled as he was, had said to Bill, "Mr. Schlatter, hell of a thing isn't it? I never thought I would see two men marry and certainly never thought one of them would be my own son."

Bill responded to him, "Mr. Benton, my sister-in-law taught this family, a long time ago, that love doesn't come in one way prescribed by someone else. She has lived her life unencumbered by anyone's expectations or judgments. Time has only proven to me how right she was and how wise she is. In time, you may find the same to be true."

The two young men now stood before me as we started the service. I began with one of my favorite stories in the Bible.

Dear friends, we have come together this day to bear witness to the blessing of this household. Heretofore recognized neither by the Church nor the State, we now recognize legally the honesty and integrity of their commitment.

As Ruth taught us, fidelity is not restricted to one man and one woman and does not need the blessing and approval of society.

Naomi said to her two daughters-in-law, 'Go back each of you to your mother's house. May the Lord deal kindly with you, as you have dealt with the dead and with me. The Lord grant that you may find security, each of you in the house of your husband.' Then she kissed them, and they wept aloud.

But Ruth said,
'Do not press me to leave you
    or to turn back from following you!
Where you go, I will go;
    where you lodge, I will lodge;
your people shall be my people,
    and your God my God.
Where you die, I will die—
    there will I be buried.
May the Lord do thus and so to me,
    and more as well,
if even death parts me from you!'

Sallie then stood to read her favorite poem—*The Divine Image* by William Blake.

To Mercy, Pity, Peace and Love.
All pray in their distress;
And to these virtues of delight
Return their thankfulness.

For Mercy, Pity, Peace and Love,
Is God our father dear:
And Mercy, Pity, Peace and Love,
Is Man his child and care.

For Mercy has a human heart

Pity a human face:
And Love, the human form divine,
And Peace, the human dress.

Then every man, of every clime,
That prays in his distress,
Prays to the human form divine
Love, Mercy, Pity, Peace.

And all must love the human form.
In heathen, Turk or Jew;
Where Mercy, Love and Pity dwell,
There God is dwelling too.

Billy, still seated, played "Great is Thy Faithfulness" on his harmonica. Then I continued with the questions for the boys to answer.

I ask each of you if you will reaffirm the vows you have already made to the other. Will you have this man to be your husband; to live together in the covenant of marriage? Will you love him, comfort him, honor and keep him, in sickness and in health; and be faithful to him as long as you both shall live?

Together they responded, "I will." Then each said to the other:

My friend, I take you to be my husband, promising with God's help to continue my fidelity and to be loving and faithful so long as we both shall live. I offer you this ring as a symbol of our continuing and unending love and fidelity. Amen.

I concluded, saying:

By the powers vested in me by the State of Texas, this family and the power of love that fills this place, I confirm upon you the legal state of matrimony, as you have reaffirmed your vows in the presence of all here who love and support you—now and always. Let us go forth in peace.

And, you may kiss—if you've a mind to.

The foreman stood to give an order. "After the kiss, we need a big group hug. Everyone gather round."

Noah said, "Uncle Billy. You're a mess."

I asked, "Could this wedding end any other way?"

Noah got the recipe from Lupe for Elma's cake and added his own colorful, artistic flair to its decoration. The assembled, ending the day—in the same way it had begun—with hope, love and gratitude.

Epilogue

Noah would go back to his own home now. It seemed rather strange for such a young man to have his own place, but he had grown up early. We always knew he was only on loan to us.

It was not easy doing something else we knew we needed to do when he moved up the ranch road. Kola and Koala would go with him. They had instantly—instinctively—taken to the boy who had come shattered and frightened following his mother's murder and helped in his healing. We could have made them stay, but we knew they had chosen their bedmate and it wasn't either of us.

The house seemed empty. Following the big day, Billy and I sat sprawled on our respective ends of the couch. Neither of us said a word. We just moved our eyes around the room as though something new would appear, or perhaps see something we'd overlooked for a long time—our lives being filled with dogs and the boy for so long.

Finally, Billy spoke. "When I stood on that outcropping and asked for your intentions, I never thought we'd raise a boy."

I waited to see if more was going to follow. When nothing did, I said, "I didn't either. How do you think we did?"

He answered, "We had a lot of help."

"Yes, we did."

He added, "The boy turned out all right, but I'd have to give most of the credit to Mom, Dad and Sallie. They schooled him."

I said, "And Sallie passed on being Sallie to him, the same way she passed on being Sallie to you."

Billy agreed, "That's right, which means all I had to do was honor Sallie. And of course, Mom and Dad, too."

"The foreman taught him how to work."

Billy replied, "We both taught him that."

I inquired, "I can't tell—are you just not wantin' to take any credit? You seem to always find someone else to lump in or pass it on to."

"It wasn't deliberate," he replied.

"You know how I always say I never feel led, and yet when I look back, I feel I've been led all the way."

Billy reflected, "That's how Noah ended up here. He was led."

I stated the obvious. "He was led to *you!*"

He added, "Like I was led to Sallie, and we were led to each other."

"I'd say that's true."

He said, "And how we've all been led together in that chapel today."

"There is no crystal ball for that, is there?" I asked.

Billy replied, "None I've ever looked into."

"You've looked into crystal balls?"

"Symbolically," he replied.

"I remember you sayin' dogs are a lot less worry than boys."

Billy said, "I stand by that."

"But I guess they're worth the worry?" I asked.

"I don't know if they all are, but ours was."

"Too true. Too true," I said.

He asked, "Do you think the boy will marry?"

"He's made it plain he wants to have someone in his life."

Billy said, "I don't reckon he'll have any trouble finding someone."

I replied, "I'm sure he'll grab whoever it is before they slip away."

He said matter-of-factly, "He's all Geermann in that regard. He'll see a good thing and not let go."

"Like your mom."

"And like me," Billy added. "We never did really teach the boy how to argue. He'd better hope he doesn't end up with someone good at it."

I said, "I guess in that regard, we didn't prepare him."

He replied, "I don't mind that we never could find anything to argue about."

"It's never bothered me, either."

He stated flatly, "There we go—agreein' again."

"We are good at agreeing."

Billy sighed. "I think he'll be all right. I don't see him wantin' to look for someone who likes to argue."

I replied, "No, I don't think so either, though you did tell him he was smart enough he might be good at it."

He added, "I never did really believe that."

"I think he knew you didn't."

We both sat quietly for a time, turning over in our minds, memories of the boy.

Finally, Billy said, "We might have to either get us our own dogs or another boy."

I noted, "We already agreed, dogs are less worry."

He speculated, "And with a boy, we might not be as lucky the next time."

"There aren't many like Noah in the world."

"Too true. Too true," he said. "What do you think is the most important thing we taught him?"

I replied, "I think you know the answer to that."

"If the heart is open, love finds a way in."

I added, "That, my friend, is the mystery of the universe."

Billy said, "The mystery is why people ever close their heart in the first place."

He stretched out his hand towards me, and I took his hand in mine. He was quiet for a minute and then said, "Jaime, until death us do part."

"Billy, until death us do part."

And then he added, "Or, I guess, it could go on after that."

I affirmed, "Indeed, it might."